'Dr Tremayne, thank you for coming.'

Anne could almost believe he was a gentleman. One whose coat was three years out of fashion, but a gentleman for all that.

'My aunt wishes to consult you.' Anne smiled. 'You must have made an impression on her, though I cannot think why when she was in a dead faint most of the time.'

He looked as though he were about to laugh, but then he pulled himself together. 'Miss Hemingford, are you bamming me?'

'Indeed, I am not. I would not presume on so short an acquaintance.'

He wondered if she would do so on a longer acquaintance, and he allowed himself to imagine them teasing each other, laughing together, happy in each other's company. But, suddenly remembering Sophie, he brought himself back to reality.

Born in Singapore, **Mary Nichols** came to England when she was three, and has spent most of her life in different parts of East Anglia. She has been a radiographer, school secretary, information officer and industrial editor, as well as a writer. She has three grown-up children, and four grandchildren. *Marrying Miss Hemingford* features characters you will have already met in *The Hemingford Scandal*.

Recent titles by the same author:

THE HONOURABLE EARL
THE INCOMPARABLE COUNTESS
LADY LAVINIA'S MATCH
A LADY OF CONSEQUENCE
THE HEMINGFORD SCANDAL

MARRYING MISS HEMINGFORD

Mary Nichols

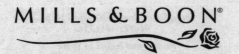
MILLS & BOON®

First published in Great Britain 2005
Harlequin Mills & Boon Limited,
Eton House, 18-24 Paradise Road, Richmond, Surrey TW9 1SR

© Mary Nichols 2005

ISBN 0 263 84385 8

Set in Times Roman 10½ on 12¾ pt.
04-0905-81155

Printed and bound in Spain
by Litografia Rosés S.A., Barcelona

MARRYING
MISS HEMINGFORD

Chapter One

1815

The funeral cortège was a long one; the old Earl of Bostock had been respected, if not greatly loved, in the Lin-
colnshire village from which he took his name. He had
lived to a great age, over eighty, so it was said, and had
outlived wife and sons, and the only family left to mourn
were his grandson Harry, now the new Earl, Harry's wife,
Jane, and his twin sister, Anne. She, most of all, mourned
the passing of her grandfather. In his latter years the Earl
had become almost a recluse, irascible, opinionated and
intolerant where everyone but his beloved granddaughter
was concerned. She had been the apple of his eye, the joy
of his old age and his constant companion. And now he
was gone.

Anne watched from the window as the coffin, on its
carriage drawn by black plumed horses, left Sutton Park,
followed by other carriages containing male members of
the family, some of whom were so distantly related she

had never met them before. Behind them in the procession were many of her grandfather's friends and close associates. The day was overcast, cooler than of late and threatening rain, though none as yet had fallen. It was a day in keeping with the sombre occasion.

Anne turned as her aunt came into the room. 'I thought he would live for ever,' she said, giving her a wan smile. 'I cannot believe he has gone.'

'We all have to go sooner or later.' Although she was forty, Georgiana Bartrum still had the petite figure of a girl; her features were unlined and her hair was still raven black and topped by a lace-edged black cap. 'Be thankful that he lived so long…'

'I wish I could have gone to the funeral, seen him laid to rest.'

'My dear Anne, you know ladies do not go to funerals.'

Anne sighed, doing her best not to weep; Grandfather would have considered it a weakness. 'I don't feel like a lady, I feel like a little girl, lost and bereft.'

'I know, my dear, but that will pass in time.' Her voice faltered and Anne went at once to put her arm round her.

'Oh, Aunt Georgie, I am so sorry, I did not mean to make you sad too.'

Her aunt, her mother's much younger sister, was herself in mourning for a beloved husband who had died suddenly eighteen months before, but, on hearing of the demise of the Earl, had come down from the Lake District for the funeral, determined to put her grief aside for the sake of her niece. 'You must not wish the old Earl back,' she said, dabbing at her eyes with a wisp of handkerchief. 'He was a great age and could do nothing for himself at the end. He is with his wife and your dear mama and papa now and you must think of yourself.'

Her aunt had put her finger on the problem. Twenty-seven years old and unmarried, Anne could not contemplate her future with equanimity. Harry and Jane wanted her to make her home with them, but though she loved them dearly, she did not think it would serve. Ape leader, old maid, maiden aunt were words that leapt to her mind. Why had she turned down every offer of marriage made to her when she was still young enough to be thought marriageable? Not quite every offer—there had been one she would have accepted from a perfectly eligible young man with whom she had imagined herself in love. They had been dealing famously with each other and she had been expecting an offer.

And then her brother, serving as a very young Hussar lieutenant, became involved in the scandal over Mary Ann Clarke, the Duke of York's one-time mistress, who had been using her influence with the Duke to sell promotions. It had been unpleasant at the time, but it had all blown over, although not before the gentleman in question had decided to beat a hasty retreat. Grandfather had said if he was so easily blown in the wind he was not worthy of her, which had been small comfort at the time.

That had been five years ago and since then she had been wary and refused every offer. Those who came after had not been ineligible, ugly or cruel, and yet she had rejected them all. She had made excuses not only to them but to herself: her grandfather was old and ill and could not manage without her; she looked after his household, wrote letters for him, read to him, ran errands and even fed him when he became too feeble to feed himself. She had also assumed the charitable duties on the estate and in the village that her mother would have done had she lived. And now it was too late; her grandfather was dead and she was well past marriageable age.

Now no one needed her. Jane was easily able to fulfil the task of the lady of the manor, though she pretended she would need Anne's help. But Anne could not while away the remainder of her life, doing embroidery and being a companion to her sister-in-law, however much she loved her. She loved her little nephew too, and therein lay much of her unease. She longed for children of her own with a fierce passion that made her miserable, and seeing little William, toddling about on his unsteady two-year-old legs, giggling when she held out her arms to catch him, made her want to weep. She had to make a life for herself, a life that she would find fulfilling, so that her lack of children did not become an unhealthy obsession.

'But what am I to do?' she asked her aunt. 'My usefulness is at an end…'

'Nonsense! You have your whole life before you. We must find you a husband—'

'Husband! At my age!' Anne gave a cracked laugh. 'Who would have me?'

'We shall have to see, shall we not?'

'Aunt Georgie, I do hope you are not scheming on my behalf, because I tell you now it will not work. I am not beautiful, I am too outspoken and independent and have had my own way far too long…' Like her grandfather, she was passionate about things she cared for, could not tolerate fools, hated fops, could not abide idleness and had a fiery temper when roused.

'None of which is an impediment that I can see.'

'An impediment to what?' Jane had entered the room, carrying a squirming William in her arms. The child was in a bright blue dress, which made a sharp contrast to the sombre gowns of the women. He held out his arms to Anne, who took him and sat down with him on her lap, rubbing her cheek against the silky softness of his hair.

'Marriage,' Anne said. 'Aunt Bartrum thinks she can find me a husband.'

Jane stood and looked at her sister-in-law, while William nestled his head into Anne's shoulder and began to suck his thumb. Anne was tall and graceful; she was not pretty so much as classically beautiful. Her rich brown hair and amber eyes were her greatest assets. Jane had often wondered why Anne had never married, why she had allowed the old Earl to impose on her so much. He had an army of servants to help him; she need not have made herself his dogsbody. Was she perhaps afraid of matrimony? 'Do you want a husband? You always said you did not want to marry.'

'It was Aunt Bartrum's idea, not mine.'

'I hope you do not think that you have to leave here, Anne,' Jane said. 'This has always been your home and it always will be. I should feel mortified if you thought otherwise. Whatever would we do without you?'

'Manage very well, I think,' Anne said, pretending to laugh. 'But there is nothing for me to do here, nothing important, that is. No *raison d'être*.'

'Fustian! You are you, my friend, my dear sister, my

bulwark. There are any number of things for you to do. You are simply feeling a little low.'

'And that is why I propose to take her away and provide a little diversion,' Mrs Bartrum put in. 'Anne needs to see that there is more to the world than Sutton Park and its environs. Why, she did not even go to London for the Season this year…'

'Grandfather was too ill to be left,' Anne put in.

'That I grant you, but now you must take stock and I do not think you can do it here.'

Anne gave a shaky laugh, recognising the truth of this. 'But there is a great difference between providing a little diversion and finding me a husband, don't you think?'

'One may lead to the other.'

'But the Season is over,' Jane said, taking William from Anne and handing him to his nurse, who had come to fetch him. 'There will be no one in town now.'

'And I am long past playing the field among the eligibles of the *ton,*' Anne said, watching the nurse disappear with her burden, her heart aching to have her own child in her arms. Could she marry for the sake of having a child? Why hadn't she asked herself that question years before when it might have been a possibility? 'For goodness' sake, I had my come-out ten years ago.'

'I do not propose going to town,' Mrs Bartrum said. 'I had thought of going to Bath, but that is old fashioned and full of dowagers and bumbling old men and, though I am content to live quietly and remember the happiness I once had, that will not serve for you. We need to find some life. We'll go to Brighton.'

'Brighton?'

'Yes, there are all manner of diversions there and good company. Now the war is ended, there are army officers and naval men and half the *beau monde* down from London...'

'Rakes and demi-reps,' Anne said. 'Hanging on to the coat-tails of the Regent.'

Her aunt laughed. 'But very diverting rakes and demi-reps.' Seriously, she added, 'They are not all like that. I know many who are honourable gentlemen and ladies who go to take the water and are perfectly respectable. We can avoid the disreputable. I intend to go and I need a companion...'

'But I am in mourning, I cannot go out and about in society...'

'Oh, yes, you can,' Jane said, suddenly realising that was just what Anne needed to fetch her out of the dismals. 'You know perfectly well it was Grandfather's express wish that you would not put on mourning for him and how do you obey him?' She looked at the heavy black silk gown Anne wore, with its jet buttons and black lace edging. 'By resorting to black without a speck of colour and it certainly does not become you.'

Her grandfather had indeed instructed her not to go into mourning for him. 'You have given up your youth for me,' he had said the day before he died. It had been a great effort to speak, but he would not be silenced. 'It was selfish of me to allow it, but when I hand in my accounts, I want you to feel carefree and happy. Cheer if you like.' He had smiled at her protests. 'I mean it. Do all the things you have missed. Will you do that?' She had promised to obey him. And she would, but not today. Today she felt too sad and her black clothes were in keeping with her mood. 'I know,' she told her sister-in-law. 'But I could not wear colour today.'

'No, but you can tomorrow. I know you have a light mauve that would be entirely suitable. And there is that cream muslin and a grey jaconet which are not vivid at all. I shall ask Harry what he thinks.'

'As if Harry had the first idea about ladies' fashions! Why, he is guided by you even to what he wears himself, otherwise I declare he would wear a pink shirt with a bright orange waistcoat.'

The jest lightened the atmosphere a little and they settled down to take tea while they waited for the men to return, when a more sumptuous spread would be offered. Anne, sipping her tea, was thoughtful. Should she accept her aunt's offer? It might give her time to reflect on what she should do: stay at Sutton Park being a maiden aunt to William and any other children who might arrive, until they grew up and left the nest and she became old and crotchety before her time, or venture into the world and see what it had to offer? She had still made no decision when the room was suddenly filled with men, all talking at once.

'He had a good send-off,' Harry said, joining his wife. 'And the whole village turned out to see the coffin go by. They stood in silence with heads bowed. I was deeply moved.'

Servants appeared with trays of food and full glasses and nothing was said about Anne's future until after the will had been read, the food eaten and the mourners had either departed for their own homes nearby or retired to the rooms allotted to them.

'I am relieved that it went well and the old man is at peace,' Harry said, folding his long legs into a winged chair by the hearth.

'I could not rid myself of the feeling that he was in the room, watching and listening,' Anne said. 'And I cannot for the life of me think why he should leave me so much money. My needs are simple…'

'Anne, my love, you have earned every groat of it,' Harry said. 'And I certainly do not begrudge it.'

'I have no doubt it was meant in place of the dowry you would have had,' Jane put in. 'Now, you can please yourself how you spend it.'

'Then I think I shall go to Brighton with Aunt Georgie.'

Harry demanded to know what she meant and, having had everything explained to him, said he thought it was a good idea. 'We do not want to be rid of you, Sis,' he said. 'You know this is your home, but a change of scene will do you good. And Aunt Georgie too.'

Anne smiled. The spinster and the widow, what would Brighton make of them, she wondered.

It took three weeks to make all the arrangements, not only because a suitable house had to be found to rent, but also because Anne was, in some ways, reluctant to leave home and family, almost afraid of what was in store for her, which she recognised as foolishness. She was a mature woman, elegant, intelligent, able to hold her own in any company, and she was still young enough to enjoy herself. That was what Grandfather had said, when leaving her that bequest. 'My granddaughter has made a great sacrifice to stay and see me comfortably to my end and nothing I give can recompense her for that,' he had dictated to the family lawyer, who read it aloud to the company after the funeral. 'I do not want her to grieve for me. I command her to be happy in any way she can and if this bequest can bring that about, then I hope she will make good use of it.'

She had cried then; only the second time she had shed tears since his death. The first had been when the doctor had pronounced life extinct and closed the old man's eyes. She had been unable to hold back her grief and stood encircled in her brother's arms, soaking his coat with her tears. The weeping was done now and she was going to do her best to obey his dying command. A few weeks in Brighton with her aunt and then she would think of her future.

They set off for London by post chaise, accompanied by Susan, Aunt Bartrum's maid, and Anne's middle-aged companion cum maid, Amelia Parker. They stayed at the Hemingford town house to do some shopping and completed their journey two days later, arriving in Brighton early on a Wednesday afternoon in late August.

The house they had taken was on the west side of the old town, in an area which had not so many years before been open fields, but since Brighton had become fashionable it was being developed at a frantic pace to keep up with the demands of the people who wanted to come and stay. Now there were elegant terraces of tall narrow buildings with biscuit-coloured façades and cast-iron balustrades. The one Mrs Bartrum had taken had a staircase that wound up from an entrance hall in decreasing squares to the upper rooms and which, viewed from the ground floor, reminded Anne of a dimly lit tower. But the rooms that led from it were light and airy with balconied windows at the front, which afforded a view of the sea, calm and sparkling on the afternoon they arrived.

'First things first,' Mrs Bartrum said when they had chosen their rooms and left the maids to unpack. 'We will have some refreshments, give instructions to the servants about how we like them to go on and then we will go and announce our arrival.'

'Announce it?' Anne queried, laughing. 'Are you going to send out the town crier?'

'No, you foolish girl. We go to Baker's library and sign the visitors' book and while we are there we will read the names of those who have preceded us. After that, home for dinner and then we shall see what tomorrow brings.'

Baker's library was on The Steine at the bottom of St James's Street and they decided to walk. Putting a light shawl over her lilac silk gown, Anne slipped her arm through her aunt's and they stepped out briskly along the sea front. Anne had never known such a dazzling light. It glittered on the sea, shone on the pastel stucco of the buildings, reflected in the windows and picked out the colours of other strollers' clothes like an artist's palette. And the air was so clear, they felt almost giddy with it.

'Shall you bathe in the sea?' Anne asked her aunt, noticing the row of huts on wheels that stood along the water's edge and the women standing beside them holding armfuls of cotton garments for bathers to change into.

'Why not?' her aunt said. 'There is no sense in coming to the seaside if you do not take a dip, is there?'

Anne smiled. Her aunt was game for anything. 'No, I suppose not.'

'We'll go one morning very early before anyone is about, then if we find we do not like it, we can come out and no one the wiser.'

'What else have you in mind for us to do?'

'That depends on the Master of Ceremonies. He will advise us what is going on and what is most suitable for us. That is why we sign the visitors' book: it tells him we are here.'

Anne found herself laughing. 'You mean he is a kind of matchmaker?'

'Not at all.' She paused. 'Unless you want him to be, then of course he will make sure you are introduced to the right people.'

'I positively forbid you to speak of me, Aunt. I will not be paraded like a seventeen-year-old newly escaped from the schoolroom.'

'I would not dream of it, my dear. There is no need.'

Anne looked sideways at her. Her aunt was looking decidedly complacent and she wondered just what she was up to. She felt no alarm; let the dear lady have her fun, for that was all it was. A diversion, wasn't that what she had said?

Even in the old part of town, there were new houses interspersed with old and Anne began to wonder what the original fishing village had been like fifty years before and what had become of its inhabitants. There must still be fishermen, because their nets were laid out to dry on a wide grassy bank next to the sea and one or two boats were pulled up at the water's edge, but of their owners there was no sign. She supposed they set out very early in the morning and, once their catch had been landed and sold and the nets put out to dry, disappeared for a well-earned rest.

They picked their way over the nets and found the library where Mrs Bartrum spent some time perusing the visitors' book and making notes, while Anne borrowed two books, then they set off to explore a little further. They wandered up Old Steine, looked at the house where Mrs Fitzherbert, the Regent's mistress, lived and a little further on came to the Pavilion, his seaside home. It had begun as an ordinary villa and had been extended and glorified over the last twenty years until it looked like an Eastern palace, with white painted domes and colonnades, and it was still being altered and embellished. 'At least, it gives work to the people of the town,' Anne said, as they moved away.

They returned home by way of North Street and Western Road and sat down to a dinner of fillets of turbot, saddle of lamb and quince tart. Mrs Carter, their cook, was a find, but then the agent had only to mention the Earl's name and the best was forthcoming, be it house, servants or horses. They had hardly finished their meal and settled in the drawing room with the tea tray when the Master of Ceremonies was announced.

Dressed very correctly in dark breeches and white stockings, long tail coat and starched muslin cravat, he came in, bowed and was offered tea, before anything was said of the purpose of his visit. Anne suppressed her curiosity and waited.

'Now, madam,' he said at last, producing a sheaf of papers from a bag he carried. 'I have here a list of next week's events. There is a ball at the Castle Inn Assembly Rooms on Monday and a concert on Tuesday. The Old Ship has a ball every Thursday, and there are several lectures and, of course, the usual games of whist in the afternoons. But I see you are in mourning, so perhaps…'

'I am, sir,' Mrs Bartrum said. 'And shall be until the end of my days when I shall hope to join my dear husband in heaven, but that is nothing to the point. My duty is clear to me and that is to put aside my grief…' she dabbed at the corners of her eyes with her handkerchief '…for the sake of my niece. She is my only consideration. We intend to join in with whatever activities you deem suitable. My niece, as no doubt you have realised, is unmarried.'

Anne thought she was long past blushing, but this statement sent the colour racing to her face and she gave her aunt a disapproving look, before she set him straight by saying. 'But not, sir, in need of a husband.'

'I understand,' he said, looking at Anne and smiling knowingly, which made her squirm, though she held her tongue for the sake of her aunt.

He stayed long enough to go through other events on offer and ticked off those they decided to attend, then took his leave.

'Aunt, I am very displeased,' Anne said as soon as they were alone again. 'I asked you not to make an issue of my being unmarried. Now he thinks you want him to find a match for me.'

'I simply stated that you were single,' her aunt said. 'Besides, we can find our own company. I saw Lady Mancroft's name is in the visitors' book; she is an old friend of mine and knows simply everybody worth knowing.' She rose from her chair. 'Now I think I shall go to bed. The sea air has made me quite sleepy.'

Anne followed her a few minutes later and went to her own room, where Amelia helped her out of her dress and left her to finish her toilette alone. Once in her night-gown, she stood at the open window and looked out over the sea. The moon had tinged the horizon with gold, which played on the sea in a long jagged line, making it glitter like a jewelled necklace on dark velvet. She could hear the waves lapping on the shore, could smell the tang of salt and fish and seaweed. It was a very different world from Sutton Park, a magical world when anything could happen. She smiled as she turned away and climbed into bed. She was sure her aunt meant to find a match for her and though one-half of her resented it, the other half was tingling with anticipation, which was, she told herself severely, very foolish of her and could only lead to disappointment.

It was very early when she woke, and unable to stay in bed, she rose and dressed and went downstairs to find the maid preparing breakfast. 'Mrs Bartrum instructed me to take breakfast to your rooms,' she said. 'I didn't expect you down...'

She was obviously flustered and Anne smiled to put her at her ease. 'Oh, do not mind me, I like to be up be-times. Take my aunt's and Miss Parker's up to her. I'll have mine in the morning room, then I think I will take a stroll.'

* * *

She had long ago stopped worrying about having a chaperon everywhere she went and, half an hour later, she was walking along the sea front. There was a little more wind than there had been the day before, which tipped the waves with white foam, but in spite of this the bathing machines were doing good business.

They reminded Anne of gypsy caravans. They had four large wheels, which elevated them four or five feet from the ground, and were entered by a flight of steps at the back that had a kind of canvas hood. Once the bather was inside, she changed into the costume given to her by the attendant and the horse drew the whole contraption into the water where the vehicle was turned round, so that the bather could descend the steps straight into the sea, still under the shelter of the hood. Thus the proprieties were observed and none of the lady's fine clothes were even dampened. Even at a distance Anne could hear the women's shrieks as they immersed themselves. Further along the beach the same service was being offered to gentlemen bathers.

She carried on to The Steine, noticing that the fishermen's nets and the boats had gone. There were sails on the horizon, but she could not tell what kind of boats they were, nor if they were coming in to land. Behind her the road was becoming busy; there were carriages and carts going about their business and pedlars setting up their stalls. What alerted her she could not afterwards say, but she turned suddenly to see a fast-moving curricle mount the walkway and clip a small child, sending her sprawling. Anne was running almost before the little one hit the cobbles. The curricle, driven by an army officer, went on without stopping.

The child could not have been more than five years old. She wore a flimsy cotton dress and very little else, no shoes, no coat. Anne fell on her knees beside her. She was unconscious and was bleeding from a wound to her head. Anne's first fear that she might have been killed gave way to relief when she saw the slight chest moving. She looked around as if expecting help to materialise but though a crowd had gathered, no one seemed particularly helpful. 'Does anyone know where she lives?' she asked.

'Take her to the poorhouse infirmary,' said one. She could tell by his clothes that he was one of the gentry; he had a fashionable lady on his arm who shuddered in distaste and pulled him away. He went meekly, leaving Anne fuming.

'There's a doctor nearby,' a young lad said, pointing towards an alley between tall narrow buildings. 'You'll know 'is place by the brass plate on the door.'

Anne scooped the child up in her arms and, supporting her head with one hand, hurried in the direction of the pointing finger. The little one, being half-starved, was light as a feather. 'You will be fine,' she murmured, hugging the child to her, though she was filthy and smelled of stale fish and her blood was seeping into Anne's clothes. 'The doctor will make you better and then I'll take you home to your mama. Where do you live?' She received no reply because the child was still deeply unconscious.

The alley was so narrow the sun could not penetrate it and there was hardly room for two people to walk side by side, but she was aware that the lad who had given her directions was pounding just in front of her. 'Here it is, miss,' he said, stopping beside a door on which was a painted notice announcing Dr J. Tremayne. Anne had her hands full and so he banged on the door for her with his fist.

It was opened by a plump woman in a huge white apron who immediately took in the situation. 'Bring her in, bring her in,' she said.

Anne followed with her burden as she was led along a corridor and into a room that was lined with benches and chairs, but no other furniture. In spite of the early hour, there were people waiting, old, young, crippled, deformed, all poorly clad, all grubby. She was about to sink into one of the chairs, when the woman said. 'Better bring her straight through.'

She ushered Anne into an adjoining room, which was evidently the doctor's surgery, for there was a bed, a desk with a lamp on it, two chairs and a large cupboard, most of it extremely shabby though perfectly clean. Of the doctor there was no sign.

'Put her on the bed. I'll fetch Dr Tremayne. He's having his breakfast before he starts. They all come so early and he'd come straight from his bed if I didn't insist he had something to eat and drink first.'

She disappeared and Anne gently laid the child on the couch. She was trying to staunch the bleeding with a towel she had taken from a hook on the wall, worrying that the little girl was so pale and lifeless, when she heard the door open and close behind her and turned to face the man who had entered.

She had expected a middle-aged man with thinning hair and a rumpled suit. What she saw was the most handsome man she had seen in a long time. He was older than she was by a year or two, tall and spare, with thick dark hair, much in need of a barber, and a tanned, almost rugged complexion. She might have been right about the crumpled suit, except that he wore no coat and was in his shirt sleeves. Nothing could have been further from the dandies who strolled in and out of London drawing rooms during the Season than this man. In spite of a slight limp he exuded masculine strength, and she felt her breath catch in her throat.

He barely glanced at her as he went over to the child and began examining her with gently probing fingers. Anne wondered whether she was expected to go or stay, but her heart had gone out to the little scrap of humanity and she wished she could do something to help. She hesitated. 'Will she be all right?'

'Let us hope so.' He still had his back to her and clicked his fingers at the plump woman who had followed him into the room. 'Padding and a bandage, Mrs Armistead, if you please.' These were put into his hand and he carefully bandaged the head wound and put some ointment on the grazed arm and leg, ignoring his audience. When she saw the child's eyelids flutter, Anne breathed an audible sigh of relief.

'You may sigh,' he said sharply, proving he had been aware that she had stayed. 'What were you thinking of to allow a child so small to run out alone? Have you no sense at all?'

Anne was taken aback until she realised that he had

mistaken her for the child's mother, which just showed how unobservant he was. The little girl was in dirty rags whereas she was wearing a fashionable walking dress of green taffeta, a three-quarter-length pelisse and a bonnet that had cost all of three guineas. The thought of that extravagance in the face of this poverty made her uncomfortable. She looked at Mrs Armistead, who lifted her shoulders in a shrug.

'I am not the child's mother,' she said, and suddenly wished she was. She could dress her in warm clothes, give her good food, care for her as her mother evidently did not. 'I never saw the child before today.'

'Oh.' Alerted by her cultured voice, he turned from his ministrations to look at her for the first time and she saw deep-set brown eyes that had fine lines running from the outer corners as if he were used to squinting in strong sunlight, but the eyes themselves were cold and empty and his expression severe. She smiled, trying to evince some response from him.

'Madam.' He bowed stiffly, hiding the fact that he had been taken by surprise. What he saw was not only a tall graceful woman of fashion, but also an oval face of classic proportions, narrow though determined chin, wide cheeks, broad brow, and lovely amber eyes full of tender concern. He held her look for several seconds, battling with his anger over the neglect of the child and his natural inclination to blame the woman who had brought her to him. She was obviously one of the fashionable set that had taken over Brighton, destroying the fishermen's cottages to build their grand villas, relegating the poorer inhabitants to dismal tenements in the murky, malodorous back lanes. There was still a fishing trade in Brighton, but it was dwindling in the face of the onslaught of the rich who wanted service more than fish. On the other hand she had cared enough to soil her clothes and bring the child to him. 'I beg your pardon for my error.'

'I was walking along the promenade when I saw her knocked down by a furiously driven curricle,' Anne explained. 'The driver was apparently unconcerned, for he did not stop. I was advised to bring her here.' This explanation was given in a breathless voice, quite unlike her usual self-assured manner, though why he should have such a profound effect on her, she did not know. It was not like her to feel the need to justify her actions.

'It is as well you did.' He straightened up and went to wash his hands in the bowl placed on a side table. 'She might have bled to death.'

The child began to whimper and Anne fell on her knees beside the bed and took her bony little hands in her own. 'Don't cry, little one. You are safe now.'

'Me 'ead hurts.'

'I know, dear. The doctor has given you a lovely white turban to make it better. What do you think of that?'

'Ma, where's Ma? And Tom. Tom…' She was becoming distressed and tried to rise.

Anne pressed her gently back on the pillow. 'Lie still, little one. We'll fetch them for you.' She looked up at the doctor who was washing his hands in a tin bowl. 'Do you know who she is?'

'No, but undoubtedly someone will come looking for her.' He knew he was being unfair, but he could not help contrasting the elegance of this woman with the poverty all around him. She was by no means plump, but she wasn't half-starved as the child was. And she had never had to sit for hours in an uncomfortable waiting room to get treatment for an ailment that would soon be cured if the patient had wholesome food and clean surroundings.

Anne stood up to face him. His abrupt manner was annoying her. She took a firm grip on herself. 'How can you be so sure?'

'I am usually the first port of call in this district if anyone is injured or lost.' He reached for a cloth to dry his hands. 'Word gets around.'

'Are you going to keep her here?'

'I can't. I have no beds for staying patients. I wish I had, I could fill them a hundred times a day. I shall have to send her to the infirmary unless someone comes quickly to claim her. You may have noticed I have a full waiting room.'

'What can I do to help?'

He gave a wry smile. 'I never turn down a donation, madam.'

'There is that, of course,' she said, irritated by his manner. 'But I was thinking of help on a practical level. I could go and look for her mother, if you could give me some idea of where she might be found.'

This produced a chuckle. 'I think that would be unwise.'

'Why?'

'If my guess is correct, it is a slum. Filthy, unsanitary and stinking. You would ruin your fine clothes and heave up your breakfast, neither of which this child has nor ever has had.'

'Do you take me for a fool?' she demanded, forbearing to point out that her coat was already ruined. 'One look at that poor little mite is enough to tell me what kind of home she comes from. But that doesn't make it any less of a home to her. And it is the child I am concerned with, not my own convenience.' She stooped to stroke the little one's tear-wet cheek and her brusque manner softened. 'Don't cry, sweetheart, we'll find your mama. Do you know where she is?'

'On the beach. With the huts.'

'She must be a dipper,' Mrs Armistead said. 'A bathing attendant.'

'But surely she does not leave the child alone while she works?'

The woman shrugged. 'Sometimes it can't be helped.'

Anne, remembering the little girl had mentioned Tom, turned back to her. 'Who is Tom?'

'Me bruvver. He looks arter me.'

'And where is he?'

'Dunno.'

Anne fumed against the boy, but kept her anger from her voice. 'What is your name?'

'Tildy Smith.'

Anne patted her hand, stood up and addressed the doctor. 'I am going down to the bathing machines to find her mother. Can you keep her here until I come back? I don't want the poor little mite to go to the infirmary if it can be helped.'

'Mrs Armistead will take her to the kitchen. There's a couch in there, but if her mother does not come for her in an hour, or two at the most, I shall have to send her to the infirmary. If my patients learn that I am making a hospital of my home, they'll expect the same service and I have to draw the line somewhere.'

He sounded so weary Anne immediately forgot her annoyance and smiled. 'I'll have the mother back before that; if I cannot find her, then I will take the child myself.'

'You?' The contempt in his voice made her hackles rise.

'Why not? I found her and brought her here. I feel responsible.'

'How can that be? You did not run her down, did you?'

'Indeed I did not! And if I ever find the man who was driving that curricle, I shall tell him exactly what I think of him. He could have killed her.'

'But he did not. And thanks to you, she will be none the worse in a week or two.' He was beginning to revise his opinion of her; she truly cared and she might be good for a generous donation; that fetching bonnet must have cost a pretty penny. Better not antagonise her. 'My name is Tremayne, by the way.'

'Yes, I noticed it on the plate by the door,' she said, wondering what the initial stood for. 'I am Anne Hemingford.'

'How d'you do, Lady...?' His pause was a question.

She smiled, offering her hand. 'Miss Hemingford.' She could have said the Honourable Miss Anne Hemingford, but decided against it. He already thought she was too big for her neat kid boots.

He shook her hand and watched her as she strode purposefully from the room, wondering if he would ever see her again. Women of quality, as she so obviously was, often sympathised with his aims, professed themselves interested in his work and even came to look round, but when they saw the patients he attracted—the poor, the lame, those misshapen by hard work and an inadequate diet, filthy because sanitation in their tenements was unheard of—they soon lost interest. He didn't care; he was grateful if they made a donation that might allow him to pay the rent for a week or two longer and buy a few more medicines, before they disappeared off the scene. Was Miss Hemingford any different?

Her look of tender concern had been genuine enough, but it had been mixed with a steely determination that made him smile. Perhaps that was the clue to why she had not married; she was too dictatorial. But did she have any idea of what she was at? If she came back herself instead of simply sending Tildy's mother, then he would know she was sincere. For the first time he became aware of his stained shirt and untidy hair. He never seemed to have time to visit the barber and though he changed his shirt every day, it was soon grubby again. He promised himself to make time to have his hair cut.

Anne hurried through the waiting room, more crowded than ever, and out into the narrow lane, breathing deeply. It was not only the strange smells: a mixture of blood, sweat, putrefaction and harsh soap, which had been overpowering, but the whole atmosphere of the place and the demeanour of the man who ran it. He had had a powerful effect on her. Not since she was a seventeen-year-old had any man made her shake like she was shaking now, with embarrassment that he might have detected it, with anger that he could be so cool towards her and with the feeling that she was being pitched into something over which she had no control. And *that* had not happened in a very long time. She had always been in control of herself, her life, even of her grandfather and he was an earl, so why should a tiny little girl and a strange man take that away?

If she had met him in someone's upper-class drawing room, dressed in pantaloons and morning coat with pristine starched cravat and his hair carefully coiffured, she would have taken him for a gentleman. He was educated and self-assured, but at the same time he seemed oblivious of his good looks and certainly unconcerned about his clothes. His cravat was unstarched and was nothing but a simple knot and his shirt was spotted with blood. It was evident his work was the most important thing in his life. Was he married, she wondered, and how could a wife compete with such dedication?

Back on the sea front, it took only a few minutes to find some steps down to the beach, where she picked her way over the shingle to where the bathing huts were lined up. Many of the contraptions were already in the water, but Anne approached the first one on the sands. 'I am looking for Mrs Smith,' she told the attendant.

'We take it in turns, ma'am,' she was told. ''Tis fairer that way. If you want to take a dip…'

'No, you misunderstand. I am looking for Mrs Smith, the mother of little Tildy. Her daughter has been involved in an accident…'

'Oh, tha's different.' She looked over the water to one where one of the women stood waiting to help her customer back into the hut. 'Martha, this 'ere lady says your Tildy's met with an accident.' Her voice easily carried and the woman hurried out, holding her arms above the surf as she waded back to dry land.

'What's 'appened to 'er, what's 'appened to my Tildy?' she demanded breathlessly. 'Where is she?'

Almost before Anne had finished explaining what had happened, Mrs Smith had asked her colleague to see to her customer and was off up the beach to the promenade with Anne at her heels. She burst breathlessly into the waiting room where Mrs Armistead was conducting the next patient into the surgery. 'Where's my little girl? Where's Tildy?'

Mrs Armistead pointed along the corridor and the distraught woman rushed off to the back region of the house, still followed by Anne.

Tildy was lying on the couch playing with a rag doll. A little colour had returned, but the white bandage made her head look enormous. Mrs Smith rushed over and fell to her knees beside her. 'Tildy, Tildy, what 'ave you bin up to now?' She leaned back to look at the little girl. 'I'll whip that Tom within an inch of 'is life, so I will.'

'Weren't 'is fault, Ma. Pa fetched 'im.'

'Why? Your pa knows Tom 'as to mind you. And even if he left you, you should 'ave stayed at 'ome.'

'I know, but 'e said they'd caught a monster and I wanted to see it.' Catching sight of Anne, she smiled. ''Allo, lady. Ma, tha's the lady what picked me up.'

Mrs Smith turned to Anne, who realised she had misjudged the woman; she evidently cared very deeply about her child. She was, Anne realised, young, younger than Anne herself, and thin as a reed. Once she had been beautiful, but the hard life she led, out on the beach, prey to wind and salt spray, had darkened and coarsened her complexion. But her eyes were a brilliant blue. 'I thank you, ma'am, with all me 'eart.'

'Think nothing of it. Do you think you can manage? I mean, you do not think Tildy should go to hospital?'

'No, I don't. People who go in there, come out with more trouble than they went in with, *if* they come out at all. I'll look after her.'

'But don't you have to go to work?'

'Tildy is more important. We shall just 'ave to 'ope her pa finds the shoals until she's well enough.'

'He's a fisherman?'

'Yes.'

Anne fished in her reticule and found a guinea and some small change. 'Will this help?'

'Only if you want to buy fish with it. I don't tek charity.'

'No, of course not. Very well, sell me fish; lobsters and crabs and anything else that's going. And if there's change, I'll take a dip in the sea and so will my aunt.'

'I should give you the fish for your help, not sell it,' the woman said doubtfully.

Tildy had been listening to this and could not keep quiet a moment longer. 'She could buy the monster.'

Anne laughed. 'I don't think I should know how to cook a monster.'

She turned as Dr Tremayne came into the room, rather like a whirlwind, all blow and hurry, his hair in more disarray than ever, but it made no difference, Anne's heart began to jump in her throat and it was all she could do to maintain an outward show of composure.

'You found her, then?' he queried.

'Yes.' She held his glance, searching his face. His brown eyes told of something she could not quite fathom; it might have been weariness, but it was more than that—sadness or bitterness perhaps. Was it because of the horrors of what he had seen as a doctor, frustration for the ills of the poor people he treated, which one man alone could not cure, or something in his past? Whatever it was made her feel uncomfortable, as if she were responsible. 'I must go, my aunt will be wondering what has become of me, I only meant to be out an hour or so.' She paused. 'I shall arrange to make a donation as soon as I can.'

'Thank you.' He did not know what else to say. He had misjudged her, but what did it matter if he had? He was merely a physician struggling against the odds in the poorest part of the community and she was a woman of means, that was obvious. Once he might have been her equal, not any more.

'Where shall the fish be sent?' Mrs Smith asked.

Anne gave her the address, wondering what cook would say when she was presented with a week's supply of fish all at once. She could not remember if her aunt was fond of fish, though they had both enjoyed the turbot the night before. She turned to Tildy. 'Goodbye, Tildy. Be a good girl now, and when you are better, perhaps your mama will bring you to see me.' She kissed the child's forehead, smiled at Mrs Smith, who tried to thank her, then held out her hand to the doctor. 'Goodbye, Dr Tremayne. I shall tell my friends of your good work. It deserves to be recognised.'

'Thank you.'

She retreated hastily before she could let herself down by telling him she hoped they would meet again, which would have been far too bold. She hurried from the house and made her way home as briskly as she could.

Justin Tremayne watched until the door had closed on her, then turned to Mrs Smith. 'Look after that child, madam. She needs rest and…' He stopped. What was the good of telling her she also needed good food? 'Send for me if you have the slightest cause for concern. Head wounds can be funny things. She was lucky Miss Hemingford brought her here so quickly.'

'I know, sir, I know.' She opened her palm to show the coins Anne had given her. 'How much do I owe you?'

'Nothing,' he said. 'You spend that on a good dinner.'

She thanked him and picked up the little girl. He put his finger out to touch the child under the chin and for a moment his eyes softened. 'Take care.'

'You're a fool,' Mrs Armistead said, as soon as they had gone. 'You can't live on air, you know.'

'Neither can they. And Miss Hemingford has promised a donation, so we can carry on a little longer.'

He only hoped she had meant it. After all, she had promised to return with Tildy's mother and she had done that and perhaps that meant she was the exception to the rule and was a young lady who kept her word. If and when the donation arrived, he would write and thank her for it, which was only courtesy, after all, and then perhaps… He shook himself and went back to his surgery to call in the next patient.

Chapter Two

'What am I supposed to do with it?' Mrs Bartrum asked. She and Anne and the cook were looking in dismay at a box full of mackerel, herring, whitebait, crab and lobster that had been dumped on the kitchen table.

'I never ordered it,' Mrs Carter said, in an aggrieved voice. 'Why would I ask for that amount unless you were going to hold a supper party and you didn't say anything to me about any such thing, ma'am.'

'No, Mrs Carter, I had no plans for one.'

'The boy who brought it insisted he had come to the right address and he wouldn't take it away again.'

'No, I don't suppose he would,' Anne said, trying to stifle her amusement. 'It is a gift to me.'

'A gift? Whatever for?' her aunt demanded. 'Who do you know in Brighton to give you a gift, and such an extraordinary one as this?'

Anne, who had slipped into the house the day before and changed her bloodstained clothes before joining her aunt, had not seen fit to tell her about the previous day's encounter. She didn't know why she had said nothing; it was not in her nature to keep secrets, but her meeting with Dr Tremayne had been so disturbing she wanted to keep it to herself, at least until she had analysed why he had made her heart beat so fast. If she had been young and silly, she might have said she had fallen in love with him on the spot, but she was not young and silly and so it must surely have another cause.

Her aunt was looking at her, expecting an answer, and so she was obliged to explain that she had helped the child of a local fisherman and this was his way of saying thank you. 'She was hurt in an accident with a curricle. I took her to a doctor and went in search of her mother,' she said.

'I can see the child would need help,' her aunt said. 'But were there no gentlemen about who could have done so? It is unseemly for you to be associating with common fishermen.'

'I never met the fisherman, Aunt, only his wife. She is a hard-working woman who wanted to reward me…'

'Surely you can do a good turn without being rewarded?'

'Of course I can, but it would have hurt her pride to refuse. I didn't realise she would actually send it, nor so much. I thought she would probably forget the minute I had left.'

'So now we have a box of fish that we cannot possibly eat before it goes bad.'

'If we knew anyone to invite, we could give a supper party,' Anne said.

'You are right,' her aunt said suddenly. 'I think it is time we began our social calls. Mrs Carter, take some of the fish for yourself and give some to the other servants and find a tasty recipe to use the rest. It gives us very little time, but a supper party it will have to be. Come, Anne, change your dress. We will call on Lady Mancroft first.'

Her ladyship had taken a house in St James's Place, not far from the homes of the elite who occupied the houses in the vicinity of the Pavilion. She was 'at home', which meant her elegant drawing room was filled with friends and those newly arrived in the town, like Mrs Bartrum and Anne. She was a tall, heavily built woman, wearing a diaphanous high-waisted gown in a pea-green colour over a slip of darker green and a matching satin turban with three tall feathers fastened to it with a jewelled pin.

'Georgiana!' she cried when she saw Mrs Bartrum. 'So you are back in society.' Being so tall, she had to bend to kiss Aunt Bartrum's cheek and then stood back to appraise her. 'You are looking well. I declare widow's weeds become you, which they don't everyone, to be sure. What brings you to Brighton?'

Mrs Bartrum looked suitably doleful at the mention of her mourning, but quickly recovered. 'I have brought my niece for a visit. She has not been here before and needed a little diversion.' She took Anne's hand and drew her forward. 'May I present Miss Hemingford.'

Lady Mancroft lifted her quizzing glass to peer at Anne. 'Granddaughter of the late Earl of Bostock, aren't you?'

'Yes, my lady.'

'Not in mourning?' There was a hint of reproof in her voice.

'Grandfather expressly forbade it. It was his dying wish.'

'But that doesn't mean the poor girl is not grieving,' Mrs Bartrum put in quickly 'She looked after him dutifully and I believe she deserves a little respite.'

'Then we shall have to do our best to amuse you both. Now, let me introduce you to everyone.'

She led them round the company, naming everyone and explaining who they were in relation to the aristocrats of the day—the cousin of a duke, the daughter of a marquis, a baronet, a banker with no claim to fame except his enormous wealth, Sir Somebody-or-Other, Lady This and Miss That—so that in the end Anne's head was reeling. She supposed she would remember them all given time.

'And here is my son, Charles,' her ladyship said, pulling on the sleeve of a Hussar major who was in animated conversation with another gentleman. 'Charles, come and say how d'you do to Mrs Bartrum. You remember we met her when we went up to the Lakes on a walking tour.'

He turned and bowed. He was a tall man of about seven and thirty, with a shock of blond curls and pale blue eyes. 'Your obedient, ma'am. It was several years ago, but I do remember how gracious and hospitable you were.'

Mrs Bartrum acknowledged this flummery with a smile. 'This is Miss Hemingford,' she said, drawing Anne forward. 'Bostock's sister.'

Her aunt's mention of her relationship to the Earl of Bostock brought home to Anne very forcefully that Harry was now the Earl and her grandfather was no more. It saddened her, but she managed a warm smile. 'Good afternoon, Major.'

He executed a flourishing leg. It was, Anne noted, a well-shaped leg clad in the blue pantaloons of the 10th Hussars, the Prince of Wales's own regiment. She was reminded of the curricle that had knocked over Tildy Smith; the driver of that had been wearing the same uniform, but she realised almost at once that Major Mancroft was not the man. 'Your obedient, Miss Hemingford,' he said. 'May I present my good friend, Captain Gosforth?'

The man he had been conversing with gave Anne a low bow. He was dressed in a brown frockcoat and biscuit-coloured trousers, held down by a strap under his shoe. He had a rugged complexion, gingery hair and hazel eyes, full of good humour. After the usual civilities had been exchanged with Mrs Bartrum, he asked, 'Have you taken to the water yet, ladies?'

'No,' Mrs Bartrum answered him. 'But we are planning to do so.'

'Nothing like it for effecting a cure,' he said.

'A cure for what?' Anne asked.

'Oh, almost anything. Gout, the ague, stomach disorders, consumption, flux…'

'I do not have any of those things, Captain.' It was said with a smile and a twinkle in the eye.

'No, naturally not. I did not mean—'

'I think you are being gammoned, Walter,' the Major put in. 'But taking a dip is not only a cure, Miss Hemingford, it is very invigorating.'

'Then we shall certainly attempt it,' Mrs Bartrum said. She turned to speak to Lady Mancroft. 'I am having an informal supper party tomorrow evening, just a small affair with a hand or two of whist afterwards. It is short notice, I know, but perhaps you and Lord Mancroft might care to come? And you, Major Mancroft and Captain Gosforth.'

'Who's your cook?' boomed Lord Mancroft. He was a very big man, not only in height but in breadth, and had a vast belly.

If Mrs Bartrum was taken aback by the question, she did not show it. 'Her name is Mrs Carter, my lord. She came highly recommended and so far I cannot fault her…'

'Mrs Carter, eh. Then you may expect us. I would give up supper with the Regent for one of her dinners. How did you manage to acquire her?'

'Our agent hired her.'

'We have a French chef,' Lady Mancroft explained. 'And he will brook no interference, otherwise we might have tried to add her to our staff…'

'I'll wager Mrs Carter would not have gone,' Anne whispered to her aunt behind her fan.

Mrs Bartrum, prompted by Lady Mancroft, included Mrs Barry and her two daughters, Annabelle and Jeanette, Sir Gerald Sylvester, an acquaintance of Lord Mancroft, and Lieutenants Cawston and Harcourt, both officers of the 10th Hussars.

'That's settled then,' Mrs Bartrum said, and, after bidding goodbye to the company, she and Anne took their leave.

'We shall have to live up to Mrs Carter's reputation now,' Anne said as they strolled home. 'Will the fish be enough?'

'In quantity there is no doubt of it, but we cannot feed them on fish and nothing else. We will have to have a roast or two and a chicken dish, boiled ham and several sweets.'

'You did say it was to be informal.'

'So it shall be. Small, select and exquisitely cooked. I will not have Mrs Carter compared unfavourably with a French chef. And they do say the way to a man's heart is through his stomach.'

Anne stopped in mid-stride and turned to face her aunt. 'Which man?'

'Oh, there are several possibles. Did you not find Major Mancroft very handsome?'

'He was not ill looking, but…'

'Oh, I know he is only the son of a baron, for all the superior airs Lord Mancroft assumes, but you have left it a little late to catch a true aristocrat…'

'*Too* late, my dear aunt. I told you I did not want you to find me a husband.'

'I am not. But if one should appear, we should not look a gift horse in the mouth.'

Anne laughed. 'But Major Mancroft is not a horse.'

'No, but you know what I mean. I am simply pointing out the possibilities. And there is Captain Gosforth. He was a naval captain, you know. Widowed…'

'How do you know?'

'I made it my business to find out. His wife died some years ago while he was away at sea. They had no children. He was invalided out at the beginning of the war and is now a gentleman farmer…'

'You mean one who does not get his hands dirty or his boots muddy except on the hunting field.'

'Of course he would not. Anne, how provoking you are. You know I would never think of inviting a yokel to supper. He is related to Lord Downland, I think, though I am not sure of the exact relationship, but he is perfectly acceptable.'

'Maybe he has his sights elsewhere.'

'With you in the room, no single man has any business looking elsewhere.'

Anne burst out laughing and hugged her aunt's arm as they continued their walk. 'Oh, Aunt Georgie, you are as good as any medicine.' And suddenly she was remembering Dr Tremayne again. Was he single? Surely a man as dedicated and busy as he was would need a wife to help him? She had at first thought Mrs Armistead was his wife until he had addressed her by name and in a voice that one would use to a servant, so she supposed she was his housekeeper or perhaps a nurse to help with his patients, but one who also made sure he had regular meals.

One thing was certain, he was not afraid to dirty his hands, nor his clothes come to that, and he had spent five minutes in the same room with her before he had even deigned to notice her. He had a hard outer crust, but that was assumed, she was sure of it, because when he was dealing with Tildy, his whole expression had changed and his eyes had softened and become full of concern. Like her, he loved children. She smiled; it was a good thing her aunt did not know what was occupying her thoughts at that moment.

'Why are you smiling?'

'I was thinking of Lord Mancroft's praise of Mrs Carter,' she fibbed. 'She must be famous in Brighton.'

'Judging by the size of his lordship's waist, I would say he was an expert in culinary appreciation, wouldn't you?'

'Oh, no doubt of it,' Anne laughed, then added, 'Shall

we take a dip tomorrow? Mrs Smith, the mother of that little girl, is a bathing attendant and she said she would look out for us.'

'You seem to have found out a lot about her in a short time, Anne.' There was a note of censure in her voice and Anne found herself on the defensive.

'Not at all. I know very little. The child told us her mother worked on the beach, so I went in search of her. The husband is a fisherman and there is also a boy called Tom. I imagine it was he who brought the fish to us. Tom was supposed to be looking after Tildy while his mother worked, but he went off to help his father.' She laughed suddenly. 'He had apparently caught a monster.'

'A monster? What kind of monster?'

'I have no idea. I assumed it was a larger-than-usual fish.'

'Well, it is of no moment,' her aunt said. 'You did what you could to help them and that should be an end of it.'

'I would dearly like to know who that officer was driving the curricle. How anyone can run down a child and carry on as if nothing untoward had happened I do not know. It was wicked. He might have killed her.'

'Anne, I know you have a tender heart and I would not have you any other way, but you cannot fight everyone's battles for them. Put it from your mind. You are here to enjoy yourself.'

Anne did try to put it from her mind, but whatever she was doing, the memory of that tiny child lying unconscious in the road kept intruding, and when she wasn't thinking of Tildy, she was thinking of Dr Tremayne and, try as she might, she could not banish him. Perhaps if she were to see him again, she might realise that he was not an Adonis, nor clever, just a very ordinary man, not even a gentleman, a physician who worked among the poor because he was not good enough to minister to the rich and earn the substantial fees they were prepared to pay. But that did not mean she could not sympathise with his work. And she had promised a donation. Instead of sending it through a third party as she had intended, she would take it herself when she could get away from her aunt without arousing suspicion. She had a feeling that Aunt Bartrum would not approve.

The remainder of the day was spent in making plans for the supper party. Her aunt drew her into every decision, from the bill of fare and the wine, to the table decorations and the clothes they should wear. Mrs Bartrum would be dressed in unrelieved black, but the gown she chose was of silk, elegantly cut with a low décolletage and deep satin ruching round the hem and it fitted her slight form to perfection. Widow or not, she was still a very attractive woman. But Anne's choice was another matter. 'Let me see what you have brought with you,' her aunt said.

She was sitting on Anne's bed, while Amelia pulled gowns out of the cupboard and her trunk, which had not yet been fully unpacked. Anne had never been one for finery; living at Sutton Park with her grandfather, she rarely needed to dress up and only when she went to London for the Season, did she bother about her wardrobe. She had not done so this year, so it had not been replenished, except for the two ball gowns her aunt had insisted on buying when they were passing through London. 'There are at least two balls every week in Brighton,' she had told her.

'And you never know, if the Prince is in residence, he might invite us to the Pavilion.'

'I do not think I should like to go.'

'Me neither, but an invitation is a royal command and we would have no choice.'

'In that case we will avoid anyone with any connection to the royal gentleman.'

But it was not ball gowns that interested her now, but something to wear for their supper party when she hoped Anne would make a lasting impression on the single gentlemen present. 'Black, grey, mauve, dark blue,' her aunt intoned as the gowns were brought out for her approval. 'Have you nothing with any colour in it?'

'Grandfather has been gone less than a month, Aunt, and I cannot, in all conscience, wear bright colours. Besides, they do not become me…'

'Well, this dove-grey crepe will have to do. You can dress it up with lace and silk flowers. We will go out this afternoon and see what the shops have to offer.'

Anne, who had been used to being independent and doing things her own way, felt as though she were losing control of her life. If she were not careful, her aunt would have her married off to the first eligible man who showed an interest. The difficulty was that Aunt Bartrum was such a dear, so well meaning and unselfish, she would be bound to be offended if her niece appeared awkward. There was nothing for it but to go along with her until something happened that meant she would have to stand her ground, then she would have to be firm.

They rose early the next morning and set off for the beach accompanied by Susan and Amelia to help them undress and to look after their clothes while they were in the sea. Mrs Bartrum was complaining good humouredly about having to rise before half the town had even been to bed, but Anne, who loved the time just after dawn when the birds were singing and few people were about, simply laughed and said she would be able to catch up on her sleep that afternoon before their guests began to arrive.

The tide was out when they reached the beach and they picked their way carefully over the newly washed shingle to the bathing machines, some of which were already in the water, and others were drawn up in a line, each with its attendant. Anne, seeing Mrs Smith, made her way over to her. 'How is Tildy?' she asked her.

'She is on the mend, ma'am, thank you for asking. She had a real bad headache for a time, but it passed and the wound is healing. I'm right thankful you came along when you did.'

'I did nothing, Mrs Smith. It was Dr Tremayne who did most.'

'Oh, yes, ma'am. The man's a saint, he never turns anyone away and he hardly ever takes money for what he does. I don't know what us poor folks would do without him.'

'Then you must be very thankful for him and hope he continues for a long time to come.' She was aware of her aunt standing beside her, drinking in the conversation, and knew she would be in for a quizzing later.

'We pray for that, ma'am, but he has to rely on what people give him to carry on. I believe he is finding it 'ard.'

'We shall have to see what can be done to help,' Anne said, smiling at the woman. 'And talking about giving, I want to thank you for that box of fish. But there was no need to send so much.'

'Course there was. Tildy is worth more 'n a box of fish to me. Besides, you pai—'

She was not allowed to finish before Anne stopped her. 'Mrs Smith, my aunt and I would like to take a dip in the sea, would you tell us what we have to do?'

The woman called the next of her colleagues in the line to look after Mrs Bartrum while she served Anne. They were each given a brown cotton gown and climbed into the huts with their maids to help them undress. Anne put on the shapeless garment and tied it with a cord round the waist and set a mob cap over her hair, before calling out that she was ready. The horse set off at a steady plod pulling the hut over the wet shingle and into the sea. 'How deep do you wish to go?' Mrs Smith asked.

'Deep enough to immerse myself totally, if you please.'

When the hut came to a stop, facing the English Channel, the door was opened and Anne realised that all but the top two steps had disappeared into the water. Gingerly she stepped down, feeling with her toes and hanging on to Mrs Smith, who led her down. The water was icy cold and made her gasp. 'It's freezing.'

'It always feels cold when you first go in. You will not notice it after a minute or two,' Mrs Smith said. 'Best thing is to get in quickly.'

It was what she had done as a child when bathing in the river at Sutton Park with Harry and Jane, but she could not remember it being as cold as this. She jumped off the last few steps, letting out a single shriek as the cold water hit her almost bare flesh, felt her dress balloon around her, then settle about her body. The more genteel ladies simply stayed under the cover of the hood, but that was not enough for Anne; she struck out towards her aunt's machine. 'It's lovely,' she called. 'Come on in.'

Aunt Bartrum was a little timid and did not venture far from the safety of the bathing machine where she was hidden, but Anne set out for deeper water, where a few hardy heads bobbed above the surface. As a child she had done everything her brother had done, climbing trees, riding, shooting, swimming; Grandfather had often said she was as much of a boy as Harry was. He had warned her, and so had Amelia in later years, that men did not like women who excelled in physical outdoor pursuits, but she did not see why she should curb her pleasures simply to attract a man. If she took a husband, he would have to love her for what she was. The thought that she might even consider marriage took her by surprise. Was her aunt already wearing her down? She would be silly to allow that, it could only lead to disappointment.

'Miss Hemingford?'

Startled, she looked up to see the disembodied head of Dr Tremayne not six feet away, his wet hair springing into tight curls all over his head. Treading water, he lifted a bare arm in greeting, making her wonder what he was wearing; the water was not clear enough to see, for which she was grateful. Even thinking about it made her heart beat at an alarming rate. 'Dr Tremayne, fancy seeing you here.'

'I am here most mornings. I find it refreshing before the rigours of the day.' He laughed suddenly. 'At least, I begin the day clean.'

'And cleanliness is next to Godliness, so I am told,' she said, treading water beside him.

'I do not know about that, but what I do know is that dirt spreads contagion and disease and it behoves me to set a good example.'

She was aware that this was not the sort of conversation a well-bred young lady should be having with a man, certainly not in their present state of undress, but she could not bring herself to turn away from him. He fascinated her. 'Oh, I am sure you do.'

'You are a long way from the beach, Miss Hemingford,' he said, looking back towards the bathing huts. 'Should you have come so far? The tide can be very strong…'

'I am a good swimmer, Dr Tremayne. Have no fear, you will not be obliged to rescue me.' She laughed, but he did not respond and she wondered if he ever smiled. 'I—I can keep going for hours.'

'You do say.' His tone was amused, almost disbelieving.

'I do and, to prove it, I will race you to that rock.' Before he could respond, she was off, cleaving powerfully through the water.

He kept up with her stroke for stroke, and it was not until they reached the rock that she realised she could not clamber out because what had been a shapeless garment when she put it on, would have a very definite shape now, clinging to every curve of her body: breasts, hips, legs.

'I must return to my aunt,' she called out to him, making for the shore. 'She will be wondering what has become of me.'

'And I must return to my patients. Good day to you, Miss Hemingford.'

He swam away from her towards a cove below the cliffs and she could see he was wearing breeches, but nothing else. Even in the cool water, she felt herself going hot. She turned and swam back to where Mrs Bartrum floundered in three feet of water. Her aunt was not alone.

Major Mancroft was beside her, wearing a loose-fitting jacket and trousers of the same rough cotton as her dress, which was a relief, for she had heard that the men often swam naked. 'Miss Hemingford, good morning,' he called as she approached. 'I have been endeavouring to persuade your aunt into deeper water.'

'No, no,' the lady said, thoroughly embarrassed. 'I am perfectly at ease here.'

'Madam, you will become cold if you do not move around a little,' he said, moving closer. 'Pray, let me assist you. Take my hand. There is nothing to worry about. We are unobserved from the shore and no one thinks anything of it when ladies and gentleman meet in the water. It has a calming influence, you know.'

Anne laughed. 'Is that another of its cures?'

Her aunt was shivering. 'I think I have been in the water long enough for a first encounter,' she said, turning back to the bathing machine where Susan waited at the top of the steps with a large towel. 'I will dress and wait for you on the promenade. Do not hurry, if you are enjoying yourselves.' And with that she disappeared under the hood.

'I, too, have had enough for my first dip,' Anne told the Major, making for the machine she had been using, glad of the shelter of the canvas hiding her as she climbed the steps and hurried inside.

The horse was put back into the shafts and the little vehicle was pulled up on to dry land, and half an hour later she stepped down, fully dressed again and feeling thoroughly refreshed. She would come again if the weather remained calm.

When she regained the promenade, she discovered Major Mancroft, once more in uniform, had arrived before her and was sitting on a bench talking to her aunt. 'Ah, Miss Hemingford, I thought I would wait and escort you home. I am not on duty today.' He rose and offered both arms and the ladies took one each and strolled along the sea front, talking easily as they went, with Amelia and Susan falling in behind them.

'Did you see service in the Peninsula, Major?' Mrs Bartrum asked.

'Alas, no. I am on the staff, which is why I am in Brighton at the moment. In case his Highness needs me.'

'Is he in residence?'

'He is expected, I believe.'

'And does Lady Mancroft come to Brighton every year?'

'Almost ever year. My father finds sea water very efficacious for his gout, you know. He drinks it with milk every day.' And when Anne pulled a face, added, 'I believe there are other ingredients, even more unappetising.'

'I think I will confine myself to bathing in it,' she said.

'I agree wholeheartedly. Perhaps we shall meet in the water again before long.'

'Perhaps,' she agreed, thinking of Dr Tremayne.

He declined an invitation to come in for refreshment when they arrived, saying his mother was expecting him, but he looked forward to having supper with them that evening, and with that he bowed and departed.

'He really is most agreeable,' her aunt said, as they divested themselves of their outer garments and went to the morning room for a light nuncheon. 'But I was mortified when he approached me in the water. I am quite sure that it is not the thing, for all he says people think nothing of it. No doubt he thinks he has stolen a march on his friend Gosforth. If they see themselves as rivals, it could make our stay very interesting.'

'Rivals, Aunt?' Anne teased. 'You mean for your hand?'

'Do not be ridiculous, Anne. How can you say such a thing? I am a widow and shall remain one to the end of my days. It was your hand I was thinking of.'

'You promised not to matchmake.'

'Nor will I. There is no need, the gentlemen will come flocking.'

'If you are right, they will be torn between my fortune and your sweet nature.'

'Then we shall have some fun, shan't we?' Her aunt, mischievous as always, laughed.

After they had eaten, Mrs Bartrum declared that bathing in the sea had made her tired and she wanted to be at her very best for the supper party, so she proposed to lie on her bed for an hour or two and suggested Anne do the same. But Anne was full of energy; besides, she had a secret mission she wanted to accomplish. She waited until her aunt's bedroom door had closed and Amelia had settled down in the parlour to stitch the lace and flowers on her evening gown, then left the house to visit the bank where Harry had arranged she could draw on funds as she needed them. She drew a hundred guineas in cash and, weighed down by the clinking coins, set off for Doctor Tremayne's house.

The waiting room was as crowded as ever and she wondered if she was wrong to interrupt him at his work, but when Mrs Armistead told him she was there, he instructed the woman to conduct her to his private room at the back of the house and he would be with her as soon as he could.

Mrs Armistead led her to a small drawing room, bade her be seated and asked if she would like refreshments, but Anne declined. 'I can see you are very busy,' she said. 'I shall be quite content to wait until the doctor can see me.'

'Do you wish to consult him? There is no need for you to come here; he would visit you at home.'

'Oh, I am not ill, Mrs Armistead, I never felt better. But you may recall I promised a donation. And to tell the truth, I am fascinated by the doctor's work and should like to know more.'

'I am sure he will be happy to accommodate you.' It was said a little stiffly and Anne realised she had sounded pompous, as if she meant to inspect the place before handing over money; that was not what she intended at all. But before she could put matters right, the woman had excused herself and disappeared.

Anne looked round the room. It was very small and ill

furnished with two stuffed chairs whose arms were worn, a table that had once been highly polished but was now stained and dull, some dining chairs and a bookcase. She rose to inspect the titles of the books it contained. The doctor's taste in reading was broad to say the least. There were medical tomes, philosophical works, books on flora and fauna, tales of the sea, books of poetry and the novels of Sir Walter Scott and even two of Jane Austen's. She was leafing through a treatise on the efficacy of sea water when the door opened behind her and Justin Tremayne entered.

The books and the room itself faded from her vision as she turned to face him. He had retrieved his coat and put it on, but otherwise he looked just as he had on their first meeting. He was every bit as handsome, his brown eyes just as cold, his jaw just as firm, but his swim seemed to have done him little good; he looked so thin and tired, she had an unexpected urge to mother him, to make him sit down and rest and provide him with nourishing food. His opening words soon disabused her of the idea he was an overgrown child.

'Madam, I understand you wish to inspect my premises. The two rooms in which I work and the kitchen you have already seen on your earlier visit, and now you have had time to look round the drawing room. There is nothing else but my bedroom. Do you wish to see that? I have to tell you the bed is probably unmade and my garments strewn about—' He stopped abruptly when he noticed the look of astonishment on her face.

'Dr Tremayne, you quite mistake the matter. I have no wish to inspect your premises, much less intrude on your domestic arrangements. My interest is purely in the work you do. I admire it greatly and would like to do something to help.'

He bowed, unsmiling. 'My apologies, ma'am.'

'Oh, please, do not call me ma'am, it makes me sound so old.' It was said with a friendly smile that quite unnerved him. He had taken her for an interfering do-gooder who wanted to take over his charitable work and run it for her own gratification, but perhaps he had been wrong.

'Miss Hemingford, I beg your pardon. Please be seated.' He picked up a little brass bell and rang it vigorously. 'I will ask Mrs Armistead to bring us some tea.'

'Only if you were planning to stop for some yourself. I have no wish to take you from your work.'

'He needs to take a rest, Miss Hemingford.' Mrs Armistead had come quickly in answer to the bell and had heard her last remark. 'I have great trouble making him stop to eat at all.'

'Tea, please, Janet,' he said wearily. 'And some of those little biscuits you made yesterday.'

'You look tired,' Anne said, as Mrs Armistead left them. She seated herself in one of the stuffed chairs, knowing he would not sit himself unless she did. 'Could you not take on some help?'

'If I could find someone who would work for nothing, I would gladly do so,' he said, collapsing in a heap in the other chair. 'But as no one is prepared to do that, I struggle on alone.'

'Why do you do it?'

'Now there's a question!' His expression was lightened with a genuine smile. 'I suppose because the work is there, crying out to be done, and someone ought to do it. Brighton is full of wealthy people, aristocrats many of them, able to pay handsomely for medical treatment for whatever ailments their imaginations conjure up, so it attracts the ambitious physician out to make his mark in the world, but they are not the only ones to fall ill. The poor are suffering too. Their ailments, unlike those of the rich, are often the result of too little food and not over-indulgence—' He stopped, realising he was almost certainly talking to one of the wealthy upper class he was denigrating. 'I beg your pardon, you do not want to hear this.'

'Indeed I do.' He had a mellifluous speaking voice that she could have listened to for hours, whatever he had to say. She ignored the other voice, the one in her head, which told her she should not be holding a conversation with a man, not even a gentleman, alone in his rooms. She was independent enough and old enough to do as she pleased. And though Aunt Bartrum would not approve, Aunt Bartrum need never know.

Mrs Armistead brought in the tea tray and withdrew, saying she had some cleaning up to do in the waiting room, if they were to be ready for the second onslaught in the evening. When she had gone, Anne offered to pour the tea and he nodded agreement.

'How did you come into this work, Dr Tremayne?' she asked as she handed him a cup of tea and sat down again with one for herself.

'Believe it or not, I was a naval surgeon until two years ago when I sustained a wound that forced me to leave the service. I needed something to make me feel wanted and useful and set up practice here in Brighton.'

So that was the reason for the limp, though it did not seem to incapacitate him unduly. 'Why Brighton?'

He shrugged, unwilling to explain he had simply been wandering up and down the south coast, wanting to be near the sea, but unsure where to settle. He could not go home to Devon; home was where his brother was. And Sophie. He did not want to see them and he was equally sure they did not want to see him.

'I was visiting the town and saw the need,' he told Anne. 'A child, very like little Tildy, had been attacked by a dog on the beach and was badly mauled. Luckily it wasn't rabid. I did what I could for her and took her to hospital. Her injured face haunted me and when I discovered she had been sent out begging by her parents, I was incensed. I stormed off to visit them, but as soon as I met them, I realised they were not entirely to blame. They were both in the last stages of famine. The father had consumption and could not work and the mother had recently been delivered of another baby, which had not survived, and she had the fever. There were two other children, both younger than the one I had treated. Two older ones were working in service, but they earned little more than their keep and were unable to send home more than coppers. That little girl was the breadwinner for the family.'

'And so you began a one-man crusade?'

'You could say that. I did what I could for them and that led to others seeking my help and so I started this practice and, before I had time to blink, I was overwhelmed with patients.' His smile was no more than a twitch of his lips, as if smiling was something he did not practise very often, but it was an attempt at one and she felt encouraged.

'Mrs Smith told me you never turned anyone away.'

'How can I, Miss Hemingford? I am a healer.'

'And do you rely totally on donations?'

'I have a naval pension and a small private income, but it is not enough. I beg, Miss Hemingford, that is what I do. I write letters to wealthy people, I write to the newspapers, I ask charitable organisations for donations and, on the few occasions I am called to treat someone who can well afford my services, I charge them an exorbitant fee. So far we have survived, but…' He shrugged expressively.

She put her teacup on the tray and opened her reticule to withdraw the bag of money she had brought with her. 'I thought you would prefer cash to a bill,' she said, laying it on the table.

'Thank you,' he said, making no move to pick it up and see how much it contained. It was acceptable, whatever the amount. 'You are very kind.'

'I wish I could do more. In fact, I intend to do more.'

'Miss Hemingford,' he said, looking perplexed, 'why?'

'For the same reason you have given me for what you do, because the need is there…'

'I wish others felt as you do. Most people think that if they pay their poor rates, they have done all that can be expected of them.'

'I am not most people, Dr Tremayne.'

'No.' She was most definitely not 'most people'; she had the face of an angel, the figure of a goddess, soft expressive eyes and a pink complexion, which was something rarely seen among the people he usually dealt with, who were raddled with illness and gaunt with hunger. He had no idea how old she was, but she was certainly no silly schoolgirl, but a self-possessed mature woman, as unlike Sophie as it was possible to be. Sophie, beautiful, spoiled, faithless Sophie, whom he had once loved. He pulled himself together; it was all in the past and he had since learned to live simply and concentrate on the problems each day brought.

So why did the woman who faced him now make him want to rush out and buy himself a new suit of clothes and a dozen cravats, so that he could meet her on equal terms? What a ninny he was! He had no money to buy suits, hardly had enough to buy a handkerchief. And in any case it was better spent on medicines and bandages. 'I am grateful for any help,' he said.

'I suppose taking on a pupil would not serve?'

'It would be better than nothing, but so far none has turned up. Those whose fathers can pay fees, do not like the long hours, the unhealthy environment in which most of my poor patients live and they are afraid of catching something…' He paused. 'Are you not afraid of that your-self, Miss Hemingford?'

'I enjoy the rudest of health.'

'I am glad to hear it. I should hate to think of anyone as lovely as you are, falling victim to any of the common diseases to be found in my waiting room.'

'Dr Tremayne!' She blushed crimson at the compliment.

'I beg your pardon. I am afraid I am too outspoken at times. You may blame living on board a man o' war and then among people who tend to say what is in their minds without troubling about convention.'

She smiled. 'You are forgiven.'

'I meant what I said.'

'In other words, you wish me anywhere but here.'

'Yes. No. Oh, dear, you are confusing me. Clever women always confuse me.'

She threw back her head and gave a joyous laugh. 'First I am lovely and now I am clever. You will quite turn my head, Dr Tremayne. I implore you to change the subject before I become too big for my boots.'

He looked down at her neat buttoned boots and realised they had cost more than he spent on housekeeping in a month. What did he think he was at, flirting with a lady of her calibre? Oh, he might have been able to hold his own a few years back, when he was still living at home, recognised for the gentleman he was, and even later when promotion was still a possibility, but not now. His poverty was all too apparent and she was only playing with him. He could imagine her going back to her fine friends and saying, 'I had the most extraordinary encounter with a strange pleb this afternoon…'

'I mean to try and find you an assistant,' she said, when he had been silent so long she wondered if he would ever speak again.

'And how do you propose to do that?'

She laughed. 'Pay him.'

'But you cannot do that. It would be a long-term commitment…'

'And do you think I am incapable of making such a commitment?'

'Not at all,' he said hurriedly. 'But I do not think pin money will suffice, unless—' He had been going to say unless she was extremely wealthy, but stopped himself in time; the state of her purse was no concern of his. 'Surely you have family and advisers looking after your money who have to approve the way you dispose of it?'

'None,' she said. 'I am a free agent and I have more than I shall ever be able to spend.'

So she was wealthy. He was not sure if he was glad or sorry for that. Apart from her name, he knew nothing else about her. Who was she? Where had she come from? How could a single woman as young as she was control her own money? Surely she was not one of those demireps who pranced about Brighton on the arms of their aristocratic lovers, glad to have risen above the lives they were born to? Was it conscience money she was offering? He did not want to believe that. For the first time in years, he found himself admiring a woman, but stopped himself before his foolishness let him down again. She was beautiful, but Sophie had been beautiful too and what had that signified except a cold, calculating heart.

'I think you should go away and think about this very carefully before you do something you might regret,' he said.

'Oh, I intend to. I shall make the most stringent enquiries, have no fear. You will not be burdened by a cabbage-head or an idler.'

'I was not referring to the assistant, Miss Hemingford.'

She rose to go. 'Oh, I know that, Dr Tremayne.' She laughed as she offered him her hand. 'But my mind is

made up and those who know me best will tell you I am
not easily diverted from my purpose.'

He could well believe that, he decided, as he took her
hand and raised it to his lips before going to the door and
opening it for her. He walked beside her down the corridor and passed the open door of the waiting room, already
filling up with new patients. 'You will be hearing from me
again,' she said. And without waiting for more protesta-
tions she stepped out into the street.

As soon as she turned the corner, she stopped and
leaned against a wall to stop her knees buckling under her.
Had she really had that extraordinary conversation? Had
she really promised to find him an assistant and pay his
wages? How, in heaven's name, was she going to do that?
She must be mad. She knew nothing about doctors or
their assistants or where they could be hired. And, as for
making stringent enquiries, she had no idea what questions to ask to verify an applicant's suitability. And inside
her, in the place where her conscience resided, she knew
it had all begun as a ploy to keep talking to him, to enjoy
his company, to look at that gaunt but handsome face and
to wonder what it would be like shining with health. She
had been imagining him among the people she associated
with, fashionably dressed, his hair trimmed, his cravat
starched, dancing with her at a ball, riding with her on the
Downs, accepted by her friends as a gentleman. She *was*
mad. Such a thing was not possible.

But that did not stop her from thinking about him and
his plight. All the way home, she turned the problem of
the assistant over in her mind. She had not come to a so-

lution when she entered the house, nor when she arrived in her room to find Amelia in a taking because she had been gone so long and it was time to dress for supper. 'Susan went to dress Mrs Bartrum an hour ago,' she said. 'And now there is no time to arrange your hair in the style we decided.'

Anne smiled and allowed herself to be dressed and have her hair coiled up on her head and fixed with two jewelled combs; she was hardly aware of Amelia's grumbling. Her mind was in an untidy room in a back street, drinking tea and making outrageous promises to a man who seemed to have mesmerised her.

Chapter Three

The first of the carriages drew up at the door as Anne went down to the drawing room and there was no time for Mrs Bartrum to question her niece about where she had been, for which Anne was thankful. She knew her aunt would be horrified to know she had been visiting a man—not even a gentleman—and been entertained alone in his room. If she knew Anne had given him money and promised more, she would have apoplexy, so it had to remain a secret. It was a pity, because Anne longed to tell someone about it and ask advice about hiring a doctor's assistant.

What, for instance, did an assistant do? Did he treat the sick himself or only do the menial tasks such as dosing someone for the ague or binding a cut finger? Any competent person could do that, surely? And how much were they paid? Would her bankers have something to say when she asked for a regular amount to be paid from her account every month? Would they insist on knowing why and investigating the recipient? Questions like that bred more questions, but she had to put them aside to stand beside her aunt and receive their guests.

Lord and Lady Mancroft arrived with the Major, magnificent in his regimental dress uniform, then the widowed Mrs Barry with Annabelle and Jeanette, whom she hoped someone would take off her hands before much longer. Lieutenants Cawston and Harcourt arrived on foot, followed by Sir Gerald Sylvester, who came in a cab. Sir Gerald, fifty if he was a day and thin as a bean pole, was got up in a dark blue evening suit, a blue shirt whose collar points grazed his cheeks and supported a pink starched cravat with an enormous bow. His waistcoat was heavily embroidered in rose and silver thread and his breeches were so tight fitting, Anne wondered if he would be able to sit, much less eat. Captain Gosforth arrived last, in a black evening suit, white shirt and brocade waistcoat, and hurried over to bow and make his apologies to his hostesses, which meant he was standing beside them when supper was announced.

'May I?' he asked, offering his arm to Mrs Bartrum.

Graciously she laid her fingers on his sleeve, leaving Anne to be escorted by Major Mancroft, who was quickly at her side. His parents followed and everyone else paired up to go into the dining room, the Barry girls with the two lieutenants and Mrs Barry with Sir Gerald. They all knew each other; indeed, it was Anne and her aunt who were the strangers to the company, but Anne did not mind that; it gave her the opportunity to observe their guests. None of them, she realised, was likely to be acquainted with a young physician looking for a first post. Such a being would be beneath their notice.

'I took your advice,' she said to Captain Gosforth as the soup was served by the two footmen her aunt had employed for the evening. 'I took a dip in the sea this morning.'

'And how did you find it?'

'Very refreshing. I shall certainly go again.'

'And did you see the commotion on the beach?' Lieutenant Cawston asked.

'No. Was there a commotion?'

'I was strolling along the sea front when I saw a crowd round a big white tent, so I wandered over to see the cause of it.' He paused, realising he had the attention of everyone. 'One of the fishermen had caught a large sea creature in his net and was preparing to make an exhibition of it, hence the tent. There was a notice on a board inviting the public to view the merman at tuppence a time.'

'Merman! There is no such thing!' Lord Mancroft scoffed. 'Nor mermaids either.'

'Oh, I don't know,' Walter Gosforth said. 'When I was sailing in the south seas, there were stories of strange sea creatures who were said to have the head and upper body of a human and the tail of a fish. They were supposed to lure sailors on to the rocks with their singing...'

'Oh, do you think the Brighton fishermen have really caught one?' Jeanette Barry asked, wide-eyed.

'Of course not,' her mother said. 'It is no doubt something they've constructed for gullible people to gape at.'

'I do not think they have constructed it,' Anne said. 'I heard about it yesterday from the child of the fisherman that caught it. She said it was a monster.'

They all turned to look at her and she began to wish

she had not spoken. 'You remember, Aunt, I told you about the little girl who was hurt.'

'Do tell us the tale,' Annabelle said. 'How did you come to be in conversation with a fisherman's daughter?'

Anne was obliged to tell the same story as she had related it to her aunt, which was not very exciting when all was said and done, certainly not to her listeners, who had no interest in the doctor to whom she had taken the little girl. 'We are indebted to the child's mother for the fish we are eating,' she said. 'She wanted to thank me and that was all she had to give.'

'So there really is some kind of strange creature on the beach,' Mrs Barry said.

'Yes, but it was not described to me as a mermaid or a merman, simply as a monster…'

'Probably a whale,' Major Mancroft said.

'But surely there are no whales off our coast and, if there were, would it not be too big for the fisherman's nets?' Anne asked. 'They would never be able to haul it aboard their vessel.'

'Only one thing for it,' Captain Gosforth said. 'We shall have to pay our tuppence to have our curiosity satisfied.'

'It's a trick,' Lady Mancroft said, wrinkling her long nose in distaste. 'A few hundred gullible people at tuppence each would line the pockets of those chawbacons very nicely, don't you think?'

'They are very poor,' Anne said mildly. 'Who can blame them for wanting to supplement their income?'

'Why not make an outing of it?' the Captain suggested. 'I shall be delighted to pay for everyone here to see it.'

'Then could we not take a picnic with us?' Annabelle suggested. 'We could find a quiet situation on the cliffs and the gentlemen could light a fire. It would be such fun.'

Everyone agreed enthusiastically. Mrs Bartrum, who was still wondering how to use up all the fish she had been given, offered to bring shrimps and herrings to be cooked over the fire, and that led Lady Mancroft to donate slices of cold roast beef and a side of ham and Mrs Barry to offer to bring orange jelly and her special biscuits, the recipe for which was a closely guarded family secret. 'And I will bring wine,' Major Mancroft offered. 'The mess has a particularly fine selection.' He paused. 'In case the Regent should arrive unexpectedly, you understand.'

'I will put my chaise at your disposal to convey the servants and hampers ahead of us,' Lord Mancroft added. 'Then, if any of the ladies feels disinclined to walk back, they may ride.'

And so it was settled, and all because of Mr Smith and his monster catch. Anne had taken no part in making the arrangements, she was happy to agree to whatever they decided; her thoughts were elsewhere. Talking of the fisherman and little Tildy had reminded her of Dr Tremayne, working away in his consulting rooms, dishevelled, hard up, caring and proud. Oh, she knew he was proud all right. In spite of his shabby room, his untidy clothes, his lack of proper equipment and medicines, he was a man who stood upright and looked you in the eye, even when admitting that he begged. He did not beg on his own behalf, but for those poor souls who had no one else to help them. He said he had been a ship's surgeon, but why had he gone to sea in the first place? Treating seamen wounded by war was very different from mending the heads of little girls and giving an old man medicine for a chronic cough. She *had* to see him again and learn more.

The rest of the meal passed in small talk: the doings of the Regent, hardly seen in public since he was so badly received at the victory celebrations earlier in the year: the peace talks going on in Vienna where the allies were carving Europe up between them; the fate of Napoleon, now banished to the remote island of St Helena, and the fear of riots and insurrection as the soldiers returned home to find there was no work for them. Anne wanted to hear more about that, but her aunt quickly suggested it was time for the ladies to withdraw and instead she found herself talking about the latest fashions over the teacups in the withdrawing room.

When the gentlemen joined them, the older members of the company sat down to whist while the younger ones were prevailed upon to sing or play. Walter Gosforth stood beside the piano to turn the page of music as Anne played her piece. 'Splendid, Miss Hemingford,' he said, when she finished and everyone applauded. 'I heard you had a prodigious talent and now I know it to be true.'

Anne laughed. 'No one but my aunt could have told you that, and I do believe she is biased.'

'She is a very vivacious lady. I did not like to ask, but how long has she been a widow?'

Anne looked at him sharply and smiled. 'Nearly two years, Captain. It was a very happy marriage…'

'Oh, I do not doubt it,' he murmured. 'Someone more agreeable than Mrs Bartrum would be difficult to find.'

'I could not agree more,' she said, hiding a smile. 'She

also has a very pleasant singing voice. Shall I prevail upon her to sing for us?'

'Oh, please do. I will be delighted to accompany her on the pianoforte.'

The whist game was drawing to a close. Lady Mancroft was gratified to have won and her rather haughty expression had softened. Anne approached the table and was in time to hear her aunt telling Major Mancroft that her niece had been laid very low by the old Earl's death, but she would soon be in spirits again. 'She is a considerable heiress,' she said. 'And very independent in mind and spirit, which cannot be altogether good for her. I think she needs someone to guide her, someone as strong as she is—' Seeing Anne, she stopped in mid-sentence.

'Aunt, we should be pleased if you would sing for us,' Anne said. stifling a desire to laugh at her aunt's less than subtle hints. 'Captain Gosforth has said he will accompany you.'

'In that case, of course I shall oblige. Major, do you take a turn about the room with Miss Hemingford.'

'Delighted,' he said, rising and bowing to Anne.

'You know, Major,' she murmured as her aunt went to consult Walter Gosforth about the music and they moved slowly round the room, 'I do not need someone to guide me, my aunt is mistaken in that.'

'I did not think you did, Miss Hemingford. But it does no harm for your aunt to think so, does it? She is a delightful lady and truly devoted to you.'

He was a kind man, she realised. 'I know. I would not dream of contradicting her.'

Mrs Bartrum sang one solo and one duet with the Captain, which had the effect of sending Major Mancroft to her side, offering to play a duet with her. She declined and suggested he should ask Anne.

It was all very amusing. Anne could see that the Major and the Captain were vying with each other to be noticed by her aunt and yet the lady herself seemed unaware of it. Not for a minute did Anne think either of them were rivals for her own hand, which meant she was saved the business of having to discourage them. By the time the party broke up with everyone promising to meet on The Steine after attending morning service next day, she was feeling exhausted. It had been a long, long day.

The front pews of the parish church of St Nicholas were full of the *beau monde,* dressed in their finery, intending to see and be seen. At the back, also in their Sunday best, were the working people of Brighton: fisherfolk, bootmakers, chandlers, harness makers, candlemakers, hatters, seamstresses, all the people who worked in the background to cater for the visitors who flocked there every summer as soon as the London Season was over. Sitting alone, neither with the elite nor the artisans, was Dr Tremayne. He was wearing a plum-coloured frockcoat, grey pantaloons, a clean white shirt and a white muslin cravat starched within an inch of its life. He held a tall beaver hat on his knees. Everything about him was neat and clean; he had even made an attempt to control his dark curls.

Anne and her aunt arrived late and most of the pews were full. Anne touched Aunt Bartrum's hand and indicated the vacant seat beside the doctor. He was kneeling to pray, but rose and moved along to make room for them and it was then she noticed that, though his boots were polished to a mirror shine, the heels were down and the soles worn paper thin. Poor man! But she knew she must not pity him, must betray no sympathy except for his work. 'Good morning, Doctor,' she whispered, settling herself beside him. 'I trust you are well.'

'Very well, thank you, Miss Hemingford.' He had wondered if he might see her in church and here she was, sitting so close to him he could almost hear her breathing, could certainly smell the faint perfume she used—attar of roses he thought it was—could reach out and touch her gloved hand if he were rash enough to try it. Her face was half hidden behind the brim of her bonnet, but he could, when he ventured to take a sidelong glance, see the delicate bloom on her cheeks.

He had been thinking of her a great deal since she left his house and was exasperated with himself for doing so. Every word of their conversation had repeated itself in his head, every movement she made remembered with startling clarity, like the way she had tilted her head and smiled when laying that bag of money on his table. He had not looked at it until after she had gone and had then been taken aback by the amount. Had she been condescending, looking down her autocratic nose at him, being generous because she could afford it and it made her feel good and virtuous? How he hated that idea. He had admitted to begging on behalf of his patients, but that did not mean he had no pride. He was stiff with it.

'And Tildy? Have you seen her again?' Her voice was no more than a murmur, unheard by anyone else.

'Yes, I have been keeping an eye on her. She continues to improve.'

'I am glad.'

They could say no more, because the parson began his slow walk up the aisle to begin the service, but Anne was acutely aware of the man beside her. They sat a foot apart, but the space between them seemed to vibrate, joining them by invisible ties that moved as they breathed, making them act in unison. They knelt to pray, stood to sing, listened, or pretended to listen, to the sermon, which seemed to go on and on. For once Anne did not mind.

She was wondering again how she could find the man an assistant. Why were they so hard to find? Was it simply that they disliked working among the lower orders where the chances of advancement were non-existent? She would need to find someone as committed as Dr Tremayne himself—where was such a one to be found? If the Doctor had been right, they were disinclined to accept low wages to help the poor, but surely that was what doctoring was all about? A woman would have more sympathy.

There were nurses and people like Mrs Armistead and handywomen who attended births and deaths, some of whom were filthy and too fond of the bottle, some of whom were clean and efficient, but there were no lady doctors. She wondered why not. She supposed women were considered too sensitive to pain, too revolted by blood and disfigurement, too ready to weep, to be able to work calmly. And in the eyes of men who were their superiors in every way, they did not have the brains to understand about anatomy and physiology. In Anne's opinion that was nonsense.

Women endured the pain of childbirth and could understand it in others, often watched their little ones die, were as stoical in adversity as men and they made good nurses when their kinfolk fell ill, so why not? And there were women who were quite clever enough to do the studying needed. She smiled secretly to herself; Dr Tremayne had called her clever. She sighed; allowing women to become doctors was something not to be thought of. The sound of shuffling and coughing broke in on her reverie and she realised, with a start of surprise, the service was over and Lord and Lady Mancroft were leaving the church, watched by those in the back pews who would make no move until their so-called betters had gone.

Mrs Bartrum rose and set off after them, leaving Anne to follow. She emerged into the sunlight almost side by side with Dr Tremayne. At the church door, the rector stood watching everyone leave, his rheumy eye noting absences that would be pointed out to the miscreants later in the week. He bowed to Lord and Lady Mancroft, who deigned to smile before passing on to chat to others in the churchyard. 'Dr Tremayne,' he said, catching sight of Justin. 'I am glad to see you once again among my flock. It does not set a good example when you absent yourself from church.'

'I cannot come when I am needed elsewhere,' Justin said, tight-lipped.

'Six days shalt thou labour—' the parson began, but he was not allowed to finish.

'People fall ill every day of the week, Reverend.'

'Quite.' He paused, looking at Anne, who had stopped

when Justin stopped. 'Are you not going to introduce me?' he asked, still addressing the doctor though his eye was taking in every detail of Anne's dress and demeanour. 'It behoves me to know the names of all my flock.'

Justin had been aware that Anne was standing nearby, how could he not? But the idea that the parson thought she had attended church with him disconcerted him. 'Reverend, you are mistaken…'

'I am Miss Hemingford,' Anne said quickly. 'My aunt, Mrs Bartrum, has taken a house in Brighton for the summer.' She nodded towards her aunt, now in animated conversation with Lady Mancroft, the curling black feather on her bonnet wagging in time with her jaw.

'Oh, I see my error. I beg your pardon, Miss Hemingford.'

'There has been no error, Reverend,' she said, slipping her hand beneath Justin's elbow. 'We are friends of Dr Tremayne. Please excuse us.' And with that, she put enough pressure on Justin's arm to make him walk forward.

'Why did you do that?' he protested, obeying the tug of her hand because he was too much the gentleman to embarrass her in front of the parson.

'Who does he think he is, preaching to you?' she demanded in a whisper. 'Looking down at you like that. Why, you have more good in your little finger than he has in his whole body.'

'The Reverend and I fight a verbal duel whenever we meet,' he said, half-pleased, half-miffed at her championing of him. 'I am not a kitten who needs a mother cat to defend it.'

She released his arm and laughed. 'I did not think you did, but I enjoyed adding my contribution.'

They joined Mrs Bartrum, who was looking at Anne in astonishment. How could she possibly know someone in Brighton well enough to take his arm in public? It must be an old family friend, chanced upon by accident. She prepared herself to be civil, but made a note to speak to Anne later about her behaviour. 'Aunt, may I present Dr Tremayne. You remember, I told you about the little girl who was injured. It was to Dr Tremayne I took her.'

Mrs Bartrum's welcoming smile faded, but, unwilling to make a scene, she inclined her head in acknowledgement but did not offer her hand or speak. Justin fumed inwardly, blaming Miss Hemingford for the embarrassing situation in which he found himself. A few years before he would have held his own, but not now. He had chosen his path and he had to walk it; if it meant being looked down on by people like Mrs Bartrum and lectured at by parsons, then he had to put up with it. He bowed. 'Your obedient, ma'am.' The next minute he had clapped his hat on his head and was striding away.

'Oh, Aunt, you have frightened him off,' Anne said.

'I should think so too! Whatever were you thinking of, taking his arm like that? I really am quite mortified. There is Lady Mancroft with her mouth open in astonishment and Captain Gosforth pretending not to notice, though I know he did.'

'Oh, Aunt, don't take on so.' She took her aunt's arm and they began to walk from the churchyard. 'It was all very innocent. The parson insulted poor Dr Tremayne, bowing and scraping to me when he realised you were my aunt and ringing a peel over the doctor for not going regularly to church. I had to do something to extricate him.'

'Why? You do not know him and he is not a gentleman.'

'Oh, he is,' Anne said, steering her aunt towards The Steine where they had arranged to meet the others who were going to see the monster and to join the picnic. Lord and Lady Mancroft had left in their carriage and would no doubt meet up with them again later. 'I believe he is a very fine gentleman.'

'He lives and works among the lower ranks.'

'By choice, Aunt, and I admire him for it.'

'One can admire someone without becoming familiar with them. Anne, I despair of you. It is no wonder you have not found a husband if you cannot tell a gentleman from a mushroom.'

'Dr Tremayne is certainly not a mushroom,' she said. 'He is making no pretensions to be something he is not. He told me he was a ship's surgeon in the war and sustained a wound that meant he could not go to sea again. He decided to help the poor instead.'

'You seem to have learned a great deal about him in a very short time, Anne. I understood you had only met him briefly.'

'So I did,' Anne said, feeling guilty about that second visit to the Doctor, but, judging by her aunt's reaction to being introduced to him, she was glad she had said nothing of it. 'But it took no longer for him to tell me than it did for me to tell you.'

'Why did he tell you?'

'Because I asked him. I was interested in the work

he was doing. He spends nearly all his time and money on it.'

'No doubt he was boasting to gain your sympathy.'

'No, he is not a boastful man. And in any case I learned some of it from the little girl's mother. She said he was a saint.'

'Saints are rare beings on this earth, Anne. For all you know, he may be the very opposite. He may have pretensions to be a gentleman and how do you know he does not have some dark secret in his past?'

Anne hesitated only a moment before replying, admitting to herself that she did find Dr Tremayne a little mysterious. His poor dress and mode of living belied his courteous manners and cultured way of speaking, which was, she supposed, what her aunt had meant. 'Fustian! You have been reading too many of those romantic novels you are so fond of.'

'I could say the same of you, Anne, making the man out to be a saint, indeed! He is a man, an ordinary man, not even a gentleman, and you will ruin your reputation if you are not more selective in those you consort with.'

'Consort, Aunt?' Anne laughed. 'I pass the time of day with a perfectly respectable man and I am consorting…'

'It is how it will be interpreted by society.'

'Then society is a ninnyhammer!'

'Anne, I beg you to be more circumspect. You will have us gossiped about.'

Anne conceded her aunt was probably right and, though she did not care for herself, she would not for the world have hurt or embarrassed her sponsor. 'I am sorry,' she said, squeezing her aunt's arm. 'I did not think.'

They said no more because they had reached The Steine where their friends were gathering. It was an open grassy area, used by fishermen to dry their nets and by the *beau monde* to congregate to walk and gossip. Neither side welcomed the other. According to the wealthier inhabitants of the town, the nets were an eyesore and the ladies often caught their heels in them and there were plans afoot to stop the fishermen drying them there. Naturally the fisherman maintained they had been using the open space for generations and it belonged to them. Being Sunday, there were no nets out and no sign of the fishermen.

'Are we all here?' Lord Mancroft called out, standing beside his carriage ticking off everyone on his fingers.

'We are one missing,' Annabelle Barry said. 'Major Mancroft is not here.'

'Here he comes,' Lady Mancroft said, as the Major drove up in his curricle.

'Mrs Bartrum, would you like to ride with me?' the Major called out as he pulled up beside them.

'No, thank you, Major, I shall walk with everyone else.'

'What about you, Miss Hemingford?'

Anne also declined.

'In that case, I will walk too.' He called to one of the men servants to take the curricle back to the stables and then to join the others at the picnic spot to help set it out and start the fire, while everyone went to see the merman. 'I'll wager a sovereign to a groat it is nothing of the kind,' he said.

No one was prepared to take him on and, once the servants had been dispatched, the whole party set off across Grand Junction Road to the beach.

Anne found herself being escorted by the Major. 'Do all the officers drive curricles?' she asked him.

'Those that have enough blunt to keep the cattle do,' he answered. 'Life in camp can be prodigious boring, you know. And racing horses or curricles is become the thing to do.'

'In the streets?'

'That's frowned upon, Miss Hemingford. It could be dangerous when there are people promenading.'

'But it does go on?'

'Doubtless there are some hotheads who are prepared to risk it, but usually it is done very early in the day before anyone is about.'

'Before anyone of quality is about, you mean. The fisherfolk rise very early, you know.'

'So they do, but they are not long on the streets, are they? They go to sea and when they return they sell their catch and disappear like rabbits into their burrows.'

She decided to ignore his deprecating remark, being more concerned with asking her questions. 'Was there a race last Thursday?'

'I have no idea. Why do you ask?'

'That little girl I spoke of last evening was run down by a speeding curricle which did not stop. It was driven by an officer in the 10th Hussars. I recognised the uniform.'

'I cannot believe one of our officers would behave so casually, Miss Hemingford. Perhaps he was not aware of what he had done.'

'How could he not be aware? The child was flung to the ground and badly injured.'

'Anne, I beg you not to prose on so about those people,' her aunt put in. 'It is not your concern.'

'But I am concerned. The man should be reprimanded and all racing banned within the boundary of the town.'

'That may be, but there is nothing you can do about it,' her aunt said. 'I doubt anyone would admit to being the culprit.'

'No, but I shall recognise him and his equipage if I ever see either again.'

The Major smiled. 'Oh, dear, that sounds like a threat, Miss Hemingford.'

'Anne, please desist,' her aunt commanded. 'We are out to enjoy ourselves and I do not want dissension.'

'I'm sorry, Aunt. I won't say another word.'

Mrs Bartrum went off to walk beside the Captain, who had been marching ahead in order to pay everyone's entrance fee as he had promised. The muslin-clad Barry girls were chatting excitedly, Jeanette on the arm of Lieutenant Harcourt and Annabelle with Lieutenant Cawston, leaving their mother and Sir Gerald to follow more slowly with Lord and Lady Mancroft. Her ladyship was not at all sure she wanted to view this creature, whatever it was, and was already hanging back. It was dead, so there was nothing to fear, her husband told her, to which she retorted that she was not afraid of it, simply worried about catching some horrible disease from the peasants who stood around watching their so-called betters with ill-concealed amusement.

As Anne approached the entrance, she realised that the woman taking the money was Mrs Smith. She smiled at her. 'I believe Tildy is still improving, Mrs Smith.'

'Yes, ma'am, and soon she'll be running about and in as much mischief as ever.'

'And do we really have a merman in here?' She indicated the tent, where a man in thick fustian breeches, an open shirt and bare feet, stood to lift the flap and let a handful of people in at a time.

Mrs Smith smiled and shrugged. 'To be truthful, we don't know what it is. No one has ever seen one before. But I thought if we charged people to see it, I could pay Dr Tremayne. He has been so good, treating Tildy and coming to see her every day and not a penny piece will he take from us.'

'And have many people come to see it?'

The woman laughed. 'They do say curiosity killed the cat. We had lines of people here all yesterday afternoon and ever since we opened again this morning.'

'Is it not putrefying?'

'It started to, but we have packed it in ice and it's not too bad if you do not stay in the tent too long.'

Major Mancroft, who had been listening to this conversation, suddenly laughed. 'Ah, then there will be no opportunity to examine it in detail.'

'Would you wish to?' Anne asked.

'Only to decide the outcome of the wager.'

'Oh, that,' she said dismissively. 'I do not see how you can establish the properties and description of a merman when no one has ever seen one.'

They were ducking under the flap of the tent as they spoke. It was gloomy inside and the smell of fish overwhelming, in spite of the ice packed round the creature. Seven or eight feet long, it was lying in a tub of rapidly melting ice. There were stakes and ropes round the tub so that none could approach near enough to touch it, not that any of the grand people in their fine clothes would want to do that. It was enough to see it and recoil in horror.

The head certainly looked very human. It had a round face with the large glassy eyes, what appeared to be small ears and a huge droopy moustache that covered the mouth. Its body was greyish and there appeared to be a tiny hand, but it had been badly mauled, either by another creature, or by the manhandling it had received when brought aboard the fishing vessel, so it was impossible to tell what its original shape had been. Its tail was certainly that of a large fish.

'It's a fish,' the Major said dismissively.

'Or a baby whale.'

'A walrus,' said someone else.

'But the head is like a man's. It has hair on its face and little ears.' This was Jeanette Barry.

'You are letting your imagination run away with you,' her mother said. 'Come, I have seen enough. The heat and stench in this tent is enough to bring on the vapours. I need some air.'

She turned to go, allowing others to file past, and it was then Mrs Bartrum swooned clean away.

Captain Gosforth, who had heard Anne's cry of distress, reached her first, scooped the lady up in his arms and carried her outside, where he laid her gently on the shingle. 'Dear madam,' he said, fanning her face with a large handkerchief. 'Do open your eyes.'

Her eyes remained obstinately closed and her breathing was ragged. Anne flung herself on the shingle beside her. 'Oh, Aunt, do wake up, I beg you.' She looked up at the rest of the party all grouped round her, all gaping, not knowing what to do. 'She hasn't had a seizure, has she? Oh, I could not bear it. She should never have gone into that tent.'

The Captain ran to the water's edge and dipped his handkerchief in the sea, which he handed to Anne, who mopped her aunt's forehead. She moaned and blinked, said, 'Oh, dear,' and fainted away again.

'Give her air,' Major Mancroft cried, shooing everyone away. 'How can you expect the dear lady to come about when you are crowding in on her like that?'

'I've brought the doctor.' Mrs Smith suddenly appeared beside Anne. 'He'll know what to do.'

The next minute a breathless Justin dropped on the shingle beside Mrs Bartrum. He put his head on her chest and listened. 'Nothing untoward there,' he said. 'Her heart is beating strongly. Her clothes need loosening.'

'What, here?' Lady Mancroft exclaimed. 'You cannot possibly undo her gown now with everyone watching.'

'Then don't watch,' he snapped without looking at her. 'Take all these people away.' He turned to look at the company and spotted the Captain looking at him in astonishment. 'Tremayne?' Gosforth queried in surprise.

Justin smiled grimly. 'Yes, Captain, as you see.' He turned back to Anne. 'Miss Hemingford, I could examine the lady better at my house…'

'Then let us take her there at once.'

'I will carry her,' Major Mancroft said, unwilling to let his rival have that honour a second time, but Gosforth, for once, did not have his mind on Mrs Bartrum but was watching the doctor, shaking his head from side to side, as if he could not believe what he was seeing.

'We have a cart,' Mrs Smith said. 'It smells a bit…'

'Fetch it,' Justin said, and when it arrived took off his coat and laid it in the bottom so that Mrs Bartrum was not dirtied by fish scales, though there was nothing that could be done about the smell. Anne walked beside it as the men manhandled it up the beach and on to the road, glad that her aunt was still not fully conscious; this undignified mode of travel would have mortified her. Once on the road it was easier and a few minutes later Mrs Bartrum was lifted off and carried into the doctor's consulting room. The Major and the Captain, having been ushered out by Mrs Armistead, stood in the waiting room, wondering what to do while everyone else had remained at the end of the narrow street, reluctant to venture down it. 'Please, do go on with the picnic,' Anne said. 'The servants will have it all prepared and there is no sense in standing around here. I am sure all will be well.' She did not wait to see if they went, but hurried to join her aunt and shut the door on them.

Mrs Armistead was already taking off her aunt's outer garments and undoing her stays. 'Why women need to lace themselves up so tight I shall never understand,' Justin said, washing his hands in the bowl on a side table; he washed his hands frequently, Anne noted. They were long fingered, well manicured, smooth. 'Just asking for trouble.'

Anne was taken aback, not only by his words, but by the swift way Mrs Armistead was stripping her aunt of her clothes in front of the doctor. It just was not done for a lady to be seen in that state of undress by anyone other than her husband—sometimes not even him—and that included doctors. Diagnosis was usually done with question and answer; if that did not suffice, the patient was examined with hands fumbling under skirts and petticoats. 'Don't do that,' she said, putting her hand on Mrs Armistead's arm. 'My aunt—'

'Is a woman like the rest of us,' Mrs Armistead retorted. 'How can the doctor tell what is wrong if he cannot see and touch?'

As soon as the last of the lacing had been loosened, Mrs Bartrum took a huge breath and her eyelids fluttered open. 'Ah,' Justin said, standing over her. 'Now you can breathe, madam, you are feeling better, is that not so?'

'Where am I?' She struggled to sit up, and seeing her state of undress, gave a little cry and fainted again.

'Now see what you have done,' Anne said, picking up her aunt's gown and covering her. 'How could you be so unfeeling? She is not one of your common sailors, nor a peasant, to strip her of her dignity.'

'She has not been stripped of her dignity, merely her outer garments,' he said. 'But as it is patently obvious that her swooning was the result of too tight clothing, combined with the heat and smell in that tent, I do not need to examine her. Mrs Armistead, you may help the lady to dress. And, as my presence seems to embarrass her, I will take myself off.'

He turned about and left the room, just as Mrs Bartrum moaned and regained her senses. 'Anne?' she queried weakly.

'Yes, Aunt.' Although Anne was still seething, she

spoke gently and took her aunt's hand. 'You fainted clean away in that tent on the beach. We could not bring you round. Doctor Tremayne was sent for and we brought you here. He says—'

'I heard what he said. I did not swoon again, but I was so mortified I could not look at him.'

'Oh.'

'Now help me dress and let us get out of here'

'Aunt, you did have your stays laced very tight…'

'Of course I did. How else could I keep my figure?'

'But if it makes you faint…'

'I have never done it before.' She turned to Mrs Armistead, who was helping her dress. 'Go on, woman, I'm not made of china. Lace me up again.'

When at last she was dressed again, with a slightly larger waist, Anne left her to go in search of Dr Tremayne.

He was sitting at the table in the drawing room, making notes, but looked up when she knocked and entered. He pushed the notes to one side and rose. 'Miss Hemingford.'

'Doctor Tremayne.'

They fell silent. The clock ticked loudly in time with Anne's heartbeat. She did not know what to say to him. She had been embarrassed and outraged on her aunt's behalf, knowing how the dear lady would feel, and yet, she knew in her heart, he was right. How could doctors diagnose and treat their patients properly if they were not allowed to examine them except at a distance? She wanted to storm at him and thank him in the same breath.

He stood looking at her, waiting for her to say something. He had thought she was different from the rest of her kind, sympathetic, not minding that her clothes were bloodied; she had talked to him about his work, said she wanted to help, had given him money and defended him, though he hadn't asked her to, but what had that amounted to? Nothing when it came to understanding him and how he went about his work. A large part of it was educating people to look after their bodies and not abuse them, but he was fighting a losing battle over that, just as no one listened to him when he maintained cleanliness was essential to good health. What had made him think Miss Hemingford would be any different?

'I came to thank you.'

'I did nothing.'

'Not for want of trying. Would you please send your account to this address?' She handed him one of her aunt's calling cards. 'It will be paid promptly.'

She was as stiff with pride as he was, he decided. 'There will be no charge.'

'Your coat was ruined.'

'Mrs Armistead will clean it.'

'I remember you said that you charged the rich who could afford it, in order to finance your work with the poor. You should make no exceptions or you will continue to struggle. We shall expect an account.'

'I do not ask for payment unless I have earned it, Miss Hemingford.'

She should have left then, turned on her heel and gone without another word. Words could be used as weapons, could convey anger, impatience, contempt, could hurt and she was seething with a desire to utter them. She stood three feet, perhaps four, from him, but it might as well have been miles. The chasm between his life and hers was too deep and too wide to be bridged. And she had been a fool to think that it could. 'I do not wonder that you have no patients except the poor,' she said. 'They are obliged to put up with your incivility if they want treatment, but fortunately my aunt does not.'

He looked hard at her, wondering why she stayed. 'Then may I recommend she consults a doctor more to her liking.'

'That is your advice, is it?'

'It is.'

'And presumably you charge for advice?'

He laughed suddenly, but it was a hollow sound. 'Why are you determined to give me money? Is my poverty so obvious?'

'I am not concerned with your poverty or otherwise,' she snapped. 'I was thinking of Tildy Smith and all those like her.'

'Very well, I shall send your aunt a bill, but I shall not press for payment if she declines to honour it. Now, if you will excuse me, I have work to do.'

'You have no patients today.'

'I have patients every day, but on Sundays they do not come to me. I go to them if they need me.' He indicated the papers on the table, the inkstand with its pot of ink, his quills and sharp knife. 'And I have notes to write up.'

'Then I will not detain you, but do you mind if my aunt sits in your waiting room while I go to find a cab? She should not be walking home.'

'Of course.' He bowed and went to open the door for her.

But there was no need to go looking for a cab. Major

Mancroft had returned with his curricle and proposed to convey Mrs Bartrum home in that. 'We abandoned the picnic,' he said. 'Everyone was concerned for dear Mrs Bartrum, and no one felt like going on with it.'

'I am sorry for that,' Mrs Bartrum said. 'I am completely recovered, as you see.'

'Nevertheless, I shall convey you safely home and then let everyone know how you are. They will be congregating at the Assembly Rooms for tea later this afternoon.'

'Then I shall join them.'

'Aunt, really, you ought not—' Anne began.

'Fustian! A little rest and a change of clothes is all I need. I have never been one to make a fuss over my health and I do not propose to start now.'

Anne remembered Doctor Tremayne's advice. Had he been hinting there was something wrong with her aunt, or was he simply being over-cautious, or giving as good as she had served out to him in angry words? She did not want to alarm her aunt, but perhaps she ought to see a doctor, one that knew how to treat susceptible ladies.

But her aunt seemed so well, and, by the time she had rested, had two cups of tea, eaten a honey cake and changed into another gown, she seemed her old self. Anne concluded that her aunt knew more about her own health than anyone else. Later Major Mancroft arrived in a light chaise to escort them to the Assembly Rooms at the Ship and Anne decided to try to put the enigmatic doctor from her mind.

Chapter Four

The Old Ship's Assembly Rooms, consisting of a ball-room, dining room and card room, were crowded with those who considered themselves Quality, all talking loudly and with evident authority on every subject under the sun, one of which was the so-called merman on the beach. It appeared that everyone had paid their twopence to be admitted, but by the time the latecomers had filed through the tent, the ice had melted and the stench of rotting fish was unbearable and they admitted to hurrying through and seeing nothing but two round eyes and a grey jelly-like mass.

'It was all a bubble,' Lord Mancroft said, slurping his tea noisily. 'And we ought to demand our money back.'

'But it was Captain Gosforth who paid for us,' Mrs Bartrum said mildly, smiling at the gentleman in question, who was dressed in the latest military-style coat and strapped pantaloons, all the better in Anne's eyes for being unadorned. 'I am sorry I did not see it.'

'You missed nothing,' Lady Mancroft said. 'I wish we

had not bothered. If we had gone straight to our picnic, we could have had an enjoyable afternoon. Instead…' She paused. 'My dear Georgiana, I was mortified on your behalf when they carried you back to that doctor's house on a cart. I wonder at Miss Hemingford allowing it.'

'What else was I to do?' Anne asked. 'Aunt Bartrum needed help…'

'Oh, I give you that, but you could have sent for Dr Wells. He is my physician and one you would not be ashamed to entertain in your drawing room. He would have come in a carriage…'

'And how long would he have taken to arrive? Half an hour, even if he was at home, which he might not have been on a Sunday. Besides, though I was not the one to send for Dr Tremayne, I believe him to be competent.' Anne's innate sense of honesty made her defend him even when she was annoyed with him.

'Indeed, he is,' the Captain said. 'At least he was competent when it came to treating wounds, injuries and the kind of sickness found aboard a man o' war, but as to doctoring in those squalid surroundings, I find that a little strange…'

'Do you know him?' Anne asked, trying not to sound too curious.

'Did once. Served on my ship. A gallant officer. When we were in the thick of a sea battle, he was there, doing his work, calmness itself. I did not know what had become of him after he was wounded and left the service. Why did he not go home to his wife?' He paused in an effort to remember. 'I collect he had a wife, though perhaps he was only contemplating marriage. I am tempted to renew our acquaintance and find out what he has been up to.'

Anne heard his words and her heart gave a little jump and then settled in her breast like a stone. If the doctor was married… What difference did it make? He was nothing to her. She was simply interested in his work and anxious to help; whether he was married or not had no bearing on that all. But if he was married, where was his wife?

'What is that to the point?' Lady Mancroft said. 'You should not have conveyed Mrs Bartrum to that dreadful tenement. Goodness knows what pestilence she might have picked up.'

'The rooms and the doctor were spotlessly clean,' Anne said. 'I would not have allowed it else.'

'Neither will be there much longer,' Sir Gerald put in, taking a lace-edged handkerchief from his sleeve and wafting it about as if waving away the memory of the stench of the place. 'I heard the builders are going to pull the street down. The land is wanted for more houses for the Quality.'

'But surely they cannot do that?' Anne asked, unable to hide her dismay. 'What will happen to Dr Tremayne's business?'

He shrugged his superfine-clad shoulders. 'He will have to find other premises.'

'But where? He needs to be close to the poor people he serves. And what about the tenants in the neighbouring houses, surely they will not be put out on the street?'

'They, too, must find somewhere else. Good thing too. How can respectable inhabitants be expected to endure the stink of fish on their doorsteps, not to mention the sight of their rags? And the doctor encourages all manner of low life to visit him…'

Anne opened her mouth to protest but her aunt's hand on her arm stayed her. 'I think we have said enough on the subject,' she said. 'Shall we speak of other things?'

'I believe there is a ball here tomorrow evening.' Anne obeyed, but her mind was still on the problems of the doctor. Was Sir Gerald right? And if he was, where would the poor man go? And what would happen to his patients, Tildy Smith and all those like her?

'Indeed, there is,' Lady Mancroft said. 'Shall you come?'

Anne pulled herself together to answer. 'If my aunt feels up to it.'

'Why should I not?' her aunt demanded. 'There is nothing at all wrong with me, as that foolish doctor was obliged to admit. I shall certainly attend and so will you, Anne. Now, I propose to take a turn around the room. Major Mancroft, may I take your arm?'

He rose with alacrity and offered his arm and together they set off to perambulate the circumference of the room.

Captain Gosforth sat down beside Anne in the seat vacated by her aunt. 'Miss Hemingford, I do most earnestly hope Mrs Bartrum has recovered from her misadventure.'

'I believe she has, Captain.'

'That is a great relief. I feel responsible. I should never have suggested visiting that tent; it was not the place to take someone of such fine sensibility.'

'I am sure she does not blame you, sir.'

'Oh, how relieved I am to hear that. Do you think she would consent to another picnic? Perhaps on the Downs. There are some pleasant spots near my home.'

'You must ask her yourself, Captain.' It was said with

a smile, which he took for encouragement, and he hurried off to prise the lady away from the Major.

Anne was thoroughly amused by the behaviour of the two gentlemen. Her aunt was a dear and they obviously appreciated her qualities. Anne did not believe for a moment that they were toadying to Mrs Bartrum to enlist her support in the pursuit of Anne herself, which was what her aunt believed. 'I'll not discourage them,' Aunt Bartrum had told her. 'Then I shall be better able to judge which will make the most suitable match for you.'

'Perhaps neither of them wants me and I should hate them to think I entertained expectations…'

'My dear Anne, I do hope you are not going to be difficult. They are both very eligible. The Major is Lord Mancroft's heir and though Captain Gosforth has no title, his family is an old and respected one and he is well up in the stirrups. And where else are you going to find a husband so late in life?'

'Aunt, I am not looking for one.'

'Of course you are.' This had been said with such firm conviction, Anne had not the heart to contradict her.

By the time everyone had drunk tea, eaten cakes and biscuits and mulled over all the latest gossip, it was time to go home to prepare for whatever evening entertainment had been arranged. By then Anne and her aunt had become on nodding terms with most of the people in the room and, according to Mrs Bartrum, their stay in Brighton looked set fair to have a happy outcome.

'I think I shall come out of full mourning and wear half-mourning for the ball tomorrow night,' she told Anne as they rode home in the carriage Captain Gosforth had put at their disposal. 'For your sake, of course.'

'Of course,' Anne murmured with a smile. 'Have you decided what to wear?'

'Purple with silver trimming,' she said. 'That should be suitable and it will go well with your lilac ball gown.' She paused. 'And I think we should hire a carriage and a groom for the duration of our stay. I should not like Captain Gosforth and Major Mancroft to come to blows over who should provide us with transport.'

Anne laughed. 'Aunt, I thought that was what you wanted, rivalry between the two gentlemen.'

'Rivalry, yes, but only in a civilised way. I should hate duels or fisticuffs…'

'Oh, I am sure it will never come to that.'

'I have told them both that I will not favour one over the other and the choice will be left entirely to you.'

'And what did they say to that?' Anne asked, highly diverted. She was sure both men were laying siege to her aunt, who was a very attractive lady and looked far younger than her forty years, and she was wealthy to boot.

'They seemed a little bemused, but said if I put such store by your judgement, then so would they.'

Anne laughed. 'Oh, Aunt Georgie, what am I to say to that?'

'To me? Why, nothing at all. But I do hope you will not reject them both out of hand. I cannot think who else will offer.'

No, Anne thought, no one would offer for her, certainly not the man who had been on her mind ever since she met him. It was only three days ago, but it seemed like a lifetime. She imagined him going about his work, sleeves rolled up, hair awry, compassionate towards those who needed his help, arrogant when faced with the pretensions of polite society, of which she was a member. She had wanted to convince him she was different, that she cared about the poor and vulnerable, cared about his work, but all she had done was confirm her prejudice and ignorance. And, if she were honest with herself, it was him she wanted to impress, not his patients. And all because he was handsome and mysterious; even Captain Gosforth thought so. She laughed at her own foolishness.

They had stopped outside their house and the coachman jumped down to open the door and let down the step. 'When will you need me again, ma'am?' he asked as they alighted. 'The Captain said I was to put myself and the equipage at your disposal any time you required it. He said he can just as easily use his tilbury if he needs a conveyance.'

'I do not think we need trouble him,' she answered. 'I intend to hire a vehicle for our stay. We cannot always be falling back on the generosity and good nature of our friends. We should not long remain friends if we did.'

'I will tell my master,' he said and, having seen them to their door, touched his hat and took his leave.

Anne laughed as they let themselves into the house. 'The Major will hear of the Captain's offer and then he will come forward with something even more elaborate,' she told her aunt. 'A coach and four, perhaps, with a postilion and liveried footmen.'

'That might be doing it too brown.' Mrs Bartrum smiled as she drew off her gloves, untied her bonnet and took off her pelisse, all of which she handed to her maid. 'But perhaps riding horses. Should you not like to go riding on the Downs?'

'Yes, but we can hire hacks.'

'Why do that when we can have them without the expenditure of a single groat? It will be a measure of the gentlemen's earnest when we see how far they will go…'

'Aunt, you are very wicked.' Anne took off her outdoor things and handed them to Amelia Parker before following her aunt into the drawing room.

'Aren't I?' She giggled like a seventeen-year-old. 'How do you think I chose my dear Mr Bartrum? I had any number of suitors, but he was the most dogged of them all. I could not shake him off.'

Anne could not imagine the mild-mannered Henry Bartrum being persistent; he had always given in to his tiny energetic wife in nearly every particular. Perhaps the pursuit had worn him out and, once he had made the conquest, he had decided to rest on his laurels. 'I am sure you did not really want to shake him off,' she said.

'Of course not. I should have been heartbroken if he had turned out not to be as single minded as I had hoped, but you know, if he had not, then he would not have been the man for me and I would have come to realise that. I commend the strategy to you, my dear. It cannot fail.'

'But supposing I find myself falling in love with someone who shows no interest in me at all? If he were indifferent to me and not at all prepared to lavish presents and praise on me, how would your strategy serve me then?'

Her aunt looked alarmed. 'Have you?'

'Have I what?'

'Fallen in love.'

'No,' she said quickly. 'I only said, supposing…'

'If, knowing your virtues and aware of your fortune, the gentleman showed no interest, then he would be a lost cause, my dear, and my advice would be to put him from your mind.'

'You do not think I should make a push to make him notice me?'

'No, I do not. It would be less than dignified and not the actions of a lady. My goodness, if he still failed to notice you, how mortified you would be.'

Anne forced a laugh. 'Yes, wouldn't I? I would want to crawl away into a hole and hide.'

'Anne, why all the questions? Is there someone…?'

'No, no, I was simply thinking about your advice and other possibilities. I was only wondering what you would do in those circumstances.'

'And now you know.'

'Yes, indeed.' She paused, anxious not to be quizzed. 'What are we doing this evening?'

'Mrs Harcourt, the lieutenant's mother, is holding a soirée. She is a foolish woman who has taken up residence in Brighton because she cannot bear him out of her sight. If Jeanette Barry accepts him, she is going to have to take the mother with him. I said we might not go. Neither the Captain nor the Major are going to be there. And we have the ball tomorrow night and so much else arranged for the rest of the week, it would be better to spend a quiet evening at home. Do you agree?'

'Certainly I do. It has been a very tiring day and you are perhaps not quite up to the mark.'

'There is nothing at all wrong with me, Anne, and I will not be treated like an invalid…'

'But you fainted.'

'It was the heat and lack of air in that tent.' She smiled ruefully. 'And that impudent young doctor was right: I was laced up too tight. Silly of me at my age.'

'It is not your age that makes it silly, but the fact that you have the figure of someone half your age and do not need to.'

'Oh Anne, you are the best medicine in the world. I do not need doctors when I have you.'

'You don't think you should see Lady Mancroft's physician? She did recommend him most strongly.'

'No. If I see anyone at all, it will be Dr Tremayne.'

'But, Aunt,' Anne protested. 'He was rude and insensitive…'

'He was also right. I do not want someone to pander to my whims and charge me a fortune for medicine whose only recommendation is that it tastes vile.'

'Oh.' Her aunt could be very capricious when she chose; she had looked down her nose at Dr Tremayne when she met him after church and she was certainly not at all pleased with him when he grumbled about her corset, and yet she was prepared to consult him again. 'I thought you did not like him. You said you thought he must have some dark secret in his past, though why you should say it, I do not know. He seemed perfectly straightforward to me.'

'He is certainly not afraid of speaking his mind.'

'What is wrong with that?'

'Nothing at all, but it suggests a familiarity with society that only the best physicians would dare to assume—' She stopped suddenly. 'Why are you laughing?'

'He is impertinent to you and that commends him to you more than his knowledge of medicine. Aunt, how can you be so whimsical?'

'I meant it probably signifies he is higher in station than he appears.'

'Do you think so?' Anne tried to keep the eagerness from her voice. 'But would a man of any consequence go to sea as a ship's surgeon?'

'Probably not. Unless something happened to send him from home. Perhaps in disgrace.'

This was something she had not considered. But try as she might, she could not imagine the doctor doing anything dishonourable or disreputable. Except, of course, for requiring his female patients to undress. She could imagine ladies of the *haut monde* being outraged by that. 'Aunt Georgie, I do believe you are curious.'

'Not at all. Why should a penniless doctor interest me, except in so far as he knows his business?'

'No reason at all.' She paused. 'So, are you going to consult him again?'

'Will it set your mind at rest if I do?'

'Yes, I think it will.'

'Then I shall ask him to call tomorrow.'

Would he come? Anne wondered. After all, they had had cross words and her aunt had hardly been grateful for his help. He might prefer to stay at home and treat those who were more appreciative. And if he did come, would it be to deliver another homily about tight clothing? Should she absent herself or stay to defend her aunt? Not that she thought her aunt needed defending, she was quite capable of standing up for herself. But she did want to see him again, if only to ask him if it was true he had been given notice to quit and how she could help him.

Justin was unprepared for a summons to attend Mrs Bartrum, nor was he inclined to go. The man on the couch needed immediate hospital treatment for a leg crushed by a lump of falling masonry from a villa he was renovating, the waiting room was full and he had a long list of home visits, including one to Tildy Smith. Head wounds were notoriously difficult and she still needed watching. He had no time for silly matrons who put vanity above health. On the other hand, if he went he might see Miss Hemingford again. It grieved him that they had quarrelled, not least because she might change her mind about helping him. Or so he told himself, though he was not altogether convincing.

'I cannot go now,' he told Mrs Armistead. 'If it is urgent, the lady must seek help elsewhere.'

She went off to relay the message and came back with the information that it was not a pressing matter and a call at his convenience would be appreciated.

'Then tell the messenger I will go later this afternoon.' He paused to look up from binding the man's leg. 'Janet, will you oblige me by pressing my best coat and laying out a clean shirt and cravat?'

'Yes, Doctor.' She nodded at his patient. 'What about him?'

'Get Joe Badger to take him to the infirmary in his wagon. There's money in the tin to pay him.' He had already made inroads into the money Miss Hemingford had given him, buying medicines, antiseptics and bandages for use in his consulting room, and bars of soap that he had distributed to his poorer patients, though whether they would use them was debatable.

As soon as the patient had been sent off, Justin called in the next one, a skinny little boy with sores all over his face; he was followed by a woman in an advanced stage of pregnancy. And so the morning wore on. He did his work efficiently and conscientiously, not allowing his mind to wander. When the last one had gone he took off the apron he had tied round himself, washed his hands thoroughly and went through to the kitchen to eat the meal Mrs Armistead had cooked. By then his thoughts were whirling again.

Why had he been summoned? When Mrs Bartrum was in his room, he had forgotten the protocol of dealing with a lady from the upper echelons of society and treated her as if she were one of his commonplace patients; she had been mortified and Miss Hemingford had been furious, as well they might be. So, who had suggested sending for him? Was Mrs Bartrum in need of medical attention or was it some ploy of Miss Hemingford's? There was only one way to find out.

He finished his meal and went up to his bedroom to change. His clothes were clean but shabby because he could not see the sense in dressing himself up in finery to administer to the poor and the money saved was better spent on something worthwhile. Once, he would not have felt like that, once he would have been ashamed to be seen in anything but the latest fashion, his hair curled, his cravat tied exactly so, his boots gleaming. He found himself thinking of what might have been, if only…

He might have been at Sevenelms with a wife and children, he might have been a distinguished scholar researching into some important aspect of medicine, he might have been an eminent doctor teaching future doctors his theories on the way disease was spread, he might have been able to command huge fees and a great deal of respect. But it hadn't happened and all because of Sophie's perfidy. It was strange that he was no longer resentful of that; she had done him a favour, enabled him to see where his talents lay, taught him the meaning of true Christian charity. And he would not have met Miss Anne Hemingford. Did the fact that she had sprung so readily to his mind mean that he was beginning to forget his hurt and humiliation at the hands of another woman?

Why Miss Hemingford should have impressed him so much he did not know, but she had. She had a beautiful face, glorious hair and a figure to match, but that was only the beginning. There was a depth in her amber eyes that betokened intelligence and compassion—more than that, a steely determination too. She could be top lofty and imperious one minute, and kneeling down in the dirt to comfort a child the next. She thought money could buy anything, even his gratitude… He laughed at himself. It certainly did that—he was too impecunious to turn his nose up at any donation, let alone a hundred guineas. He finished dressing and set off for his appointment.

When he arrived, he was shown into the drawing room where Anne was sitting reading a library book. She put it down and rose to greet him. 'Doctor Tremayne,' she said, noticing that he had taken trouble with his appearance; his hair was tidy and his cravat spotless. She could almost believe he was a gentleman, an indigent one whose coat was three years out of fashion, but a gentleman for all that. 'Thank you for coming.'

'Mrs Bartrum has not taken a turn for the worse, I trust?'

'No, no, but you did suggest she should consult a doctor…'

'Only to have my diagnosis confirmed.' There was a faint smile about his lips. 'I can hardly act as my own second opinion.'

'Nevertheless, my aunt wishes to consult you.' She smiled mischievously. 'You must have made an impression on her, though I cannot think why when she was in a dead faint most of the time.'

He looked as though he were about to laugh, but then he pulled himself together. 'Miss Hemingford, are you bamming me?'

'Indeed, I am not. I would not presume on so short an acquaintance.'

He wondered if she would do so on a longer acquaintance and he allowed himself to imagine them teasing each other, laughing together, happy in each other's company, but, suddenly remembering Sophie, he brought himself back to reality. 'Then where is my patient?'

'Expecting you, if you would be so good as to follow me.' She conducted him to her aunt's boudoir where Mrs Bartrum and Susan waited for him. Having ushered him into the room, Anne left them and returned downstairs to order tea to be served in the drawing room when the consultation came to an end.

He came downstairs half an hour later. 'How is she?' she asked.

'Right as ninepence,' he said, trying to smile and not quite succeeding. Mrs Bartrum was intelligent and perceptive and, once he had finished his examination of her to which she had not protested, she had asked some probing questions that he found difficult to turn aside without being rude. He had felt like a schoolboy caught out in a prank or a young suitor being roasted by a parent about his prospects. Where was his home? What had made him take up medicine? Where had he studied? Was he married? Did he hope to be? He was tempted to retort that he was not a green boy, that he had no pretensions towards her or her niece, but it was not in his nature to be impertinent; he was brusque when occasioned demanded, but not impertinent. He smiled. 'We had a very frank discussion…'

'And?'

'Miss Hemingford, you surely do not expect me to break my patient's confidence, do you?'

'No, of course not, I only wished to know if there is anything I should be aware of…'

'If there is, your aunt will tell you.'

The maid arrived with the tea and she invited him to take some refreshment, but he declined, rather tersely, Anne thought. 'I am afraid I have no time, I have other patients to see,' he told her. Then he picked up his hat and departed, leaving her feeling deflated, as if he had known she wanted to discuss his assistant, or lack of one, and his need for new premises, and was avoiding it. And his enigmatic replies to her questions worried her. She hurried up to her aunt's room, where Mrs Bartrum was sitting at her table, playing patience. 'Well, Aunt, what did he say?'

'Nothing I did not know already.' She put the eight of clubs on the nine of diamonds and continued dealing the pack. 'He is a struggling physician with a conscience, not a comfortable state to be in, to be sure.'

'I meant about you.'

'Me? I am in the best of health.'

'Oh, I am so glad to hear it. I was afraid…'

'Goodness, child, you have no reason to be.'

'You mean you asked him to call in order to quiz him?'

'I did no such thing. It would have been ill mannered.'

'So he did not mention losing his home?'

'No, why should he? It is his business, not ours.'

'But it must be very worrying if it is true.'

'Anne, you are showing a great deal of concern for the man, I do hope there is no more to it than Christian charity…'

'Of course not, what more could there be?'

Her aunt gave her a sidelong look and collected up the cards. 'I am glad to hear it. Now let us forget him and have our tea. And then we must make ourselves ready for this evening's ball.'

Anne's head and heart had been so full of the doctor she had almost forgotten the ball. Somehow she could not summon up any enthusiasm for it, but her aunt was evidently looking forward to it and so they drank tea without mentioning Dr Tremayne again and afterwards went to their respective rooms to change into ball gowns.

It was over a year since Anne had attended a ball and

that had been with Harry and Jane, and suddenly she was looking forward to it. Amelia had spent hours sewing dozens of little silk violets on the lilac gauze, round the neckline, the little puffed sleeves and under the high waist, which was also threaded with green ribbon.

'There!' Amelia said as she finished her coiffure with more green ribbon threaded through her tresses. 'You will be the belle of the ball. I am sure Major Mancroft and Captain Gosforth will be in raptures over you. Which one do you prefer?'

'Neither.'

'But if they offered…'

'They will not offer for me, Amelia. I certainly hope they do not, for if they did, I should know it was only out of disappointment that my aunt had turned them down.'

'And you do not mind?'

'Of course not. I am not looking for a husband, and, if I were, it would not be either of those.'

'Mrs Bartrum will be disappointed.'

'So she may be, but she is also sensible of my feelings.' She smiled at her friend. 'If I marry, which is very unlikely seeing I have reached the grand old age of seven-and-twenty without an offer I could consider, the man must have more substance than those two gentlemen. He must be strong and handsome, intelligent and compassionate towards those less fortunate…'

'Perhaps that is why you have not married. Your standards are too exacting and you frightened them all away.'

'Perhaps.'

'There was a time when I thought you were taken by Lord Montford's son and there was Dr Harrison…'

'Doctor Harrison?' she repeated in surprise.

'Yes, surely you remember? You caught a dreadful chill travelling to London from Sutton Park with Jane and Harry. It was about three years ago, as I recall, before they were married. Jane insisted you stay with her to be looked after and he was sent for. He came every day, more often than I thought was necessary, and you were often alone with him…'

'Goodness, that was because I was scheming to throw Harry and Jane together and I needed his help.' She smiled suddenly. 'He had some very modern ideas about medicine, I recall. I believe he is a professor now at one of the teaching hospitals.'

'Oh, and I thought you had rejected him because he was not a gentleman…'

'I would not have cared a fig whether he were a gentleman or not if he had been right for me, Amelia.' He had been young, handsome and caring, but the spark had not been there; the spark that was necessary to ignite the flame of mutual love was missing. How she had known it was missing, she did not know then, but she was beginning to recognise it now. Though what good it would do her, she had no idea. Aunt Bartrum had said she should not make a push to make herself noticed and those cold brown eyes had not softened towards her.

But while they had been talking, it had come to her that Professor Harrison was the answer to her problem of finding an assistant for Dr Tremayne. If he did not know of a suitable candidate, he would tell her how to go about finding one. Tomorrow she would write to him and then she would endeavour to find out if there was any truth in the rumour that the doctor's house was to be pulled down, because something must be done about it if it were.

She rose and left the room, prepared to enjoy the ball and amuse herself watching her aunt's two suitors falling over themselves to be favoured. It was as if she had two separate lives; the one inhabited by her aunt and her matchmaking and the other by Dr Tremayne and his crowded waiting room. It was uncomfortable and smacked of deceit and she wished wholeheartedly the two could be merged. But she did not see how that could be brought about. Her aunt did not look upon a ship's surgeon and country doctor as her equal, even though she admitted Anne would never find a husband as high in station as she thought she deserved. Aunt Bartrum was prepared to compromise, but not that far. In any case, Anne told herself ruefully, the man himself was impervious to her.

Justin was far from impervious, but he had promised himself that no woman would ever again humiliate him as Sophie had done and he made a manful effort to thrust thoughts of both ladies from his mind. He told himself he had more important things to concern him than the fair sex. His comfortable existence, comfortable only in as much as it did not require him to think about anything but his patients, was being turned upside down. He had that morning met someone from his past, someone who could tell the world who he really was, and he had been given a month's notice to quit his home, and where he would go and what would happen to his patients he had no idea. And threaded through all was the image of a beautiful woman.

He had tried to keep her at arm's length, to treat her coolly, to pretend he was only interested in the money she might donate, but it had not worked. She was pushing memories of Sophie from his mind, insinuating herself in her place and before long he would be trapped. Again. Just when he had reached some quiet in his life, he was faced with more turmoil. Damn her. Damn all women. He would not allow it to happen.

His thoughts were interrupted by a knock on the door and a few moments later Mrs Armistead showed Walter Gosforth, dressed in pristine evening attire, into his cluttered drawing room. He rose to greet him. 'I half expected you.'

'My dear fellow, I could not see an old friend in such extraordinary circumstances and not try to discover what had caused the change, could I?'

Justin poured them both a glass of cognac and resumed his seat, indicating the other chair to his guest. 'Curious, were you?'

'Yes, I admit it. Did you go home after you left the navy?'

'Briefly. I found I could not stay. Everything had changed, I felt out of place, *de trop,* if you must know. The woman I had planned to marry had turned out not to be the one for me, after all…'

'I am sorry.'

Justin gave a grunt meant to do duty as a laugh. 'Not half as sorry as I was.'

'I can understand you wanting to get away for a time, but why come here?'

'To this hovel, you mean?'

'Well, yes, I suppose that is what I do mean.'

'To find a use for myself, to remind myself that there are others in the world a great deal worse off than I am, to lose myself…'

'And have you?'

'Until very recently, yes.'

'And has no one tried to find you? Surely your parents…'

'My mother died and my father has washed his hands of me. I have let down the family name, not only over a broken engagement, but because of the work I do. Oh, he did not mind so much while I was in the navy; second sons often choose the armed services and there was a war going on. He even managed to overlook the fact that I chose medicine, healing instead of killing, but when I came out he expected me to conform, to wish Andrew and Sophie happy and to spend my days in idleness on half-pay until I found myself another bride. I could not do it, Gosforth…'

'I am sorry.'

'Do not be. I am fulfilled.' He was aware that this was only a half-truth, but if he repeated it often enough, he told himself, it would become reality. 'But I would prefer you did not make what I have told you public. There was enough gossip at the time. And learning of my background would spoil my relationship with my patients.'

'You have my word.' He drained his glass and watched as Justin picked it up with his own and rose to refill them both. 'It cannot have been easy. What about money?'

'Ah, there you have it. I have a small allowance and my pension, which would be enough to live on, but it is not enough to support this project. I rely on charitable donations and until recently a generous landlord who chose to overlook the fact that I sometimes forget to pay the rent. Now he is selling to the developers and I am required to quit.'

'What will you do?'

He shrugged, handing over a brimming glass. 'Start again somewhere else.'

'You need help to do that. Publicity. You should put yourself about, tell people what you are doing, people who can do something about it, people with deep pockets. You should frequent the Assembly Rooms, make yourself known.'

'That is the last thing I want.'

'I did not mean as Viscount Rockbourne's son, but as the local physician promoting a brighter future for the poorer citizens of this town. It is a worthy cause.'

'That would mean neglecting my patients.'

'If you went during the day perhaps, but surely there is no reason why you should not attend some evening functions. You will moulder away and forget you are a gentleman if you do nothing but work. There is a ball tonight. Come as my guest.'

'Out of the question. I am tired and I have no evening clothes.'

'You still have your dress uniform, don't you?'

'Yes, but…' He was sorely tempted. It was two years since he had attended any kind of social function, was beginning to wonder if he remembered how to behave at one. Had he forgotten how to make inconsequential conversation, how to flirt mildly, how to dance? Would Miss

Hemingford be there? Why did his errant mind keep returning to her?

Walter had said all he meant to and rose to his feet. 'I have to go. I am expected. If you change your mind, I will see you later at the Castle Inn.'

The ballroom at the Castle was large, decorated in the classical way with pillars and mouldings and a painted frieze. Even though a ball was held there every Monday, it was still a glittering affair in which the Master of Ceremonies was all over the place, presenting gentlemen to ladies, newcomers to each other, making sure everyone had partners. Anne, like her aunt, was much in demand and she enjoyed the attention, but she could not help wishing a certain medical man was one of their number. Dressed in fashionable clothes, he would easily have held his own.

'Miss Hemingford,' Major Mancroft said, breaking in on her thoughts as they executed the steps of the minuet. 'I need your advice.'

'My advice, Major? Whatever can I tell you that you do not know already?'

'How to reach Mrs Bartrum's heart. She is always charming and amiable towards me, but she is like that to Walter Gosforth too and I had hoped for more. She will not indicate which of us she will have and I hoped…'

'Oh, Major, I cannot intervene in matters of the heart…'

'She said she would leave the decision to you.'

'She was bamming you. I have no influence with her at all and, if I had, I would not use it. If you wish to know if she will have you, you must ask her yourself.'

'When would be best? Tonight? For some reason, Captain Gosforth is absent, though he did say he would come. Should I strike while the iron is hot?'

'That is a strange metaphor to use about one's love,' she chided him. 'It sounds too aggressive when you should be all gentleness and persuasion.'

'Yes, you are right, but should I go and ask her now?'

Anne looked towards her aunt, who was in animated conversation with Mrs Barry and the dandified Sir Gerald. She was having a wonderful time and enjoying her role of matchmaker so much, it would spoil it if she were to receive a proposal for which she was not prepared. 'I should give her a little more time, Major. She was so attached to dear Uncle Bartrum, the idea of remarrying must be introduced gradually.'

'Then I shall accept your advice, but if Gosforth gets in first…'

'Major, it is not a race, not a case of first to offer first to be accepted, you know. I am sure my aunt will make her mind up according to the dictates of her heart. You must reach her heart.'

'Oh, you are so wise, Miss Hemingford. If my heart and soul had not been otherwise engaged, I am sure I should be looking to you as my life's partner.'

She laughed. 'Flummery, Major, all flummery.'

The dance ended and he offered her his arm to return her to her aunt's side, just as Captain Gosforth appeared in the doorway. 'Damn,' the Major muttered under his breath, making Anne laugh. Before the Captain could reach them, he had bowed before Mrs Bartrum and whisked her away for the next dance.

Walter, seeing the object of his hopes disappearing, bowed to Anne and extended his hand. 'May I?'

'Certainly, sir.' And before she could draw breath she was being guided on to the floor and taking part in a conversation almost identical to the one she had had with the Major. It was highly diverting. If she had not been so modest and so fond of her aunt, she might have felt miffed that neither gentleman was interested in her as a potential bride. At least it saved her the task of having to let them down gently, though one of them at least was going to be disappointed; her aunt could not marry them both.

She was so engrossed with talking to her dancing partner she did not notice the new arrival. He stood in the doorway, watching her, and his emotions were turning like the cogs of an engine, back in time, back to another ballroom and another dancing couple, laughing into each other's faces, oblivious of those around him. He felt again the fury he had felt then, the rush of blood to the head, the urge to seize the woman from her partner's arms and drag her from the room. He had not done so, of course. Nor would he now; he had even less reason to do so. But he could not stand still.

As the dance came to an end he made his way over to the couple and bowed low. 'Miss Hemingford, your obedient.'

'Doctor Tremayne!' She could not keep the astonishment from her voice. 'I…I did not know you were coming.' He was dressed in the impeccable blue coat and white breeches of a naval lieutenant. His epaulettes gleamed and emphasised his broad shoulders, his buttons shone and his breeches, tied with a ribbon above white silk stockings, displayed well shaped calves. The sight of him sent shivers running down her spine, especially as he was not smiling and his dark eyes, directed at her, were as cold and empty as before.

'He did not know himself,' Gosforth said. 'I persuaded him to come out of hiding for an evening.'

'I was never in hiding.'

'No, of course not,' Anne soothed. 'Everyone knows who you are. And I, for one, am glad to see you.'

The orchestra began to play a waltz and the Captain excused himself and hurried off to find Mrs Bartrum before she could be snatched up by anyone else. Anne was left facing Justin. He extended his hand. 'I may be a little rusty, but may I have the honour of treading on your toes?'

She laughed; he did have a sense of humour, after all. 'Indeed you may, sir, but it is your toes that will be at risk, I think.'

He swept her into the dance and she went gladly, uncaring that her aunt had caught sight of them and her mouth had dropped open; she was where she wanted to be, with the man who had held her in thrall ever since she had first set eyes on him.

He had not forgotten how to waltz, nor did his wound trouble him unduly, and before long Anne was lost to everything but the sound of the music and the feel of his gloved hand on her back. Her feet went where he led, her body swayed with his, her breath merged with his. It was as if they were one being, one entity, inseparable. Neither spoke.

He felt something stir inside him, a twisting of his gut, a lightening of his heart, a reaching out to another human being. Oh, he felt for his patients, shared their pain and anxiety, but this was different; it was painful and yet joyous, immeasurable, eternal. He looked down at her. She was smiling dreamily, her eyes unfocused. Did she feel it too? But why would she? Why would she look at a doctor with no pretensions to do anything but serve those who needed his skills and could not afford to pay for them? He could tell her otherwise, but he had too much pride to do that.

The music came to an end at last and the moment, if there really was a moment, passed. 'Thank you,' he said stiffly, bowing and offering her his arm.

She took it and they perambulated round the circumference of the room. 'You have caused quite a stir, Doctor,' she said, hoping he would not notice that her hand on his sleeve was trembling. 'Everyone is wondering how you came to transform yourself and whether they should acknowledge you.'

'You did.'

'Naturally I did. I know you for what you are.'

He looked startled, as if caught out in a guilty secret. 'What do you mean?'

'That you are a man to be admired for the good work you do, for your unselfishness in caring for others.'

'Oh. Thank you.' The words were spoken with relief and quiet sincerity. 'But it takes another of like mind to see it.'

'I have heard you are about to lose your home to the greed of the developers.'

'Yes.'

'You will fight them, of course.'

'No, I do not have the means and it would be a futile thing to do. I would rather expend my energy on finding somewhere else.'

'You need a proper hospital.'

He gave short laugh, quickly stifled. 'What I need and what I may have are two different things, Miss Hemingford.' He paused to negotiate a way around another couple. 'But Captain Gosforth seems to think that if I put myself about and conduct a public campaign for funds I shall succeed.'

If she was disappointed that he had not come to the ball especially to see her, she did not show it. 'He is right. We could have a musical evening, another ball. There are any number of ways to raise money for a good cause. All we have to do is convince people of its importance.'

'We, Miss Hemingford?' And for the first time his face was lit in a genuine smile. He had been handsome before, but with his eyes sparkling with humour, he took her breath away.

'Of course.' How she managed to keep her voice from betraying her, she did not know. She had fallen in love, really in love, for the first time in her life, the first, last and only time. He had softened enough to smile, but there were still mountains to climb, one of which was the fact that he had given no indication he returned her feelings. In his eyes, she was a wealthy philanthropist, indulging herself, trying to lay up good marks in heaven. But she did know that was the way to his heart. And even if she managed to pierce its shell, there was still prejudice and snobbery to overcome.

Aunt Bartrum would not consider his station in life

high enough and she was sure her brother would not approve. Harry had no jurisdiction over her, but she would not like to fall out with him. He and Jane were very special to her; she could not lightly discount what they had to say. And there was still a mystery surrounding the man himself, still questions unanswered, questions she had no right to ask. But it did not make one jot of difference to the way she felt. It was glorious, heart-stopping and at the same time frightening in its intensity. Her emotions were so scrambled, she didn't know whether to laugh aloud or burst into tears. Surely he knew? Surely she had given herself away?

'I intend to do all I can to help,' she said, doing her best to overcome the crack in her voice. 'The first donation shall be mine and I intend to rally everyone to support you.'

'You have already given me money.'

'Ah, but this is different, this will be an official fund-raising project.'

He laughed. She was glowing with life, ready to take on the world and it made him smile indulgently. She had brought with her the first of sign of brightness in his life for years, a ray of hope. 'I think you do not know what you are taking on, Miss Hemingford.'

'Oh, be sure I do. Now let us go and tell my aunt all about it.'

He allowed himself to be led towards Mrs Bartrum, who was standing beside Captain Gosforth. With the Captain so evidently on good terms with the doctor, she could do nothing but acknowledge Justin and listen to Anne's enthusiastic proposition. Anne knew she had boxed her into a corner, but it was in a good cause and she felt no qualms about it. The poor of Brighton, particularly the children, needed to be looked after and she meant to do all she could to see that they were. It had, so she told herself, nothing to do with the fact that she had fallen head over heels in love with Dr Tremayne.

They were all standing together in a group when there was a movement by the door, which meant a newcomer had arrived. Anne, who had her back to her, did not see her, but Justin did. His face blanched and, excusing himself on the grounds that he had a call to make, he bade everyone goodnight and hurried from the room by another door.

Perplexed, Anne stared after him and then turned to see who had entered. The woman approaching the Master of Ceremonies was unbelievably lovely and she evidently knew it and smiled easily as everyone stopped whatever they were doing to watch her progress. She had golden hair, a flawless complexion and eyes the colour of cornflowers. Her gown of cream satin shimmered as she moved and the diamonds at her throat glittered.

'Who is that?' Anne whispered.

'That,' murmured the Master of Ceremonies, who had heard her question, 'is Mrs Tremayne.'

Chapter Five

How Anne got through the rest of the evening, she did not know. She danced, made conversation, laughed, and watched the vision who had invaded her happiness with a great lump in her heart that threatened to stop it beating altogether. All her hopes had been shattered. She was engulfed with misery. Why had he not told her he had a wife? Captain Gosforth had hinted that he might have, but he should have said so himself. Surely when they were dancing he had realised how she felt about him? It was cruel and unfair and she wanted to crawl away and hide.

Of all the foolish things to do, falling in love at her age was the silliest, and falling in love with a married man was the outside of enough. She could never admit it. She had to go on as if nothing had happened, to pretend all was as it should be. She had her pride, after all, and it was her pride which must sustain her.

The long evening came to an end at last. Arrangements were made for people to meet again, to go to other functions, but Anne hardly heard them. All she wanted was to go home, to find her bed and give way to her distress.

'You are quiet, Anne,' her aunt said as they travelled home in a cab. 'Did you not enjoy yourself?'

'Yes, Aunt, of course I did. I am a little tired, that's all.'

'You should not be tired at your age. You should be able to stay up until dawn and not feel a thing. Are you unwell? Shall I send for Dr Tremayne in the morning?'

'No, no, I do not need to consult a doctor, certainly not Dr Tremayne.'

'Oh, has he displeased you?'

'No, of course not.'

'Strange, isn't it?' her aunt went on, unaware that she was twisting a knife in Anne's wounded heart. 'The doctor is living in that unsavoury tenement, apparently as poor as a church mouse, and yet there is a wife, bedecked in diamonds and silks, who suddenly appears like a ghost from the past…'

'And the doctor disappears like a bolt from a crossbow.' The laugh Anne attempted died in her throat. 'Perhaps they are estranged. But if they are, why has she put in an appearance now?'

'I am sure I do not know.'

'Did he not tell you when you consulted him?'

'Why should he do that? If he wants to have secrets, it is his business, not ours.'

'To be sure.'

'Did he say nothing to you when you danced with him? I am not at all certain that I approved of that, but as the Captain assured us he was a gentleman, I could say nothing against it, but I am sure it was noted.'

'By the Mancrofts, I suppose. You may tell them, if

they ask, that we talked of his wish to set up a hospital, nothing more.'

Her sharpness alerted her aunt and she turned to face her. 'Something has put you in the suds, Anne, I wish you would tell me what it is.'

'Aunt Georgie, I am not in the suds, I am simply tired.'

'Then perhaps you should lie in tomorrow. We are not expected at Captain Gosforth's picnic until the afternoon.'

'I know. I heard you talk of it. Who else is going?'

'I do not know. The Mancrofts, of course and I suppose Mrs Barry and her girls, and, if they are going, you may be sure the lieutenants will not be far behind.'

'Mrs Tremayne?' She could hardly utter the name without a catch in her voice, but surprised herself when she managed it.

'Good heavens, why should she be invited?'

'I just wondered.'

Her aunt gave her a knowing look, but decided not to comment. 'Major Mancroft is calling in the morning,' she said. 'He has promised to advise me about hiring a carriage and horses for the rest of our stay in Brighton. I had hoped you would accompany us.'

'Pray excuse me, Aunt. I have letters to write.'

'He will be disappointed not to see you.'

'I am sure he will recover from it, especially if he has you for company.'

'But I am not the one looking for a husband.'

'Neither am I. It is the last thing I want.'

'Oh, Anne, what am I to do with you?'

Anne reached out and squeezed her aunt's hand. 'Nothing, dear Aunt, I am past marrying. Let me be.'

They drew up at the house, paid off the cabby and let themselves into the hall where a single lamp burned on a side table. Lighting two candles from its flame, they made their way up to their rooms. Anne was glad she had told Amelia not to wait up for her; she did not want to be quizzed on how the evening had gone, did not want to talk about it at all. She pulled off the lovely gown and flung it in a corner. She had danced in it, danced a magical waltz with the man of her dreams, had been transported to heaven on the wings of optimism and been hurled back to earth with such violence she was battered and bruised. And now there was nothing but wounded pride.

She finished undressing and flung herself into bed, knowing she would not sleep. What could she do to recover her sanity? What could she do to return to being the Anne Hemingford who had arrived in Brighton, content with her lot as a spinster, unaware of the pitfalls of falling in love with the wrong man? Why could the object of her affection not have been Major Mancroft or Captain Gosforth, or even one of the other gentlemen to whom she had been introduced? Why, oh, why did she have to fall for a married man?

No one must know. She must call up all her reserves of strength and carry on as if nothing had happened. And that meant throwing herself wholeheartedly into raising money for the new hospital and finding an assistant for Dr Tremayne, perhaps more than one. And if she had to meet his wife, why, then she would smile. And smile.

Justin, walking the dark streets, was furious, so furious he could hardly contain himself. What was she doing in Brighton? Had she come to torment him? And where was Andrew? Perhaps he should have stayed to find out, but the sight of her, walking into that ballroom, her head in the air, a smile on her lips, as if she knew she would find a welcome, had filled him with horror and he had bolted. He did not want to introduce her to the assembled company, certainly not to Miss Hemingford. As far as the people of Brighton were concerned, he was a practising physician who treated the ill, the lame and the needy. He did not want to have to explain who he really was, did not want to be the subject of the tattle of the *beau monde,* who would undoubtedly make up the reason for his estrangement from his family if he did not provide them with one. What price his hospital now?

It was nearly dawn before he decided to turn his steps towards home. He would not let her spoil his plans. She was his sister-in-law, wife of his brother, nothing more. He had found a new life for himself and a new love, even if he could not tell her of it. Not yet. Not until Sophie had gone home and left him in peace again.

The house, in its narrow mean street, loomed in front of him. It had been his home and his workplace, but soon it would be no more, and in its place would be a grand villa, one of a new terrace, occupied by people like Lord and Lady Mancroft, Mrs Bartrum and Sir Gerald Sylvester, even Sophie and Andrew if they fancied a seaside holiday. But that did not mean he would give up. Thanks to Miss Hemingford, he had at last managed to interest a few influential people in the idea of a hospital and that must be his only concern. It was safe, uncomplicated and engrossing and did not leave him time to brood.

If only Sophie had not arrived. He could not understand why she had come or what she would tell his father and brother, or even if she would tell them anything. He could not believe they had sent her or even condoned her coming. Was it simply an unpleasant coincidence?

He smiled grimly as he let himself in, passed the waiting room, dark and empty now, and went upstairs to his bedroom. He had nothing to be ashamed of, not inside himself where his conscience resided, even if polite society thought differently. And he had much for which he could feel a degree of satisfaction. He would do as Gosforth suggested and go out and about, try to raise money for a hospital and keep faith with his patients and nothing Sophie could do would hurt him. He stripped off his uniform, returned it to the sea chest he kept against the wall and tumbled into bed.

Two hours later, he woke to a new day, knowing that his waiting room would be full, and if he wanted to keep Miss Hemingford's good opinion of him he had a great deal of explaining to do.

His sister-in-law arrived halfway through the morning, pushing her way past Mrs Armistead who tried to bar her way and sailing into the room where he was treating a man with a wound to his leg that was threatening to become gangrenous. He had seen enough of those in the navy to recognise the early symptoms; unless treated urgently the patient might lose his limb. He was not prepared for the perfumed tornado who invaded his sanctum.

'So this is where you have been hiding yourself,' she said, looking round with her full red lips curled in distaste. 'No wonder we could not find you.'

'I cannot think why you would wish to find me,' he said coldly.

'She would come in,' Mrs Armistead said from the doorway. 'I tried to stop her.'

'I know that, Mrs Armistead,' he said wearily, going to wash his hands. 'I'll deal with it. Will you refresh the dressing on Mr Gorton's leg for me in the way I showed you, and tell anyone else who is waiting that I will be a little delayed.' He turned to Sophie. 'You had better come through to the drawing room. I assume you have something to say to me.'

'Who is that woman?' Sophie demanded as soon as they had entered the dingy room.

'She is my housekeeper and assistant.'

'Really? I had thought you would have more taste, but I suppose being on a man o' war has made you less discerning.'

He refused to rise to the bait. 'What do you want, Sophie? I am very busy.'

'Are you not going to invite me to sit down?'

'If you must.'

She sat in one of the armchairs, her rose silk pelisse making it look shabbier than ever. 'What a place!' she said, looking round. 'Surely you could have done better than this? It is a positive slum.'

'It suits me.'

'Are you still repining?'

'Over what? Your rejection of me?'

'Oh, but I did not reject you, Justin dear, you jilted me, don't you remember?'

He had agreed to be the one to break off the engagement in order to save his father pain. Andrew was the heir and Andrew's reputation must not be stained by gossip about stealing his brother's intended bride from him. It did not matter if the second son was talked about as long as the inheritance remained unsullied. He had been so angry and hurt at the time, he had not cared who would be publicly blamed. All he wanted to do was escape from a situation he found intolerable. And now she had turned up again, curling her lip at the way he lived.

'You know that's not true,' he said quietly. 'Like a dutiful son, I did as I was asked. I left my home, cut myself off from my family so that Andrew could comfort you in your distress and marry you when the gossip died down. I assume that is what happened.'

'Yes. But it was a mistake. I made a dreadful mistake. I should have stayed with you.'

Why did he find that difficult to believe? 'Are you not happy?'

'No, I am miserable.'

'Why? You have everything you could wish for. You have the heir, the estate is in good heart, you will never want for blunt…'

She smiled slowly. 'I know, I do not need to be told that, but I do not have you, do I? Oh, Justin, I was wrong. I realise that now. All I want, all I ever wanted was you…'

A year ago, even a month ago, he might have been heartened to hear her say that, although he would never have admitted it. She was his brother's wife and that, as far as he was concerned, was the end of it. He looked into her empty blue eyes and found himself comparing them with a pair of amber ones and wondered how he could have been such a fool. 'You made your choice and we must both live with the consequences. Now, if you will excuse me, I am very busy.'

'Busy scraping a living as a country doctor, and not very successfully if the state of this place is a measure of it. Justin, are you not ashamed of how you live? Your papa would be mortified if he could see it.'

'How is my father? He is not ailing, is he?'

'No, he is well, but wishes you would come home. When I tell him how I have found you, he will insist upon it.'

'How did you find me?'

'His physician told me about a paper you wrote, something to do with antisepsis in surgery, so he said, but it meant nothing to me. He traced you through the publisher.'

'He had no right to do that.'

'If you wanted to keep your whereabouts a secret, you should have used a *nom de plume*. Even then I did not realise how you were living. I thought you would at least be working among people of your own rank.'

'I go where I am of most use.'

'But you still go to balls and mix with the *ton*.' She paused. 'Who is she?'

'Who is who?'

'The beauty in the lilac gown you were dancing with. I watched you from the doorway for a long time before you saw me. Very engrossed with each other, you were.'

He stared at her, wondering why he had ever imagined

himself in love with her. She was beautiful, there was no denying it, but the beauty was only skin deep. She would not kneel on the ground to comfort an injured child, would not worry about the Mrs Smiths of the world, as Miss Hemingford did, would not even deign to speak to them. Miss Hemingford's beauty was in her whole being, in her compassion and understanding; it came from within. 'A friend.'

'A friend, eh? One of the numerous demi-reps who inhabit this town, no doubt.'

He kept his temper with a visible effort, clenching his fists at his sides. 'Miss Hemingford is a lady.'

'So that's her name. Well, well. And does she know how you live?'

'Of course she does. Everyone in Brighton does.'

'I'll wager she does not know you jilted me.'

'I am hardly likely to noise that abroad, am I? Especially when it isn't true.'

'The world thinks it is.'

'Not my world, not the one I live in now.'

'But they could find out.'

'You would tell them?'

'I do not need to. You know what gossips are like. They know my name, they saw you run when I arrived, their curiosity will be whetted, they will not rest until they have dug out the whole sorry episode…'

Justin's heart sank. She would cause trouble, he knew it. His brother ought to have curbed her, made her see that it was better to let sleeping dogs lie, not wake them up to bark all over town. 'Where is Andrew?' he asked.

'Where would he be but at home in Sevenelms?'

'He let you travel alone?' he queried in surprise.

'He could not stop me. He wants you home.'

'To salve his conscience, no doubt.' He had left home to ease their path, but that evidently had not been enough, though what else he could have done he did not know.

'I did not think you would be so bitter.'

'Bitter!' He found himself shouting and lowered his voice. 'Have I not grounds for bitterness? I lost not only the woman I hoped to marry and the love I had for my brother, but my home and my good name. That hurt most of all, and going back will not cure that, it will make matters worse. Now please leave me. Return to Sevenelms and tell them you could not persuade me.'

'You will change your mind.' She smiled, a feline smile that made him think of a purring cat, pretending not to see the mouse, but ready to pounce as soon as it dropped its guard. Well, she would learn that he was no mouse and she could no longer wind him round her thumb as she had used to do.

He had been a fool; she had used him to get close to his brother and now she was trying to use him again. But for what purpose? What did she hope to gain? She would never risk the scandal that leaving her husband would bring about. Rank, consequence, status, whatever it was called, were of prime importance to her. It was why she had left him for his brother in the first place. So, what was she after? She already had everything.

'Go home,' he said wearily. 'There is nothing for you here.'

'I will go if you come too. Then everyone will realise you have been forgiven and we are a united family again.

We could—' she stopped when she saw his ferocious look, then added quickly '—be friends.'

'No.'

'Then I shall just have to stay here until you change your mind.'

'I am unlikely to do that.' He opened the door to indicate the interview was at an end. 'I am afraid I am too busy to escort you to your hotel.'

'Oh, do not trouble yourself over it, Grimes is waiting with the carriage at the end of the street.'

He conducted her to the street door, more to make sure she left than out of courtesy. She turned on the step and, reaching up, put her arms about him and kissed him on the lips. For a single moment in time, his memory conjured up the emotion he had felt when she had first kissed him. He had gone to London for the Season, not particularly to look for a wife, but simply to enjoy himself and see what the capital had to offer. She had recently had her come-out and was much in demand, being beautiful and bright with an engaging manner, and he had soon become enamoured and determined to make her his wife. When the opportunity arose to escort her to a prestigious ball to celebrate some naval victory, he seized it joyously. After supper they had strolled in the grounds of the mansion where it was being held and he had proposed. It was then she had flung her arms about his neck and kissed him, making him the happiest man in the kingdom.

For that split second of time, he was young again and she was the embodiment of his dreams. He felt himself respond to the pressure of her lips, felt the warmth flood through him and was ashamed of his reaction. He pushed her angrily away, aware of her smile of triumph. 'I knew you had not forgotten,' she said softly.

'Go!' he said. 'Leave me alone.'

'I am sure you do not mean that, Justin dear,' she said. Then she laughed and turned to go, calling over her shoulder, 'You will come round, I have no doubt of it.'

When she had gone, he breathed a huge sigh of relief and went back to his office, where he collapsed into the chair by his desk, pale and shaking. How could he have allowed her to pierce his guard? And the worst of it was knowing she had contrived it very skilfully. It was bad enough having to quit his premises, having to beg for funds to keep him going, without the added worry of wondering what Sophie was plotting and why. If the old gossip reached Brighton, he might as well say goodbye to his hospital. And Miss Anne Hemingford's good opinion. He composed himself and rang the bell for his next patient.

Anne had decided to take a dip in the sea while her aunt was out, but the intrepid early bathers had gone and only the fashionable matrons were splashing about at the edge of the surf. If she had hoped to encounter the doctor again, she was disappointed. She did not stay long in the water, but on coming out saw Mrs Smith and Tildy beside one of the other machines and went over to speak to them.

'Hallo, lady,' Tildy called to her.

'Hallo.' Anne smiled and squatted down beside the child and took her bony hands. 'I see you have lost your turban.'

'Yes. I am better now.'

'Thanks to you and Dr Tremayne,' Mrs Smith added.

'Have you seen him lately?'

'Two days ago. He came to check on Tildy and look at a cut on my husband's hand. He's always cutting himself; his hands get cold, you see, when he's using a knife. This time the cut became infected on account of handling that putrefying monster…'

'Oh, dear, poor man. Did you ever discover what it was?'

'No, but I'm sorry the lady fainted. I hope she recovered.'

'Yes, she is perfectly well. Did you raise a lot of money?'

'Seven pounds. The doctor did not want to take it, but I insisted.'

'You heard about his house being pulled down?'

'Yes. Dreadful it is. I don't know what we will do without him.'

'Perhaps it won't come to that. Some of us are planning to raise funds to help him. If we raise enough, we hope to provide a proper hospital and other doctors to help him.'

'That is wonderful news, miss.'

Anne bade them both goodbye and left them, more determined than ever to put aside her personal feelings for the good of the community. Having been the one to suggest the hospital, she could not now stand by while others did the work. She must steel herself to meet the doctor to discuss the practicalities. Nothing could be done without consulting him. Deciding there was no time like the present, she crossed the road, making for the doctor's house.

She was just in time to see Mrs Tremayne emerge, followed by the doctor and, as her footsteps slowed and stopped, she witnessed that kiss. She was too far away to hear what was said, but she did not need to hear the words. That kiss was not one given and received by an estranged couple, far from it. Turning on her heel, she stumbled away.

Aunt Bartrum was delighted with the new park phaeton. It had her widow's lozenge painted on the doors— the Bartrum coat of arms enclosed in a diamond shape—dark blue velvet upholstery and two matched bays to draw it. The Major had even helped her to hire a man to act as groom and coachman. 'We are all set to go where we please now,' she told Anne. 'I shall drive it myself to Captain Gosforth's this afternoon.'

Anne, who had returned home and spent the rest of the morning writing to Harry and Jane and to Professor Harrison, was feeling calmer and more in command of her emotions. What she had witnessed had finally brought her to her senses. She was a spinster and would remain one and falling in love at her age was the height of folly. She would never have children of her own and so she must make do with other people's. Her nephew she adored, but he had parents who could provide all the love and comfort he needed. There were others not so fortunate and she would devote her life to those.

She went outside to inspect the new carriage. 'Do you think you can manage it?'

'Of course, I can. You are not afraid to ride with me, are you?'

'Of course not! Besides, I shall hope to take the ribbons myself for part of the journey.'

Using prize money he had earned while in the navy, Captain Gosforth had bought a solid manor house ten miles inland from Brighton. It had a substantial acreage used for crops and a vast tract of down land on which he grazed sheep, whose wool and meat were in great demand. He called himself a farmer, but Anne was sure he had never done a day's labour in his life; he had stewards and labourers to do it for him. As far as Aunt Bartrum was concerned, that was a virtue. 'He is a gentleman of excellent pedigree,' she told Anne as they bowled along in the late summer sunshine.

'Related to Lord Downland, I collect you said, though I have never heard of him.'

'His lordship may not be one of the top one hundred, but it is an old established family and not one to be ashamed of.'

'And do you prefer him to Major Mancroft?'

'My preferences are not to be considered, Anne. You must make up your own mind.'

'Oh, I have.'

'Already? Pray do not be hasty, let them dangle a little longer.'

Anne laughed. Having strange and convoluted conversations with her aunt over her two suitors was infinitely preferable to thinking about Dr Tremayne and his elegant wife. It was certainly more amusing. 'It is not me they are dangling after, but you, Aunt.'

'Do not be ridiculous, Anne.'

'Is it so ridiculous?'

'Of course it is. I will not hear another word on the subject. Now see, you have made me lose my concentration

and the horses are all over the place.' She pulled ineffec-
tually on the reins as the skittish beasts decided to go
their own way. 'My, they are strong, too strong for me.'

Anne took the ribbons from her and skilfully pulled the
horses up. 'There, they are calmer now, do you want to
take over again?'

'No, you take them. We are nearly there.'

Anne turned in at the gates of Bracken Farm and drew
up behind a row of other carriages. Walter, who had been
watching for them, hurried forward to open the carriage
door and let down the step. 'Good day to you, ladies, I
trust you had an uneventful ride, though there was no
need to go to the expense of obtaining a carriage. I would
have been delighted to send my coach for you.'

'I fancied my own conveyance,' Aunt Bartrum said,
taking his hand and stepping down. 'I like to drive myself, you know. I often did when we were at home and my
dear Bartrum was alive.'

'In that case, why did you not ask me to assist you in
its procurement?'

'Major Mancroft was free and you were no doubt occupied in arranging today's amusements,' she said lightly.
'I did not want to drag you into town needlessly.'

'It would have been a pleasure, ma'am.'

'Then I shall certainly call on you next time I need help,
Captain.' She gave Anne a look which that young lady
could only interpret as defiant. 'Perhaps my niece has a
commission for you.'

'Delighted to oblige,' he said, turning to Anne.

'I shall think of something,' she promised him, trying
not to laugh.

Walter, as a senior naval officer, had been used to organising people and making sure everything ran smoothly and
he put his talents to good use on this occasion. Mounts were
provided for Aunt Bartrum and Anne and those of his guests
who wished to ride to the venue. Small vehicles were organised for the elderly and those of a more timid nature, and
they set off in convoy to the spot he had chosen for their picnic, where a wagon packed with good food, wine and cor-
dial had been dispatched ahead with servants to lay it all out.

'Oh, the air is so clear up here,' Anne said to the Captain, as they rode side by side. They were high up on the
Downs and she could see the sea sparkling in the distance,
though Brighton itself was hidden by folds in the hills.
Down there, the man she loved was probably working,
looking after his poor patients. But what of the woman she
had seen leaving his house? Superbly gowned in a long
feather-decorated pelisse and a matching hat, she had
looked out of place in that setting. Anne could not see her
living there, supporting the doctor in his work. But perhaps she was about to take him away from it. Would that
make fund-raising pointless? But thinking of Tildy and all
those poor people in the waiting room told her it could not
be pointless, even if they had to find other doctors.

Her aunt was riding slowly, deep in conversation with
Major Mancroft, no doubt talking at cross-purposes, as
she seemed to be doing more and more lately. The Captain, left out in the cold, was endeavouring to interest
Anne in the countryside through which they passed, waving his hand to encompass the landscape. 'All in good
heart,' he was saying. 'I can offer Mrs Bartrum a comfortable life, if she were to consent to be my wife.'

Anne pulled herself back to pay attention. 'Have you asked her?'

'No, not yet. I plan to do so very soon. Do you think I may hope for a happy outcome?'

'I truly cannot say, Captain. I know she holds you in high esteem, but as a husband…' She paused. 'I think she will be taken by surprise…'

'Surely not? I have never attempted to hide my intentions.'

Anne smiled. 'There are none so blind as those who will not see.'

'Whatever do you mean by that, Miss Hemingford?'

'She is a widow who loved her husband; perhaps she has convinced herself that marrying again will betray his memory and so she is denying her true feelings.'

'I suppose you may be right. I often think about my poor Lucy, but life must go on and grieving will not bring them back. I am lonely, Miss Hemingford, and I think Mrs Bartrum must be too. We are two mature people who could deal very well with each other.'

'That may be the case, Captain, but please tread softly. I would not, for the world, have her alarmed.'

'Indeed I will.' He paused. 'You know, you are a very kind-hearted young lady, and comely with it, I wonder some young blade has not snapped you up long ago.'

Anne forced a laugh. 'Perhaps I am too particular. And marriage is a big step to take. I think I would need to know someone very well before agreeing to spend the rest of my life with him. It is all a gamble…'

'And have you never been tempted to take a gamble?'

'Perhaps when I was young I might have done so, but

it came to nothing and I am inclined to the view that it was not meant to be,' she said, realising as she spoke that if Dr Tremayne had been free and if they had continued to enjoy the rapport they had established before the arrival of his wife, then she would have gambled her all. 'I have my books and my charitable work and many good friends.'

'Speaking of charitable work, have you thought any more about Tremayne's hospital?'

'Indeed I have.' She paused and then took a deep calming breath before continuing. 'But I wonder if he will want to go on with the project now his wife has arrived.'

'His wife, Miss Hemingford?'

'The lady who arrived at the ball late last evening was his wife, was she not? The Master of Ceremonies called her Mrs Tremayne.'

'Oh, no, Miss Hemingford, you are mistaken. The lady is indeed Mrs Tremayne, but she is his sister-in-law, his brother's wife. As far as I know, Dr Tremayne is unmarried.'

She knew her mouth had dropped open and quickly shut it again. He was not married; he was single, free, unencumbered. She felt like singing it aloud, but as the tableau she had witnessed earlier that day impinged itself on her mind's eye, she realised it had not been a sisterly kiss, a peck on the cheek, but lips on lips, bodies pressed together, and it had gone on for a long time. How could an honourable man behave like that towards his brother's wife? He would not. Only a cur would do so. It gave her a disgust of him. 'Then why did he not stay and speak to her at the ball?'

'I have no idea, Miss Hemingford.'

Almost as if unwilling to pursue the subject, he left her

to round up the stragglers, calling to them to keep together or they would miss the turn. Anne rode on and joined her aunt and the Major. 'You seem agitated,' her aunt said, looking closely at her. 'What has the gallant Captain been saying to you?'

'Nothing, Aunt.'

'Nothing? I cannot believe that you have spent the last half-hour riding at his side and he has not broached the subject of marriage. Surely he hinted?'

'Hinted?' queried the Major, a broad smile lighting his face. 'Do you mean to say Gosforth is contemplating offering for Miss Hemingford?'

'Why should he not?' Mrs Bartrum demanded, apparently unaware of the reason for his surprise. 'She will make an excellent wife. Beautiful, intelligent, sensible, not to mention wealthy. The Captain could do no better.' She paused. 'Anne, why are you looking at me like that? I am perfectly sincere.'

'Oh, Aunt Bartrum, you are putting me to the blush. Pray desist.'

Mrs Bartrum turned from Anne to the Major. 'What do you think of that, sir? She is also modest.'

'I am sure you are in the right of it,' he answered.

'Are you not inclined to make a push to offer for her yourself?'

'Aunt Bartrum, I shall never speak to you again, if you continue this conversation,' Anne put in sharply. 'Now you are embarrassing Major Mancroft.'

'Not at all,' he said. 'I am flattered to think that Mrs Bartrum considers me good enough for her delightful niece…'

Anne could not stand any more. She excused herself and rode off alone. She had no idea how her aunt was going to extricate herself from the bumblebath into which she had toppled herself, but she supposed the gentlemen would make their offers, Aunt Georgie would be startled, horrified perhaps, and would either consider one of them or turn them both down. Whichever it was, it had no bearing on Anne herself, whose head was filled with another man altogether. She could not get him out of her mind; he had been there from the moment she had first seen him, through the misery of thinking he was married, until now, when she had been told he was single. If only she could get the memory of that kiss out of her mind.

She was too stirred up to ride demurely and she could tell her mount was itching for exercise. She set off at a gallop, flying over the soft turf, climbing ever higher, until the wind caught her, billowed her habit out behind her, swept away her hat and lifted her hair from its combs. Only when she pulled up on the brow of the hill and looked back, did she realise she was alone. The others had turned off the path and were lost to sight. Sighing, she turned back to find them.

For all but Anne, the picnic was a great success; everyone ate too much, some even fell asleep in the sunshine afterwards, others strolled on the grass quietly exchanging news and gossip. The defeated Napoleon Bonaparte had been banished to the island of St Helena from where, it was confidently hoped, he would be unable to escape as he had done at Elba, and Princess Charlotte, the Regent's only legitimate offspring, had, so they said, fallen in love with Prince Leopold of Saxe-Coburg.

'He is a nobody,' Lady Mancroft said. 'Only the third son of a duke. How can he be considered as a suitable husband for the heir to the throne?'

'Does it matter, if they love each other?' Anne asked. 'I think too much is made of rank.'

'How can you say so?' demanded her ladyship. 'Bloodlines are what holds society together. Without them we should have the chimneysweep marrying the heiress and their offspring would inherit the traits of the sweep. The stock would be diminished as a result. And how could such a one as a chimneysweep look after a great estate?'

'You mean we are all like cattle, to be chosen for our breeding.'

'Well, breeding will out, there is no doubt of that. Those born to a position of power know how to use it…'

'And abuse it too. The chimneysweep might look after his people better than a spoiled aristocrat who thinks of nothing but fine clothes, plentiful food and gambling. Having been poor himself, he would understand the needs of the poor.'

'Anne!' Mrs Bartrum protested. 'How can you say so?'

'It's all the fault of that doctor fellow,' Lord Mancroft put in. 'Arriving at the ball unannounced like that. Miss Hemingford should never have stood up with him. He has quite turned her head.'

Anne felt the colour flare in her face. 'Dr Tremayne is a good man…'

'But not a gentleman.'

'Oh, but he is,' Walter said quietly. 'Or I would not have asked him to be my guest.'

'Your guest?' they queried, astonished.

'Indeed yes.'

'Really?' Lady Mancroft queried, while Anne held her breath. They had already forgotten her in their curiosity, but now their gossiping tongues were aimed at the doctor. She did not want them to start them wagging against him, but at the same time she was as anxious to know as much about him as possible. She told herself that if he were to be given money to run a hospital, his character, background and qualifications were relevant. 'Then why is he practising medicine?' her ladyship continued. 'And why here, among the vermin of the old quarter?'

'I asked him that myself,' Anne said, disliking her ladyship's reference to the poor as vermin. 'He said it was because the need was there. It still is and I, for one, shall contribute to the fund to build a hospital. It behoves those of us who have the means to help those who do not.'

She did not notice Walter's look of relief as the company began to debate the pros and cons of having a new hospital and he was saved having to answer any more questions about his knowledge of the doctor.

But Anne was not spared questions, nor the peal rung over her by her aunt on the return journey.

'Anne, I am sure I do not wish to curb your generous spirit and I shall support whatever fund-raising efforts are made for a hospital, but did you need to air your radical views quite so vehemently? If you are not careful, it will give Lord and Lady Mancroft a disgust of you and the Major, for all his years, is still guided by his parents. He will not offer for you, if you do not act with a little more delicacy.'

'Aunt, I do not want him to offer for me. Indeed, I am sure he has no intention of doing so. I am second-best.'

'I never heard such a tarradiddle. Whatever gave you that idea?'

'He told me so himself.'

'Oh.' She was silent for some time, then added with a sigh, 'Then we shall have to fall back on Captain Gosforth.'

'No. Aunt, please do not refine upon it. I do not want either gentleman.'

'There is no one else,' her aunt said, ignoring Anne's plea, 'except Sir Gerald, and I do not think he would serve…'

'No, he certainly would not.'

It was the tremor in her voice that alerted her aunt to the fact that something was wrong. She turned to look closely into Anne's face. 'My dear, whatever is the matter?'

'Oh, Aunt Georgie, please do not quiz me.'

'But how am I to help you, if you will not tell me what is wrong?'

'There is nothing wrong.'

'And that is a whisker if ever I heard one. I am sorry I scolded you. I am only thinking of your good.'

'I know, Aunt, I know.' She paused. 'But you agree with Lady Mancroft, don't you? Like should marry like…'

'Anne, surely you have not been so foolish as to contemplate an unsuitable alliance?' She stopped suddenly. 'Doctor Tremayne! Oh, Anne!'

'How is he unsuitable? Captain Gosforth assured us he is a gentleman.'

'So he may be, but one who has chosen a different path. Anne, you are the granddaughter of an earl, sister to one, and though I said you should not aim too high, I did not mean you should set your sights so low as to consider a mere physician. It is not to be thought of.'

'Why are you so against him?' Anne cried. 'What did he tell you about himself when you consulted him? Was it something very dreadful?'

'He said nothing, but then why should he?'

'Mrs Tremayne is not his wife, you know. She is his sister-in-law.'

'So I understand, but what is that to the point? He is not eligible, you must realise that.' She paused, but when Anne made no comment, added, 'Has he said anything?'

'No, of course not.'

'Have you?'

'Most certainly not. I am not such a bufflehead.'

'Then nothing need be said. I would suggest leaving Brighton, but that would cause comment.' She patted Anne's hand. 'Having been the instigator of the idea to raise funds for a hospital, it would look strange if you backed out now, so the best thing I can do is to support it wholeheartedly myself, then we can enter into it together and no one will think anything of it. Do you agree?'

'Yes, Aunt. My feelings do not come into that at all. I want to help those in need, just as Dr Tremayne does. We have that in common, if nothing else.'

'Good,' her aunt said complacently. 'We must carry on and I beg you to think seriously about marrying Captain Gosforth, if the Major's affections are engaged else-where.'

She would not have been so complacent if she could have seen inside Anne's mind. Her niece was not so easily turned. She could not blow out a flame that had been kindled so suddenly and so hotly when she had thought all hope of ever being warmed by its heat had passed. Love, passion, desire, whatever anyone liked to call it, had invaded her heart, her mind, her soul and could not be quenched. But quenching it and admitting it was hopeless were two different things. She would work alongside him, help him to achieve his aims and perhaps one day... She shook herself. What was the sense of dreaming impossible dreams?

Chapter Six

Because Mrs Bartrum and Captain Gosforth entered wholeheartedly into the fund-raising, Major Mancroft felt obliged to join in too, and a working committee was set up that also included Mrs Bartrum, Lady Mancroft, Anne and Dr Tremayne. They met in a room in Tuppen's library on Marine Parade and thrashed out ways and means of raising money as quickly as possible. This included proposals for a concert at the Old Ship, a rout at Lady Mancroft's home, and horse racing and sport on the fields to the west of the town, for which there would be an entrance fee that would go to the fund. Lord Mancroft, prompted by his wife, had promised to donate prizes for the winners. And capping it all would be a grand charity ball at the Castle. It was all looking very promising.

Anne was never alone with Justin, Aunt Bartrum saw to that. Not that Anne minded; in a way she was relieved because she would not have known what to say to him. Even seeing him sitting across the library table brought back that scene outside his house when he had kissed his sister-in-law. She had felt hurt, as a rejected lover might feel, but it had not entered her head at the time that it was anything more than a husband kissing his wife. Since she discovered the truth, the memory had continued to haunt her. Whenever she thought about it, she was overwhelmed with feelings of disgust and could not meet his eyes. Whatever had made her imagine she was in love? She had had a lucky escape.

But instead of feeling fortunate she was immersed in misery. Something wonderful, something that could have raised her to heights of ecstasy, something for which she longed with all her being, had been snatched from her before it had had time to develop. She felt old, older than her twenty-seven years, old as time itself, and weary beyond imagining. But that was inside. Outside she was bright and cheerful, full of plans, offering her services in whatever capacity they were needed and accompanying her aunt on social outings. She wore herself out so that when she finally fell into bed, she was too exhausted to stay awake. But even her dreams were haunted by the man who had won her heart and disdained it.

And to make matters worse, Mrs Tremayne seemed to be everywhere. Wherever Anne and Aunt Bartrum went, be it to someone's soirée or for a stroll along the seafront, she was there. Sometimes she had only her maid for company and then there was nothing they could do but invite her to join them. Sometimes she was in the middle of a gaggle of noisy young people of both sexes, prominent among them a certain Captain Smollett, who looked vaguely familiar to Anne, though she could not place him. In no time at all the gossiping tongues were wagging over her. Why was she in Brighton? Where was her husband? What was he thinking of to allow his wife to stay at an hotel with only a maid for company?

Had she really come to support her brother-in-law in his efforts to open a hospital? She said that was the reason, but she had arrived before that project had been anything more than a dream and she was rarely in his company. That could have been because he was too busy, but the tattlemongers were adept at inventing stories if they could not get to the truth of the matter. Mrs Tremayne was becoming the talk of Brighton. As far as Justin was concerned, there had been gossip enough over that broken engagement three years before and he did not want it to resurface, especially here, where he had hoped none of it was known.

He wished with all his heart she would leave the town, but she showed no sign of granting his wish. 'You must do something before she ruins your plans, old friend,' Walter Gosforth told him one day when they met at the library where Justin had gone to consult a reference book. 'No one will support a man who is surrounded by gossip and innuendo.'

Not wishing to meet her, Justin wrote to her, suggesting she should lose no time in returning to her husband who must surely be missing her, but that only served to bring her to his door. She swept in as she had done before, ignoring the waiting patients and the protests of Mrs Armistead. Sighing, he took off his stained apron, washed his hands and led her to his drawing room.

She had no sooner sat down than she was up again in a rustle of taffeta, waving his letter under his nose. 'Justin, how could you be so insensible of my feelings as to write in such cold terms? Anyone would think I had come to Brighton expressly to upset you. How can you be so cruel? I am not your enemy.' She stopped ranting and her voice took on a wheedling tone. 'You loved me…'

'More fool I.'

'You cannot mean that. We were everything to each other once…'

'Once.'

'You are still everything to me, Justin. Living with Andrew is hell, but…' She managed a sob. 'I would try to be a good wife to him if only you would come home. If I knew I had your support, I could endure his cruelty…'

'Cruelty, Sophie? Surely not.'

'Oh, he is not violent, but he has a cruel tongue. I had to get away, just for a few days, just to see you, to remember what it was like before…'

Andrew could be sharp-tongued, as Justin very well knew, but he found it difficult to believe that amounted to cruelty. Even if it were true, there was little he could do about it. He had no intention of going home and being on the receiving end of his brother's sharp riposte and his father's disapproval of his way of life.

'It is all in the past,' he said. 'You are married to Andrew and should be at home with him, not being escorted around Brighton by rakes like Captain Smollett.'

'The remedy is in your hands, Justin. Escort me yourself. There is the day of the races and the Charity Ball at the Castle. If you escort me, then no one will say a thing against it. You are, after all, my brother-in-law and can stand in for Andrew.'

'I may not go.'

'Of course you will. Both events are meant to raise money to fund your hospital and you are duty-bound to put in an appearance.' She paused, her eyes brimming with false tears. 'Please, Justin, Captain Smollett cannot keep his hands to himself. I did not know he was like that, he was so charming at first. Now I am afraid. I need your protection.'

He knew Smollett's reputation and she could well have bitten off more than she could chew and really he did need to silence the gossips. 'If I escort you to the ball, will you go home afterwards?'

'Very well.' She sniffed and dabbed at her eyes with a scrap of handkerchief. 'I am not insensible of my duty, though it will break my heart.'

He could see nothing for it but to agree and she flung her arms about his neck to kiss him. He was trying to disentangle himself when there was a knock at the door and Mrs Armistead put her head round it. 'Doctor, I beg your pardon, but I must speak to you.'

Grateful for the interruption, he turned to smile at her. 'What is it, Mrs Armistead?'

She looked from him to the lady and then back again. 'My nephew is here, sir. He has come to fetch me. My sister has been taken very ill with a fever and she needs nursing and her husband and children need looking after. There is no one but me…'

'Then of course you must go to her. Do not worry. I can manage.'

'Thank you. There are three people in the waiting room. There's Mrs Maskell, who looks as if she is about to drop her infant any minute, a man with a mangled arm, dripping blood everywhere…' she paused to smile when she saw Mrs Tremayne give a visible shiver of revulsion '…and Mrs Smith has brought Tildy. She's scratched the scar on her head because it itched and made it bleed again.'

'I'll see to them. Off you go.'

As soon as she had disappeared Justin turned back to Sophie. 'I am afraid this changes everything. Without Mrs Armistead, I shall doubtless be too busy to attend social engagements…'

'Surely you can find a replacement.'

'At short notice, it will be next to impossible. Mrs Armistead was—is—an excellent nurse as well as a housekeeper and she was prepared to work for next to nothing. She will be hard to replace.'

'One more good reason to put an end to this nonsense. You are not a dogsbody, you are a gentleman. But look at you, grubbing around in the dirt like a labourer, advertising your poverty as if you were proud of it. It quite makes me shudder.'

'Then go away where you will not have to witness it.' He held the door for her and reluctantly she preceded him down the corridor. He paused outside the door of the waiting room from which a low rumble of conversation could be heard and he knew his patients were becoming impatient. He smiled suddenly. 'If you must stay, then you can make yourself useful. Take off that bonnet and pelisse and put on an apron. You can fill in the patients' cards. Names and directions, age, symptoms. It is easy enough. And then you can show them in when I ring for them.'

She gave a little shriek of laughter. 'Oh, Justin, as if I would stoop to such a thing.'

'It is what I do.'

'Not for much longer. I will lay whatever odds you choose that you will be persuaded to give up this strange life of yours.'

'Never. I am a doctor and a doctor I will always be, certainly while I have the strength to do the work.'

'So you say, but you have not accepted my wager.'

'Very well, I accept. A large donation to the new hospital if I am still here six months from now. I am sure Andrew can afford that.'

She laughed, sure of herself, and stretched to kiss his cheek, before letting herself out of the street door, leaving him to cope with his patients alone.

Having stayed out late at a whist party the night before, Anne and her aunt were sitting in the morning room over a late breakfast bemoaning the fact that neither had won. 'I had the most useless hands all evening long,' Aunt Bartrum said, buttering toast. 'Hardly a trump in them and then only low ones. The Major seemed to have them all.'

'Well, you know what they say, Aunt, unlucky at cards, lucky in love.'

'Well, I was that, of course. Dear Bartrum was a man in a million.'

'I was not referring to the past, but the future. Have you had no offers?'

'Anne, you are being perverse. I do not expect, nor even wish, to remarry. We came to Brighton on your account, not mine.'

'Ah, but if someone should capture your heart, you would not gainsay it, would you?'

'Stuff!' But her cheeks had gone quite pink and Anne smiled; her aunt was not as immune as she liked to pretend.

They were interrupted by a knock at the door and the maid came to tell them there was 'a person' at the door, asking for Miss Hemingford.

'What do you mean, "person", Betty? Did she not give her name?'

'She said it was Smith, Miss Hemingford.'

'Oh, not that fish woman,' Mrs Bartrum said, shuddering at the memory of that claustrophobic tent and the smell of the so-called monster. 'Anne, I do not think you should encourage her…'

'But I must see her, Aunt. I do not think she would call if it were not important. Perhaps she has a message from Dr Tremayne about the fund-raising. Or perhaps Tildy has had a relapse and I can help in some way.' The thought of anything happening to that lively child distressed her more than she could say. She turned to the maid, still waiting by the door. 'Show her into the downstairs parlour, Betty. I will be there directly.'

The girl disappeared and Anne hurriedly finished her breakfast and went to greet her visitor. 'Mrs Smith, I hope nothing is wrong. It isn't Tildy, is it?'

'No, no, Miss, Tildy's fine. It's Mrs Armistead. She's had to go to her sister who's been took bad and her with seven little ones. The poor doctor is all alone and the waiting room's that full, he don't rightly know which way to turn. I tried to 'elp, but he needs someone who can read 'n' write and 'sides, my family hatta come first. Mr Smith and the children need reg'lar meals and if I was to neglect me job…'

'I understand. Did Dr Tremayne send you to me?'

'No, but I reckoned you'd know how to find him some 'elp.'

If she was disappointed that the doctor had not thought of her himself, she quickly stifled it. 'I'll see what I can do. Thank you for telling me.'

Mrs Smith, her duty done, departed, leaving Anne with a problem. Could she do anything to help the doctor and would he welcome the interference if she did? But if Mrs Smith told him of her visit and she did nothing, what would he think of her?

She turned as Mrs Bartrum entered the room. 'Well, what did she want?'

'Nothing for herself, she was concerned for Dr Tremayne. Mrs Armistead has had to take leave and he is without help and inundated with patients.'

'What did she suppose you could do about it?'

'Go to the agency and hire help for him, I suppose.'

'Surely he could do that himself. After all, he knows what his requirements are.'

'I think he is too busy.'

'Anne, I do hope you are not going to become involved with any more of the doctor's problems. There is enough gossip about him already. You do not want to be tarred with the same brush.'

'Aunt Bartrum,' she said firmly. 'He is not the subject of gossip, his sister-in-law is and he cannot help that. And I am part of the fund-raising committee, part of the whole project—I must help where I can.'

'It will all end in tears.'

There had been tears in plenty already, but she was not going to admit that. Besides, they had all been shed now and she had dried her eyes and resolved to be sensible. 'No, Aunt. I had a silly moment, but it has passed now. I am thinking only of the doctor's patients.'

Her aunt sighed. 'You will do as you please, I know, you always have. Shall I come with you?'

'No, dearest, there is no need and I recollect you were going to visit Lady Mancroft this morning to help her with the arrangements for her rout. You may offer my excuses. I may join you later.'

The agency could find her no one suitable at such short notice. There was a young girl, a housemaid who had been part of a large household, but Anne knew she would not be suitable. The need, she explained, was for someone who could manage ill and injured people, some of them dirty and some possibly deranged or violent. 'We do not deal with that kind of person at all,' the woman who ran the agency told her in a voice that left Anne in no doubt such requests were far beneath her. 'Try the infirmary, they might know of some poor woman glad to earn a few coppers.'

Anne thanked her and left, starting towards the infirmary and then changing her mind when she remembered Mrs Smith saying people came out of there worse than when they went in. And this had been borne out by Dr Tremayne. 'They know nothing of cleanliness,' she recalled him saying at the meeting round the library table. 'They perform operations and treat wounds with the same unwashed hands they use to prepare food or empty slops.

Dirt is the biggest killer of all. That is why I want this hospital, so that we can lead by example.'

She could picture him, sleeves rolled up, dark hair awry, surrounded by patients, all clamouring to be seen, and it filled her with an urge to be there, to share his burden. She tried to remind herself that she was disgusted with him for kissing his sister-in-law in that intimate manner, but the image of him at work, as she had seen him work on Tildy, quite dispelled that. She set her feet firmly in the direction of his house.

Her imagination, if anything, had underestimated the pandemonium there. The waiting room was bursting and there was a long line of people patiently waiting at the door. She pushed her way in, amid angry protests that she should take her turn and being a nob didn't give her the right to be seen first.

Justin, hearing the commotion from the adjoining room, went to calm everyone down. His heart gave a lurch when he saw the cause of it, but then he steadied himself and smiled at her. 'As you see, Miss Hemingford, I am not in a position to receive visitors.'

'I am not a visitor. I am here to help.'

'You?' He only just managed to stop himself from laughing.

'Yes. Why not? I promised to find you an assistant and here I am. Tell me what to do.'

'You cannot mean that.'

'Indeed I do.'

'You must be mad.'

'No madder than you.'

They stood three feet apart and glared at each other,

until he gave a grunt that could have been a laugh, and said. 'Have it your own way. I haven't time to argue. See if you can organise these people. I need to look at the most urgent cases first. And I need records kept.' He nodded towards a chest of drawers. 'You'll find cards in there.' And with that he returned to the patient on the couch, leaving her to try and carry out his instructions.

She peeled off her lace gloves and stuffed them in her pocket before removing her coat and bonnet. She hung them on a hook behind the door where she found Mrs Armistead's discarded apron. It was much too big, but she wrapped it round herself, tying it tightly into her waist and turned to the queue. 'Now, let's see if we can have some order, shall we?'

Justin heard the commotion die down and then the soft murmur of her voice as she spoke to each patient in turn. He did not believe for a moment that she would last out an hour, let alone a day, but at least she was willing, more willing than Sophie had been. He had asked for her help only to goad her, knowing how appalled she would be. Miss Hemingford was not appalled, apparently not afraid, but she had not experienced the worst of it yet. She could have no idea what the work entailed and, for someone who had obviously never done a hand's turn in her life, it would come hard. He didn't know whether to be angry that she had the effrontery to think she could make a difference or bemused by her naïveté.

But it was wonderful to have her so near. He had only to call out and she would be there, her bright eyes meeting his, her smile setting his heart thudding. But he would not call her. It was a kind of test, a test of himself to see if he could work efficiently with her so close and a test of her to see if she had the stamina for it. If she lasted a couple of hours, he would relieve her, tell her she had proved her worth and send her home to her tea parties and fund-raising. He was very grateful to her for that. But as for acting as his assistant… She was mad and so was he to allow it.

He finished examining the patient on the couch, told him to rest at home and gave him a bottle of restorative, though nothing he could think of would restore the man's damaged heart. Then he picked up the bell and rang for his next patient.

He looked up as the door opened and Anne ushered in a woman carrying a baby who was so thin and weak, she wondered that the child was still drawing breath. She was filled with compassion and aware of her own inadequacy. 'Mrs Bristow, Doctor.'

'Thank you.' He smiled. 'You seem to have quietened them down.'

'Yes. I told them they would not be seen any quicker by making a fuss.' She paused as the mother sat down and began pulling the ragged shawl from her infant, who was too weak even to cry. 'Some of them admit they are not ill. They say you give them money to buy food for their children…'

'Food is the medicine they most need, Miss Hemingford. You will find a tin containing coins in the top drawer of the chest. Sixpence each usually suffices.'

She retreated, found the money and halved the queue in a matter of a few minutes, though some who had come only for the money undoubtedly needed medical attention as well and she told them to come back later when the doctor was less busy. There was one man who had cut the top of his thumb off at his work who needed immediate attention. She found bandages in a drawer and bound the stump as best she could before sending him in next. Others she felt were malingering, but she was not sure enough to send them away. Only the doctor could do that.

She worked steadily all morning, filling in cards, showing in patients, smiling cheerfully though some of the sights she saw appalled her. It was the tiny children who concerned her most. She was almost reduced to tears by the condition of some of them: thin as rakes, poorly clad, listless, without any of the bubbling energy of her nephew. In spite of the sores and the dirt, she took some of them in her arms and tried to comfort them before handing them back to the adults who had brought them in.

And then suddenly the last patient had gone and the waiting room was empty. She sank into a chair utterly exhausted, kicking off her shoes.

Justin found her with her head nodding on her chest, and smiled. Some of her lustrous hair had escaped from its pins and was curling about her soft cheeks, there was a spot of blood on her forehead where she had wiped it with a bloodstained hand, and more blood and grime on the overlarge apron she wore. She had worked like a Trojan and lightened his load considerably, but he could not allow her to continue. She had seen and done things today that no gently nurtured young lady should ever have to see and do and he had been a cur to subject her to it.

It was all because of Sophie, because of her reaction to his suggestion she should work. He had not meant it, knew she would not agree, but his annoyance with her had somehow transferred itself to Miss Hemingford and she had been the one to be punished. But, oh, how magnificently she had coped! If it were possible to love her more, he did at that moment.

'You poor dear,' he said softly.

'Oh.' Startled, she sat up to find him looking down at her, smiling a little. 'I am sorry…' She struggled to her feet, only to find one leg had gone dead, making her stumble. He reached out to catch her and the next minute she was being held in his arms.

She did not move, did not want to move. His arms were warm and comforting and she could hear his heartbeat against her ear, beating a little fast as hers was. Slowly she looked up into his face. He was gazing at her with an expression she could not fathom. There was a glimmer of hope there, along with sorrow, as if one were cancelling out the other. His dark eyes were no longer cold and empty, but soft pools that mirrored emotion so deep she felt herself drowning in it.

'What is there to be sorry for?' His voice was softly sensuous.

'For falling asleep at my post.' She gave a crooked smile. He had not released her; their two bodies were still entwined, so close they might almost have been one entity. 'That's punishable by a flogging in the service, is it not?'

'You think I should flog you?'

She laughed softly. 'Do you think I deserve it?'

'You deserve a medal.'

'Fustian!'

'I mean it. You have worked wonders, done more than I could ever have expected of you.' He held her at arm's length and looked down at her, smiling. 'A nurse in the making, but I cannot send you home looking like that.'

'I don't intend to go home yet. There might be more patients later…'

'Perhaps, but you have done enough. You are exhausted. I will show you where you can wash and do something with your hair.' He put out a hand to touch it, making the last of the pins fall out. It cascaded round her shoulders in a shining curtain of chestnut. 'Oh, dear, I seem to have released it all.'

'It was beyond repair anyway.' She flung her head back, making her heavy tresses swing about her face.

He was entranced and put his hand behind her neck to lift it, looking into her face. Her amber eyes were shining and her cheeks were glowing a warm pink, but it was her lips that were the centre of his gaze; slightly apart, they were rosy and inviting. Did she know what she was doing to him? Was she being deliberately provocative? Or was she simply an innocent, unaware of the havoc she was creating in his breast? With a low moan he lowered his face to hers, touching his lips to hers with gentle tenderness. It was all he intended, if it could be said he had any prior thought at all. He certainly took no time to consider how she might react.

If she was startled, it did not last. It seemed such a natural thing for him to do. She made no protest, did not draw away, and when the kiss deepened and his mouth crushed hers and forced her lips apart she experienced sensations that were entirely new and delightful; instead of pulling away in horror, she actively clung to him, wanting more.

They drew apart at last and stood looking at each other, as if weighing up what they had done to their fragile relationship. It could never be the same again and both knew it. How could they work together on the fund-raising committee, he the recipient of charity and she the benefactor, when there was that kiss drawing them close and at the same time forcing them apart? She was sure the effects of it were emblazoned on her face for all to see. And then she remembered another kiss, one he had given to his sister-in-law, one that had disgusted her. And now she was disgusted with herself.

'I must go,' she said, reaching for her pelisse and bonnet, quite forgetting she had offered to continue working.

'Not like that. You must tidy yourself first.'

She gave a harsh laugh. 'Or I will have the whole place talking, you mean.'

'They already gossip about me and I care little for that, but you must think of your own reputation. It is easy to misconstrue appearances.'

'Oh.' Did he mean when he kissed Mrs Tremayne? But he had no idea she had seen that, so he probably meant nothing. But had she misunderstood it? Had it been no more than an innocent show of affection? Oh, how she would have liked to believe that!

'Come,' he said, offering her his hand. 'I will show you where you can see to your toilette and afterwards I will fetch a cab to take you home.'

Because there was nowhere else, he took her up to his bedroom. It was surprisingly tidy, but then he was a naval man and she supposed sailors had to learn to be tidy in the crowded confines of a ship. He fetched a kettle of hot water that had been left to simmer on the hob in the kitchen, poured it into a bowl and found her a towel; then he left her.

He went down to the office to complete his notes. But today his attention wandered to the young lady who was even now stripping off and washing in his bedroom. He imagined her every move, the removing of her garments one by one, the soft flesh slowly revealed, a little at a time, and ached with the need of her. Something had passed between them that first day when she had brought Tildy to him, something immeasurable, something eternal. Had she felt it too? But why would she look at a doctor with no pretensions to do anything but serve those who needed his skills and could not afford to pay for them? He could tell her otherwise, but he had too much pride to do that. He had been a fool and he must never let it happen again.

He was still sitting disconsolately at his desk, his pen idle in his hand, when she returned. Unable to restore her coiffure, she had brushed her hair and tied it back with one of his cravats. 'I hope you don't mind,' she said.

'No, I do not mind. It is more becoming where it is than round my neck.'

'Thank you.' She paused, tongue-tied for a moment. 'Will you not let me help again?'

'No. I am grateful for your assistance, but you have done more than enough. Your aunt will think I have kidnapped you.'

For the first time Anne thought of Aunt Bartrum. She would indeed be worrying what had become of her. What she would tell the dear soul, she had no idea. 'Then if you would be kind enough to fetch a cab for me, I will go.'

'Certainly.' He rose, came round the desk towards her, then carefully skirted round her to reach the door. It was almost laughable, but she was not laughing. She wanted to cry. They had been so close, but now they were as distant as ever, just as if nothing had happened. Going into the waiting room, she retrieved her coat and slipped her arms into it in a kind of stupor. She stood dry-eyed and aching, though whether that was caused by disappointment, a feeling of being unfulfilled, or sheer physical tiredness she did not know. She had come to no conclusion when she heard voices and footsteps. Thinking it was Justin returning with the cabdriver, she turned towards the door, a bright smile fixed on her face.

'Look who has been sent by your aunt to fetch you,' he said.

She looked past him to see a tall gangly man with pale gold hair and clear blue eyes standing in the doorway. It was a moment or two before she recognised him and then her face broke into a genuine smile. 'Doctor Harrison!'

He bowed. 'Miss Hemingford, your obedient.'

'I beg your pardon. I should have said Professor Harrison. May I present Dr Tremayne.' She turned to Justin. 'This is Professor Harrison.' To which they responded by laughing aloud.

'We are acquainted,' Justin told her. 'George and I were at medical school together.'

'Oh, what a coincidence. I wrote to the Professor because I thought he might advise me on how to find you an assistant…'

'And when I read the name of your protégé,' he told her, 'I simply had to come and see for myself what he was up to.'

'Having a well-earned break, though it will not last,' Justin put in drily. 'I have lost my usual nurse and Miss Hemingford has been standing in for her.'

Professor Harrison smiled. 'Yes, Mrs Bartrum guessed as much. I went there first, of course, expecting to see Miss Hemingford. The good lady explained what had happened.' He turned to Anne. 'She told me she was concerned that you would do something foolish.'

Unable to prevent herself, she looked across at Justin and found him looking back at her with a half-amused, half-wry expression on his face. She felt the warmth flood into her cheeks and quickly turned away. She had certainly done something foolish, though she did not think that was what her aunt had meant. Before she could think of a suitable reply, Justin answered for her.

'She has certainly done that,' he said, his face a mask of gravity. 'She insisted on working here all morning and has exhausted herself. I was about to find a cab to send her home when you arrived.'

'I came in Mrs Bartrum's carriage,' George put in. 'Her driver is with it, so if you would like to take it, Miss Hemingford, I will stay here and talk to my old friend. Perhaps I may call on you later?'

'We are expected at Lady Mancroft's rout,' she said. 'It is in aid of the fund…' She paused, wondering if the Professor would be welcome in her ladyship's drawing room, but then she told herself he was a step above an ordinary physician and, as Dr Tremayne was expected, she could not see there would be any objection. 'Why not come too? You could come as our guest.'

'I shall be honoured.' He gave her another polite bow.

She extended her hand, which he took and held an inch or two from his lips before releasing it. Justin, when he was offered the same courtesy, actually kissed the back of her hand. His lips were warm and dry and sent shivers up her arm and down through her whole body, churning her stomach all over again, making her feel wanton. But she was not a wanton; she was a respectable spinster. She snatched her hand away. 'Good day, gentlemen. I hope your discussion is fruitful.' She pulled on her gloves, retrieved her reticule, now without the few coins it had contained when she arrived—she had put it all in the waiting-room cash box—and allowed the Professor to escort her from the house to the carriage, which he had left at the end of the street.

'When I wrote, it was advice I needed,' she told him. 'I did not expect you to drop everything and come in person.'

'I know, but by coincidence I found myself with time to spare and was thinking of taking a holiday when your letter arrived. Curiosity overcame me. I simply had to come and see what was going on.'

'Nothing is going on. You can see the doctor is completely dedicated to his work and all I want to do is help him.'

He made no comment to what had seemed a defensive remark and opened the door of the carriage to hand her in. 'I shall enjoy mulling it over with him. Please offer my respects to your aunt. We will meet again this evening.'

He stood back to watch as Daniels flicked the reins and the carriage carried her away, then he returned to his friend, who conducted him to the drawing room and poured wine for them both.

'A remarkable woman,' George said, taking a glass and folding his long form into one of the battered armchairs.

'Indeed she is.'

'How did you meet her?'

Justin explained about Tildy and the curricle. 'From then on, things just happened,' he said. 'She seemed to want to take over my life.' He paused and laughed. 'In my own best interests, of course.'

'That sounds like the Miss Hemingford I know. She once involved me in a scheme to bring together her noddycock of a brother and her second cousin, a sweet little thing but without Miss Hemingford's strength of character.'

'No doubt she succeeded.'

'Oh, yes. I was obliged to explain to Miss Jane's father that the two young ladies needed a recuperative holiday and she arranged for her brother to escort them. Very neat.'

'And the outcome?'

'Why, a marriage, of course. The brother and cousin married and since then he has inherited.'

'Inherited what?'

'Why, the title and the estate. Did you not know the old man was dead?'

'What old man?'

'The Earl of Bostock. Do you mean to say you did not know Hemingford is the Bostock family name?'

Justin was taken aback. Why had he not rumbled it? Bostock was one of the oldest earldoms in the country and the estate was vast. He had guessed she was high in the instep, but it had never entered his head who she really was, a member of one of the richest families in the kingdom. And he had had the temerity to kiss her and make her work in gore and filth! His guts curled in embarrassment at the thought of it. 'I do not live in society, turned my back on it, so to speak, and it slipped my memory.'

George laughed. 'And now she has a new crusade. What is she planning for you, my friend?'

'A new hospital.'

'Then you will almost certainly have it. Once Miss Anne Hemingford goes on the march, there is no stopping her.'

'So I have discovered, but as it is meant to help me in my work, I have no objection.'

'Just what is this work? I assume this will be no ordinary hospital.'

'No, it won't.' He paused as his stomach rumbled. 'But I'm gut-foundered. I've had nothing to eat since a hasty breakfast. If you do not mind, I'll tell you about it over a meal. My housekeeper has had to go and visit a sick sister, so we had better go out and sample the fare at a local hostelry.'

'Better still, we will stroll back to my hotel. The food there is excellent and you can tell me everything while we walk. I do not suppose you have a carriage.'

Justin laughed. 'No, I'm afraid not.' He looked at his friend's fashionable frockcoat, brocade waistcoat and intricately tied cravat and smiled wryly. George had come up in the world and left him behind. 'I need to change my clothes, if you will excuse me.'

He collected a jug of water from the kitchen and rushed up to his bedroom. The water he had poured for Anne was still there, gone cold now, and the towel she had used was draped over the end of the bedstead to dry, still smelling faintly of her perfume. He had had old Bostock's grand-daughter in his bedroom; they had been together without a sniff of a chaperon. His face burned at the memory of his erotic fantasy.

For the first time since leaving home, he half regretted turning his back on his family, which would have made him acceptable in society's eyes. But, no, he had made his decision to take the road he had and there was no going back. Pulling himself together, he poured the water out of the bowl and replaced it with fresh, then washed and searched in his chest for something suitable to wear, something that would take him to Lady Mancroft's rout after their meal.

The clothes he worked in were too shabby and his dress uniform too grand for the occasion, but under both he found a dark blue superfine tailcoat he had bought when he first returned home from the war. Although it was two years out of date, it was hardly worn and there were pale blue pantaloons and a blue-and-white-striped waist-coat in some shiny material. He found a shirt and a newly starched cravat, for which he murmured thanks to the absent Mrs Armistead, and quickly dressed. A brush through his hair and he was ready.

'Oh, I see you are civilised,' George commented on seeing him.

He grinned. 'When occasion demands it.'

'Not very often by the look of that coat.' It was said with an indulgent smile. 'When did you buy it?'

'Eighteen-twelve, I think, or it might have been thirteen. There's nothing wrong with it, is there?'

'Nothing at all, my friend,' he said, watching Justin attach a note to his door telling prospective patients that the consulting rooms would be open at eight the following morning and where he could be contacted in case of an emergency. 'Will they dare come knocking on Lady Mancroft's door, do you think?'

'Not unless the emergency is dire. They are usually considerate.' He picked up his hat. 'Shall we go?'

'Now,' George said as they walked among the promenaders on the sea front. 'Tell me how you came to be scraping a living in a slum in Brighton.'

It was a long story and Justin did not feel inclined to reveal the whole of it, but he did go into more detail when it came to his mission among the poor people of the town and his theories about cleanliness. By the time they entered the portals of the best hotel in town his friend had all the salient facts with none of the emotional turmoil that still assailed him. 'I believe there are virulent organisms at work for which soap alone is not enough,' he concluded. 'And that has led to a study of why some diseases affect the poor more than the rich, how much of it is hereditary and how much a result of the conditions under which people live.'

'All very commendable,' George said, as they made their way to the dining room.. 'I have been working on something similar myself, doing tests in the laboratory, involving my pupils, though the evidence is circumstantial and we have yet to find proof.'

'I do not intend to wait around for the old fogies to come round to my way of thinking. I mean to show I am right in the real world, the one of poverty, disease and sickness. Rates of recovery from wounds and surgery will be proof enough for me.'

They paused in their discussion to order a capon, pork chops and vegetables, and then continued tossing ideas about the hospital back and forth while they ate until George was as enthusiastic as he was. 'Have you found premises or do you mean to build?' he asked.

'I have been given notice to quit my present premises and have no time to build. Besides, it will be far too dear. I am looking for a large house to convert, one that will also give me and my staff a home. The problem is that places like that are being converted into boarding houses, which is a far more lucrative proposition for the owners.'

'Considering that the Regent has made Brighton *the* place to be seen after the London Season, I am hardly surprised. I wonder at you choosing it.'

'It chose me. You may see only the glitter of the *beau monde,* but behind that there is a community of fisher folk and artisans being pushed out of their traditional way of life.'

'And you have made them your own?'

'It happened.'

'Why? How?'

Justin paused, wondering how to tell him without divulging all the hurt and misery that had preceded it. In the end he gave George the same explanation he had given

Walter Gosforth, that the lady he had hoped to marry had chosen his brother instead. He said nothing of a broken engagement or the gossip that followed it. He had hoped that was dead and buried. 'I could not settle at home when I left the navy,' he told him. 'It was too painful for everyone concerned. I was staying a few days in Brighton when my skill as a doctor was called upon to treat a child bitten by a dog. And then his parents needed help and before I knew what was happening I found myself inundated with patients.'

'And that is fulfilling?'

His mind travelled fleetingly to Anne, but he would not allow it to linger there. 'Yes, except for a conviction that I could, and should, do more.'

'And so the idea of a hospital was born?'

'Yes. But I do not have the resources to fund it and that is why we have formed an association to raise the necessary finance, not only to find and equip the hospital, but maintain it as well. The patients themselves will pay only if they can afford to.'

'And Miss Hemingford?'

'What about her?'

'Come, my dear fellow. I am not blind. I saw how it was.'

'I told you she had been working, getting her hands dirty…' He paused and smiled wryly. 'More than her hands, her face too.'

'She is very beautiful, even more when she is dishevelled, I think,' George said. 'It is a wonder she has never married. After all, her dowry must be a great incentive to set against the fact that she is perhaps too forthright…'

'She may be forthright, as you say.' Justin felt bound to defend her, though he felt ill at ease talking about her. 'But she is full of compassion and not at all top-lofty.'

'Oh, I know that. There was a time…' He stopped suddenly and laughed. 'Wishful thinking on my part, of course, but she did show me more than mere courtesy…'

Justin was seized with something he would not admit was jealousy that his friend could speak so lightly of the woman who had won his heart. He pulled himself together. 'What happened?'

'Why, nothing. Nothing could, I was flying too high.'

'She is not like that!'

'No, but her family are.'

Justin had to admit he was probably right if Mrs Bartrum was an example. 'I believe her aunt has set herself the task of finding a husband for her.'

'Are you among those being considered?'

'No, of course not, but if you come to the rout, you will see them for yourself.'

George drained his glass. 'Then let us be off. It promises to be a very interesting evening.'

Chapter Seven

Anne was subdued as her aunt's carriage carried them the short distance to Lady Mancroft's house, which was hardly surprising after the peal Aunt Bartrum had rung over her when she returned home from the doctor's.

'Anne, whatever has happened to you?' she had demanded, catching sight of her niece trying to make for the safety of her bedroom without being seen. 'Have you had an accident?'

'No, Aunt.'

'Oh, do not tell me you have been assaulted? Oh, you foolish, foolish girl, to go out alone like that…'

'Aunt, I have not been assaulted,' she had reassured her with a crooked smile. Could what had happened be considered an assault? An assault on her senses perhaps, an attack on her emotions, but it was her own fault for allowing it to happen. 'I could not find a helper for Dr Tremayne and went to tell him so. There were so many patients waiting—'

'Anne, do you mean to say you actually *touched* them?' Her aunt sounded horrified.

'Some. The children. I felt so sorry for them. There was a little baby, half-starved it was, and a small boy. He was crying and I tried to comfort him. My hair came down.'

'So I see.' Her aunt had pressed her lips together in disapproval. 'What have you tied it back with?'

'A cravat. Doctor Tremayne lent it to me.'

'Anne!' her aunt had gasped, clutching at the jet necklace at her throat. 'I am in despair. If this gets out, we will not be able to hold our heads up in society again. Your reputation will be in shreds and mine along with it.'

She had continued in like vein for several minutes and Anne, who hated upsetting her, had apologised for her thoughtlessness and promised it would not happen again. 'Now Professor Harrison has arrived, there will be no need. I left them with their heads together, talking about the new hospital.'

'I am beginning to wish I had never heard of it. If we had not come to Brighton—'

'We would never have met Major Mancroft and Captain Gosforth, would we?' Anne had put in, in an effort to raise her spirits.

'Whatever will they think?'

'Why, nothing. There is no reason they should ever learn of it, is there?'

'I suppose not. Now, do go and change and throw that gown away, it will never clean properly.'

Anne was exhausted, physically, mentally and emotionally, but she realised it would be unwise to complain of it and so she had gone up to her room, where the maids were busy filling a bath. Having drunk a reviving cup of tea, she had bathed and dressed in a rose-and-burgundy-striped sarcenet and sat for Amelia to put her hair up, and by then she felt more like her old self. Except for the memories, memories of being held in Justin's arms, of being kissed, the soft touch of his lips on hers and the sensations that had aroused; memories like that would never leave her. And in a very few minutes she had to face him again, and in company, and whatever happened she must not give herself away.

Lady Mancroft's large ground-floor drawing room was full to bursting, which was gratifying since everyone had paid five guineas to the fund for the privilege of being there. A string quartet played in a corner but no one was listening to the music. It was far more diverting to make one's way, wineglass in hand, from group to group, exchanging gossip.

Anne made her way between them, keeping close to her aunt as if wanting her protection, which was so unlike her, she was able to smile at herself. Disjointed snatches of conversation came to her ears as they passed on their way to greet their hostess, who was holding court in the far corner of the room. 'Will he come?' and further on, 'He won't bring his mistress, will he?'

'Georgiana!' Her ladyship, being very tall, had caught sight of them above the mêlée and began elbowing her way towards them.

'What a squeeze it is,' she said, after Aunt Bartrum had greeted her with a kiss on each cheek. 'I am sure there are more people here than I invited...'

'As long as they have all paid, that is to the good, do you not think?' Anne said. 'I am pleased to see that so many people are in favour of the hospital.'

'They are here because they think a very important personage might put in a brief appearance.'

'No? He never is!' exclaimed Aunt Bartrum. She looked down at her high-waisted satin gown striped in two shades of grey, obviously regretting its simplicity. 'If I had known…'

'Charles took the opportunity of acquainting him with the aims of the association when he was called to attend him,' their hostess explained. 'He thought his Highness's approbation might serve us well. Charles said that an interest was expressed in tonight's function.'

'Then we must thank the Major for his thoughtfulness,' Mrs Bartrum said, looking round the company. 'But I do not see him.'

'I believe he is in the card room. We have arranged a few tables for those who like a small wager, but they have to promise to donate a percentage of their winnings.'

'Then I shall go in search of him,' Aunt Bartrum said. 'Anne, do you come with me.'

Anne smiled; her aunt was determined not to let her out of her sight. She need not have worried; the last thing her niece wanted, so she told herself, was a confrontation with Dr Tremayne. She refused to admit, even to herself, that she had been gazing about the room looking for him. Perhaps he would not come. If he and the Professor had become engrossed in talking about medical matters and old times, then they might have decided to forgo the doubtful privilege of fighting their way through the crowd and having to make meaningless conversation.

Major Mancroft was not playing cards because all the places were taken, but he was standing to one side watching the play. As soon as he saw Mrs Bartrum and Anne, he came forward to bow to them. 'Good evening, ladies. It is good so see you. And looking so elegant too. Mrs Bartrum, that gown becomes you exceedingly.'

'Why, thank you,' Aunt Bartrum said, almost preening. 'But do you not think Miss Hemingford is in looks tonight?'

He turned to smile at Anne. 'Indeed she is. Two jewels in this packed company.'

'I believe you have been working on our behalf and we must thank you,' Mrs Bartrum said, digging her elbow into Anne's side.

'To be sure, Major,' she agreed, endeavouring not to smile at the Major's clumsy attempts at flattery. 'We have been overwhelmed by the support given to our project through your good offices.'

'Oh, it is nothing. I slipped the information about tonight's occasion into the conversation, that is all. I doubt he will come, but even the rumour of it has swelled our funds, don't you think?' And he winked and touched the side of his nose with his finger.

'Major! That is dishonest,' Anne said, wondering how well one needed to know the Prince to be able to slip something into a conversation with him.

'Not at all. He did not say he would not come. If he had, then it would indeed have been a hum.'

'Where is Captain Gosforth?' Aunt Bartrum asked. 'I have not seen him.'

The Major's expression clouded at the mention of his rival, but it quickly cleared. 'I expect he is somewhere about. I cannot imagine he would absent himself,' he said drily. 'Not when he knows you will be here.'

'Then we shall go and find him and leave you to your game.'

'I was not playing,' he said quickly. 'Allow me to escort you.' And he offered his arm.

Aunt Bartrum nimbly skipped out of his way so that he found himself beside Anne. He could hardly turn away and she, smiling at his chagrin, put her fingers on the crook of his elbow to follow her aunt. 'I am sorry, Major,' she whispered, as they returned to the drawing room by way of the stairs and the entrance hall. 'Aunt Bartrum can be very contrary sometimes. Have you spoken to her about your intentions?'

'Not exactly. I hinted, but she always manages to turn the conversation. She speaks of you and how it is her duty to see you happily married…'

'Oh, dear. Perhaps it is time you did more than hint.'

'Oh, do you think so?' His face lit with hope, making her smile. Whether her aunt would entertain an offer from him she did not know, but it was time something was resolved.

It was at that point Anne saw Professor Harrison and Dr Tremayne come in the front door and her heart skipped a beat. The doctor looked so different from the tired, dishevelled man she had left only a few hours before. Dressed in shades of blue, not quite up to the minute, but very fine for all that, he held himself with the easy assurance of a man used to being waited on, as he handed the footman his hat. No one who did not know the truth would take him for anything other than a gentleman.

He looked across the hall and caught sight of her on the arm of Major Mancroft and his face clouded briefly. Mrs Bartrum had evidently been to work on them, judging by the way Miss Hemingford was hanging on to the Major's arm and laughing up at him. Surely she would not succumb? He wanted to rush over and tear her away. Instead he bowed. 'Miss Hemingford, your obedient.'

'Doctor Tremayne.' She inclined her head in formal acknowledgement. Whatever had been between them, if there had ever been anything between them, had gone, been blown away on a contrary wind. The cold emptiness was back in his eyes. She could not bear it and turned away. 'Professor Harrison, I am pleased to see you have been prevailed upon to join us.' The smile she turned on him was one of genuine warmth, not lost on Justin.

How could she allow him to kiss her, more than that, actively respond, and then turn to others so readily? Was she a flirt? Did she enjoy teasing? 'Major, may I present Professor Harrison?' he heard her say. 'He is a teacher at Guy's Hospital. I believe his advice on our project will be of inestimable value.'

'Then you are welcome, sir,' Charles acknowledged him with a bow. 'Do you know Mrs Bartrum?' He turned to the lady with a smile, which confused Justin even more. What was going on?

'We are acquainted,' Aunt Bartrum said, coming forward. 'How do you do, Professor. Shall we go into the drawing room? I will present to you our hostess. Come, Doctor, do join us.' And with that she almost dragged the two gentlemen away, leaving Anne with the Major.

'Oh, dear,' Anne said. 'I had hoped to leave you alone with her. Now you will have to find another opportunity.'

'I shall not find it standing out here. Shall we follow them?'

Anne could hardly say she did not want to be anywhere near Dr Tremayne because that would be a consummate lie. She longed to be near him, to be close, so close she could experience again the tremors, the excitement that coursed through her at his touch. If a touch could do that, if a kiss could make her lose all reason, how would she feel if they went even further? If they… She shivered as her imagination pictured it. How could she, a respectable well brought-up young lady, have such wanton thoughts?

'Are you cold, Miss Hemingford?' The Major's voice was so ordinary, it brought her back to earth with a bump. 'I could fetch you a shawl.'

'No, not at all.'

'Then let us hasten to Mrs Bartrum's side.'

Aunt Bartrum was in the middle of an animated group of people who were evidently enjoying each other's company. There was Lord and Lady Mancroft, a little bemused at having to entertain two doctors, even though one was an eminent professor; Mrs Barry, watching over her two chicks like a mother hen; and Captain Gosforth. 'He would be here,' the Major muttered.

They were drawn into the group, which had been discussing the impact the interest of the Regent might have on their project. 'I believe it will have an adverse effect,' the Captain was saying. 'He is far from popular.'

'Only with the proletariat,' her ladyship put in. 'Those of us with any pretence of breeding know what a fine man he is.'

'Fat,' muttered Justin, who was standing close enough to Anne for her to hear.

She smiled in spite of herself. 'Fie on you, Doctor, you must not say disparaging things about our future king, especially if he becomes a benefactor.'

'If he does, then I shall bow and scrape with the best of them, but give me leave to doubt it. His unpopularity with his people is well earned. He spends a fortune on that monstrous building while a large section of his subjects lives in abject poverty.'

'It is a beautiful building, how can you say it is monstrous?'

'Huge, like its owner, and just as impractical.'

'I give you that, but it is employing hundreds of men who would otherwise be out of work.'

He ignored her riposte. 'Miss Hemingford, I must speak to you.'

'We are speaking.'

'I mean alone. There are matters I must put before you.'

'I do not think that would be wise, sir. You might be tempted to repeat your behaviour of this morning…'

'My behaviour!' His whisper was indignant. 'It takes two, you know, and I do not recollect you protesting.'

'You took me by surprise.'

He managed a rueful grin. 'I took myself by surprise. But you are right, an apology is called for and I offer it humbly.'

He did not look particularly humble, she decided, risking a glance at his face; he looked cross. 'I accept your apology,' she murmured. 'We will speak of it no more.' She turned and smiled brightly at Professor Harrison. 'What do you think of our project to provide Dr Tremayne with a hospital?'

'Very commendable and I wish you success with it. If there is anything I can do to help, you have only to say…'

'If you could recommend one of your pupils as an assistant, that would be of most immediate help, I think. Dr Tremayne is overworked to the point of exhaustion…'

'I will say when I am exhausted,' Justin put in sharply. 'And looking after a handful of ailing civilians is nothing to spending twenty-fours hours without a break in the bowels of a fighting ship in the middle of a battle.' He regretted his words as soon as he had said them. She looked as though she had been struck. 'I am sorry. That was uncivil of me. I beg your pardon.'

'I understand,' she said quietly. 'I am a meddlesome female. You are perfectly able to put your own case.'

'But Miss Hemingford has the right of it,' George pointed out. 'You need help if you are not to wear yourself out and then you would be no use to your patients or anyone else. I will be glad to recommend a pupil to assist you, but until he arrives, I will be your assistant.'

'You?' Justin almost laughed, then, realising his friend was serious, added, 'Do you mean it? It's not the kind of work you are used to.'

'All the more reason to do it. How can I inculcate the notion of service in my pupils, if I do not practise what I preach? Besides, I am interested in your plans and would like to be involved.'

'Splendid!' Anne said, glad the uncomfortable moment with the doctor had passed. 'I shall not need to go to the consulting rooms again if you are there. To tell the truth, I think I am better employed organising our fundraising activities.' She looked across at Aunt Bartrum, who seemed visibly relieved at this statement. 'We are holding a day of horse racing and sport on the Belle Vue Fields next Thursday and a grand charity ball at the Old Castle the following Monday week. We hope by then to have a tidy sum, sufficient for Dr Tremayne to start looking for premises. I do hope you will join in. We could co-opt you on to our committee. What do you think, Lady Mancroft?'

Her ladyship, mollified that Anne had deferred to her as the senior ranking lady present, quickly included the newcomer in the discussion about how the games should be organised and Anne was able to slip away. She needed a quiet moment to compose herself.

She found the room on the first floor, which had been set aside for the ladies to refresh their toilette, and sank into the corner of a *chaise longue.*

She had fallen into a coil of her own making. From a simple wish to help the poor and ill people of the town, she had progressed to wanting a hospital and that had led to involving others with more influence than she had, and now there was a committee and half the town talking about it. Even the Prince Regent. None of that would have bothered her if it had not been for her personal feelings for the man at the centre of it all.

She was reminded of the snowballs she used to make with Harry at Sutton Park when they were children. The more they rolled them, the bigger they became. For a few minutes she relaxed and allowed her memory to linger. She could see again the hill in the park and Harry and herself, wrapped up in warm coats, mufflers and fur-lined boots, careering down it, pushing the ball of snow until it was bigger than they were. It fell apart at the bottom, shattered into a pile of white powder and they had rolled in it, screaming with laughter. In spite of having lost both parents in a dreadful coaching accident, they had been happy children. They had a home with their grandfather and wanted for nothing, except a little discipline perhaps, and someone warm and soft to cuddle. Fond as she had been of the old man, she would never have dared go so far as to embrace him.

Grandpa. Had she mourned him as she should? Enjoy yourself, he had commanded her from the grave, but her attempts at enjoyment had fallen more flat than she could ever have imagined. There was less joy than anguish. She loved a man of whom her aunt did not approve as a possible husband for her, but that was not the worst of it; that could be overcome. The worst of it was that while Dr Tremayne had kissed her and set her limbs on fire with longing, he had spoken no words of love, had regretted it with an apology, while at the same time suggesting it was all her fault. And at the back of her mind was the memory of him kissing his sister-in-law. How could she have been such a ninny?

What would Harry make of it? She had always been close to her twin, able to tell him everything. Perhaps if she went home… But how could she, when she had been the instigator of the fund raising and so much depended on it? The hospital was a necessity if poor children like those she had seen that morning were to be helped. Her thoughts went round and round, while she tried to lose herself deeper into the sofa.

She sat up with a jerk as Mrs Tremayne glided into the

room and went over to the dressing table to look in the mirror. Believing herself alone, she turned her head this way and that, touched her finger to her fair hair and smiled to herself. Suddenly catching sight of Anne in the reflection of the room behind her, she whirled round. 'Why, Miss Hemingford, I did not see you at first. Why are you hiding?'

'I am not hiding, Mrs Tremayne, I am resting.'

'Too much for you, is it? All this attention.'

'I do not know what you mean.'

'Everybody rallying round you to help open a hospital. It is a vast undertaking and one requiring a great deal of money and—what shall we say?—aplomb. I think you have bitten off more than you can swallow, my dear.'

'Oh, that! It is a little tiring, but it is a good cause and I assure you I am perfectly able to swallow whatever I chew.'

'It will never come to fruition, certainly not with Justin at the centre of it.' She took a step towards Anne to stand over her, meaning, Anne was sure, to intimidate her.

'Why do you say that?'

'Because he is only playing at being a doctor. He has these fancies, you know, but they do not last. First he must go to sea and not even as a fighting man, but a surgeon, and then he must travel, and then he suddenly decided he would like to live in a slum and experience poverty at first hand. It is all a gull, he is not poor, or anything like it, and the whim will pass just as all the others have.'

'You mean he is not a proper doctor?' The question was forced from her.

Sophie's laughter peeled out. 'It depends what you mean by proper. His behaviour is most improper, but if you mean has he qualified, then I believe he has. But that is nothing to the point; studying medicine was another of his fancies. The developers will pull his house down and he will realise how foolish he has been and return home where he belongs.'

Anne was relieved to hear that the doctor had not been duping people about his qualifications. As for improper behaviour; her cheeks burned at the memory. How much did this woman know? Had the doctor confided in her? She pulled herself together to answer coolly, 'There is nothing reprehensible in wanting to help those who are not in a position to help themselves. I am sure Dr Tremayne is sincere in that.'

Unable to intimidate her, Sophie sank on to the sofa beside her and tried a different tactic. 'Of course he is sincere,' she confided. 'That is half the trouble. He really believes what he is doing at the time. It is only when the project, whatever it is, palls and he is off again that the dear people he has involved in it realise his capricious nature. Believe me, it will happen again and you will be left high and dry.'

'I am sure you are wrong.'

'My dear, I have known him for a long time.' She gave a light laugh. 'If you have been taken in by him, I do most sincerely caution you. It would not do, you know. I do not know how deep your pockets are, but wealth alone is not enough. He would never marry beneath him.'

Anne was so furious she jumped to her feet. 'Just how far beneath him do you suppose me to be?'

'I am sure I do not know, but if you can grub around at those filthy consulting rooms of his, you cannot be far up the social scale.'

Anne began to laugh and sat down again, hugging her arms round her in her mirth, until the tears came to her eyes. There was something frenetic about it.

'Why are you laughing? I was not jesting.'

She was about to enlighten her tormentor, but then decided to not to do so. It would be a diversion to play along with her and see how she reacted when she finally learned the truth. 'Oh, no reason,' she said, wiping her eyes. 'The idea of a man choosing to live in poverty when he does not need to, I suppose. That's doing it too brown.'

'As I said, he has these notions. He may fancy acting the philanthropist, but you note he is not using his own blunt.'

'But he has done so and spent it all.'

'Gammon!'

Anne did not know what to believe. There had always been a mystery surrounding the doctor, even her aunt had said so, which might have been why she was against him. But she did not want to believe that he had deliberately misled people, that he was a fraudster. Surely she would have known, would have detected it in his manner? She found herself thinking about his manner. When he was not kissing her, melting her limbs until they were liquid with desire, he had a gentle and caring manner and there was no doubt the poor people he treated held him in the highest regard. Surely they could not all be wrong?

'I shall bring him to his senses,' Sophie said, sensing her uncertainty. 'He will come home with me to Seven-elms where he belongs, so I suggest you retrench before you are hurt. Do not encourage him in his folly.'

Anne did not answer; her tears of laughter had dried on her cheeks and made her skin feel taut. She no longer felt like laughing. There was so much to think about. Was Dr Tremayne really wealthy? Did he come from a nota-ble family? Aunt Bartrum had certainly said she thought he was higher in the social scale than he pretended, but why would anyone do that? And where was Sevenelms? Was it a village? An estate? Or simply the name of a house? If she had been duped, then so had all the good people of Brighton who had subscribed to the hospital project. And she had been instrumental in bringing that about! How mortifying that would be, not only for her but Aunt Bartrum and Harry too, if it all turned out to be a hum.

She was roused from her reverie by Sophie's soft laugh. 'Give up, my dear. A nobody of a do-gooder has no hope of capturing him.' She stopped speaking as the Barry girls came into the room, laughing at a joke one of the lieuten-ants had made.

Anne rose and left the room with all the dignity she could muster.

Back in the crowded drawing room she found her aunt in conversation with Captain Gosforth. Mrs Bartrum was laughing like a schoolgirl, her cheeks a little pink. She turned when she saw Anne. 'There you are, my dear, we have been wondering what had become of you. There is to be music and the Captain is endeavouring to persuade me to sing, but I fear I am not up to standard for a public performance…'

'Of course you are, Aunt, you have a beautiful singing voice.'

'There, what did I tell you?' Walter put in. 'I will be happy to accompany you.' He smiled and bent his head lower and Anne caught his whisper. 'Not only tonight, but always…'

So he had declared himself at last. Her aunt, whose pink cheeks became even rosier, tapped his arm with her fan. 'Captain, you go too far.'

'I beg you to forgive me. Impatience, don't you know.'

Her aunt was prevailed upon to entertain the company and then others were persuaded to sing or play and all the time Anne looked about her for Dr Tremayne, determined to face him out with Mrs Tremayne's accusations. But he was nowhere to be seen. 'Where is Dr Tremayne?' she asked the Major, as the recital came to an end amid generous applause.

'He was called away. Urgent, he said.'

'Oh.' Their confrontation would have to wait. But she was determined it would not wait too long.

The party broke up at midnight with everyone promising to attend the races. Anne, still unsure of whether to believe Mrs Tremayne, was tempted to confide in her aunt as they were carried home in the carriage, but decided against it. Until she was sure, she would say nothing.

'Do you know, that foolish man has misunderstood,' her aunt said.

'Foolish man?' she queried, still thinking of the doctor. 'What has he misunderstood?'

'That I am only in Brighton for your sake. He appears to think that, being a widow, I am in want of a husband…'

'Oh, you mean the Major.'

'No, I do not,' she said sharply. 'I mean Captain Gosforth. He has been talking the most arrant nonsense and will not believe that I have been trying to promote you. It is all very vexing…'

'Is it, Aunt? I should have thought you would be pleased…'

'How can I be pleased when I have failed you so badly?'

'But you have not failed me. I told you from the start I was not thinking of marriage; if you turn him away on my account, I shall be the one who is vexed.'

'We had to fall back on the Captain after you told me the Major was already spoken for,' she went on, ignoring Anne's protests. 'Though who it can be I do not know. I have not noticed him paying particular attention to anyone else. I believe you may be mistaken in that and he simply said that to encourage you…'

Anne was glad of the darkness of the coach to conceal her smile. Not for the world would she hurt her aunt by making fun of her. 'If that is so, then I am afraid he will be disappointed. He is an amiable man, but not for me.'

'Oh, Anne, you are not still wearing the willow for Dr Tremayne, are you?'

'No, of course not,' Anne said quickly, too quickly to convince her aunt. 'And I wish you would not prose on about him.'

'Anne, I have been hearing rumours…'

Anne's breath caught in her throat and her voice was husky. 'What rumours?'

'That he was once engaged…'

'So?'

'I believe he was the one to break it off.'

'Who told you this?'

'The Major. He had it from Captain Smollett and one must suppose that the Captain learned it from Mrs Tremayne, so it must be true.' She paused while Anne digested this information. 'I was right about his rank. He is the second son of Viscount Rockbourne.'

For the second time that night, Anne's laughter was almost hysterical. 'First he is looked down upon as inferior; then, when we discover he is a man of substance after all, he is still not acceptable in society because he has done something so dishonourable as to renege on a betrothal,' she spluttered. 'Do you not find that amusing?'

'Betrayal is never amusing, dearest,' her aunt said, putting a hand on her arm to calm her.

'No, Aunt, but I am not at all sure we should believe everything Mrs Tremayne says.' She spoke firmly, but the doubts were there in her mind and would not go away.

'What has she to gain by spreading a story like that if it is not true?'

'I do not know, but there is something havey-cavey…'

'Of course there is, he is trying to hide his shame.'

'He does not behave like a man with a shameful past. He is far too arrogant for that.'

'The trouble is that you do not want to believe it.'

Silently Anne agreed, but they had stopped outside the house and the coachman was opening the door and letting down the step, bringing an end to the conversation. Not wanting to renew it after they entered the house, Anne said goodnight to her aunt and made her way to her bed, where she lay going over every word of what Mrs Tremayne had said, mulling it over, wondering if she could possibly have misunderstood. There was only one way to find out and that was to confront Dr Tremayne and insist that he tell her. But why would he? Why would he admit to what, among the *haut monde,* amounted to a crime? Was that why he had turned his back on society to work among the poor?

She slept at last, but her sleep was disturbed by night-mares. Something grey and slimy was crawling all over her and though she tried to run from it, it followed her as she ran across the strand into the sea. She was swimming, using all her strength to escape, but although she was thrashing out with her legs, she could make no headway and the monster, which seemed to be at home in the sea, was gaining on her, swamping her and she could not throw it off.

Anne woke in a cold sweat to find all the bedclothes in a tangled heap and her pillow on the floor. A golden rapier of sunshine had found its way between the folds of the curtains and was shining on the wall beside her bed.

She smiled ruefully and left the tangled sheets to go and draw the curtains. The sky was streaked with pink and mauve around the rising sun and the sea glittered sharp as a diamond, smooth as silk. Instead of rousing Amelia, who never liked to rise early, she dressed in a blue spotted muslin gown, slipped a silk shawl about her shoulders and, after leaving a note telling her aunt that she had gone for a dip, she crept from the house, making for the beach.

Mrs Smith was beside her bathing machine, mending

one of the brown cotton gowns she provided for her bathers. Anne greeted her and asked after Tildy before paying her money and climbing into the little hut to change. Five minutes later, she had ducked under the sheltering hood and was swimming strongly out to sea. Deliberately she turned and made for the little cove beneath the cliffs from which she knew Dr Tremayne bathed.

There was no one about. She waded ashore and looked about her. The sand was firm and pale, without the blemish of a footmark. No one had been there since the last high tide. She sat down on a rock to wait.

Half an hour passed and no one came. Her disappointment was almost tangible. She told herself firmly that it was only because she was anxious to clear the air, to learn the truth in order that the hospital project could go ahead unsullied by gossip. It had, she upbraided herself, nothing to do with her personal feelings. She rose and paced the sand, wondering whether to return to the bathing machine, glancing upwards to see if anyone was coming down the path from the top of the cliffs. It remained deserted. At the top she could see a building, its windows reflecting the light from sun and sea and she wondered what it was. Suddenly making up her mind, she scrambled up the path towards it.

It was a large house, empty and deserted. Weeds choked the path to the door and the uncurtained windows were festooned with cobwebs. She went closer and, shielding her face with both hands, peered inside one of the downstairs rooms. There was no furniture, except for a table, a cupboard and a few broken chairs but, though everywhere was thick with dust, the room was light and spacious. Excitement mounting, she ran round to the other side, which fronted on to a narrow lane. There was an oak front door with a tarnished knocker and more weeds growing in the drive. She stood back and looked upwards. It had two solid brick storeys and a row of dormer windows to the attics above those. It was obvious it had not been lived in for years. Why did not bother her, but here was their hospital.

Impatient to find out who the owner was and whether it was for sale or lease, she ran back to the cliff path and skittered down its steep incline to the beach. She was not looking where she was going or she might have stopped herself, but her own momentum carried her down and straight into the arms of Justin making his way up the path. He put out his hands to hold her steady and stop her bowling him over. The suddenness of his appearance took her breath away and for a moment she could do nothing but stand facing him, her breast heaving.

He had just emerged from the sea and was wearing nothing but skin-tight knee smalls. She watched mesmerised as the water ran off his muscular shoulders in little droplets, coursing through the fine hairs on his chest. She felt an almost irresistible urge to reach out and stop one on its way with her finger, might even have succumbed if he had not been holding her at arm's length. 'Oh,' she said, shifting her gaze upwards to his face. 'I…' She stopped, unable to think of a single thing to say which did not sound mundane and utterly out of keeping with the moment.

'Anne…' His voice was hoarse as he looked down at her. The cheap cotton garment she wore was clinging to the curves of her body like a second skin, except that it did not cover her white throat and only just concealed the pink mounds of her breasts. He released his grip on her arms to reach out to touch the edge of it. She held her breath, waiting for him to push it down off her shoulders, wanting him to do it, to expose her breasts to his gaze. There was nothing in her head except a throbbing desire to meld herself with this man, to become one with him. She waited for him to fling her down on the sand and tear the damp garment from her trembling body, knowing she would do nothing to resist. But he did nothing of the sort. Instead he gave her a rueful smile and slowly lifted it back on to her shoulder. 'You will catch cold.'

She was shivering, but not with cold. She was on fire with the heat of her passion, a passion she felt sure he had shared until that moment. And now the ardour was gone leaving her raging with disappointment, desire unfulfilled. She felt the tears well in her eyes and blinked rapidly. 'I am not cold.'

He did not know how he kept his hands off her. She was so desirable, every contour of her body revealed beneath the wet costume, inviting him to explore. Her amber eyes, dilated and shining, drew him in, until he was floundering and it took a monumental effort of will to resist her, to break the spell and turn from her so that she would not see how his own body betrayed him. Did she not know what she was doing to him? His voice, when he spoke, was harsh, denying his weakness. 'What are you doing here?

'I came looking for you.'

'Why?'

She had come to confront him, to quiz him about his

broken engagement, to ask him why he had not told her he was the son of a viscount and why he had kissed his sister-in-law in that intimate way, but the accusations died in her throat. She simply did not care. He had stepped back from the brink, but that did not mean he was not affected and there would be other times. She smiled suddenly. 'I have been exploring that house.' She pointed upwards. 'It will make a perfect hospital...'

'Oh.' It was his turn to be disappointed. 'Did you know about it? Before you swam out here, I mean. Is that why you came?'

'No, I was taking a dip and saw the cove and decided to come ashore to rest before returning. If you use this path often, you must have passed the house many times. I am surprised you have not considered it before.'

He wondered how she knew he used the path and if she had deliberately come ashore to meet him. If he had not decided to curtail his swim, he might have missed her. He felt the hand of fate moving his affairs and was not sure he liked it. 'The idea of a hospital was nothing but a dream until you came.' He paused. 'Do you make dreams come true, Miss Hemingford?'

'You called me Anne just now.'

'Did I? A slip. I apologise.'

'No, don't do that, it means you are sorry for it. You are not sorry, are you?'

'Not in the least.'

'Then when we are alone, I am Anne. And you are...?'

'Justin. My name is Justin.'

'It suits you. Do come and look at the house with me.' She held out her hand and he took it and together they climbed up to the house and walked all round it. Her hand was in his the whole time, warm and comfortable and a perfect fit. He released it to try the door and both were surprised when it opened. 'Oh, do let's look round,' she said, dancing inside, her bare feet making footprints in the dust.

He followed as she skipped from room to room, exclaiming at each new find. 'The big room downstairs, and the one beside it, will make the reception areas,' she said. 'And that parlour at the back, looking out on the gardens, can be your private sitting room. The kitchens are dismal and filthy, but that can soon be remedied.' He listened without comment, marvelling at her enthusiasm, loving her with an ache in his heart that threatened to overturn his resolve.

When they had been over the whole of the ground floor, she insisted on climbing the stairs in spite of the fact that some of the wooden treads were rotting. Fearful for her safety, he took her hand again. They went from room to room and finally stood looking out over the sea from one of the upstair windows. 'Oh, it is perfect,' she said, turning to him and laughing with an exultant joy that was only marginally caused by the discovery of the house. 'Do you not think so?'

'It will need a great deal of work.' He had to keep his mind on the idea of the hospital or he would lose all control. 'Some of the wood is rotting, half the windows are broken and I noticed some tiles missing from the roof.'

'Such small matters are easily overcome. Tell me, can you not see it, clean and scrubbed and these rooms lined with beds? They have such wonderful views, they will aid the patients' recovery, do you not think? And the staff can be housed in the attic rooms.' She turned to him, glowing with enthusiasm. 'What do you say?'

He smiled. 'Yes, if the fund can afford it.'

'Oh, I knew you would agree.' And she flung her arms about his neck and kissed his cheek.

He raised his hands to hold her, changed his mind, then changed it again, wrapping his arms about her, not wanting to let go, amused by her exuberance, wishing it might always be so. He wanted to speak to her privately, to tell her about Sophie, perhaps even tell her how he felt about her, but suddenly he felt tongue-tied. Telling her would spoil the moment. He did not want to bring the sordid world of reality into the fantasy world they had created here in this empty, echoing house.

She dreamed of a hospital and it was his dream too, but added to that was another, which meant she would be at his side always, his wife and helpmate. But that would mean denying her the social intercourse of her equals, subjecting her to the life of service he had chosen and how could he ask that of her? If he was to have his hospital, to do the work he had set for himself, he could not have her. He lowered his head to brush the top of her head with his lips. 'We cannot do anything about it until we have discovered who owns it and if it is for sale.'

'Then let us do that at once.'

He looked down at her and grinned. 'Can you imagine the faces of the tabbies, if we go into town dressed as we are? They will all have apoplexy.'

Her laughter pealed out. 'And you will tell them it is because their corsets are laced too tight.'

'Oh, dear, I am not forgiven for that, am I?'

'Of course you are. Aunt Bartrum said you were right.'

'Did she? The lady goes up in my esteem.' He paused, not wanting to part from her, but knowing the idyll had to end. He had left George Harrison dealing with the early arrivals with the help of a nurse he had hired, but he could not allow him to shoulder the burden all day or his friend would regret promising his help. 'Come, I will see you safely back to the bathing machine before you are reported drowned. And then I must return to my patients.'

'Oh.' She was suddenly seized by guilt. She had been gone hours; Mrs Smith would be worried, might even have alerted her aunt. 'I must go at once.' And she tore down the stairs, out of the house and down the cliff path with him at her heels. They both waded out and dived in as soon as the water was deep enough to swim. It seemed a great deal colder than it had on the outward journey and though it only took a few minutes, she was shivering uncontrollably by the time they reached the spot opposite the bathing machines.

He stopped and moved closer to her, reaching out to take her hand. 'I shall horrify all the patrons if I emerge here, so I will go back the way I came. Make sure you have a warm bath and a hot drink as soon as you arrive home.'

She smiled as he raised her wet hand to his lips. It was the smile of a conspirator. 'I think I will not tell of our meeting. I found the house and I will make enquiries about it and bring the matter up at the next meeting of the committee.'

'And I shall be surprised and delighted.' He turned and swam back the way they had come while she waded out to the bathing machine where Mrs Smith was still placidly plying her needle on the top step. 'I am sorry I was so long,' she said, clambering up into the vehicle. 'I hope you were not concerned for me.'

'Oh, no, Miss Hemingford, I saw you leave the water up by the cove, I knew you hadn't drowned.' Her smile was so broad, Anne knew she had also seen Dr Tremayne. 'But if you don't want to catch a chill, you must let me give you a brisk rub down to warm you before you dress.'

Anne laughed aloud. 'Mrs Smith, I am not a horse.'

But she succumbed to the ministrations and when her body was pink and glowing, she dressed and strode home, optimism in every step. She had not said a word to him about the rumours, but they did not seem to matter. She loved him and she meant to have him and no one, certainly not Mrs Tremayne, would stand in her way. Together they would set up a hospital that would be a byword for excellence. If she could make his dream come true, she would be happy. She refused to acknowledge that there might be storm clouds ahead.

Chapter Eight

'Rockbourne,' said Lady Mancroft disdainfully, seating herself at the head of the table in Tuppen's library, though no one had actually appointed her as chairman. 'I have never heard of him.'

The members of the committee were gathering to finalise the arrangements for the horse racing and sports. Neither Justin nor the Professor had yet arrived and Aunt Bartrum had just repeated the gossip that the doctor was the second son of Viscount Rockbourne.

'He was Vice-Admiral Sir Joshua Tremayne,' Captain Gosforth told them. 'He was granted the title for his exploits in saving the West Indies for the British Crown back in eighty-two. The Battle of the Saints, they called it, on account of the islands being named after saints. I was there, a lowly midshipman, but it was a fierce encounter and he acquitted himself with great honour.'

'Oh, a new title.' Her ladyship was not going to give way easily. 'New titles have been scattered like falling leaves in the last few years, no matter that the recipient has no ancient family background to support it. Why, it denigrates the position of those whose antecedents go back hundreds of years. Mancroft can trace his line back to Elizabeth's time…'

'To be sure,' Mrs Bartrum soothed. 'We know that and are fully appreciative of the honour you do us by participating in our project.' Aunt Bartrum was being true to her word and was behaving as if she, and not Anne, were its instigator, notwithstanding her ladyship seemed to have usurped the role. Anne might have felt resentful, except that it served to take attention away from her and her confused feelings, and for that she was grateful.

'Well, if the Regent expresses an interest, then it is my duty to support it,' her ladyship said, stretching the truth. 'But what I cannot understand is why the doctor should keep his father's title a secret. A gentleman does not deny his rank without good reason.'

'I believe he thought it would help him to be more acceptable to his poorer patients,' Anne put in, speaking for the first time. 'He sees his mission as one of service and they might be overawed or wary of him if they thought he was one of the upper echelons of society.'

'Fustian!' her ladyship exclaimed. 'The peasantry care nothing for who or what a man is, so long as they are given their medicine. Besides, they are taught to respect a gentleman's rank. I refuse to believe that is the reason.' She paused, but as no other explanation occurred to her, added, 'And there is Mrs Tremayne…'

'What about her?' Anne's voice was sharp.

'Mrs Tremayne told Captain Smollett the doctor is estranged from his father and brother.' This was added by the Major.

'Do you know why?'

'Something to do with a broken engagement.'

'There!' Lady Mancroft was triumphant. 'What did I tell you? He is hiding something.'

'I cannot think that has any bearing on the work of the committee,' Captain Gosforth said, endeavouring to change the subject.

'But of course it has,' the lady insisted. 'If there is a scandal attached to him, then we should not be puffing him up over this hospital scheme.'

'We cannot go ahead without him,' Anne said, speaking mildly, although she was far from calm. If they decided they would no longer support the idea of a hospital, then she and Justin were lost. His interest in her was through the project and it was through the project she would convince him they belonged together. But she could not quite banish Mrs Tremayne's accusations from her mind, even though she had made up her mind to pay them no heed. 'It was his idea.'

'That is nothing to the point. This committee was formed to raise money for a hospital for the poor, no more, no less, and if we decide Dr Tremayne is not a suitable person to head it, then we can appoint someone else. Professor Harrison, for example. I believe he has more standing in the medical world.'

'I think that is despicable,' Anne protested. 'We should not be gossiping about the doctor, especially when he is not here to defend himself.'

'Why is he not here?'

'I expect he has been delayed. His waiting room is always full, which is why the hospital is so necessary, and in my opinion he is the ideal person to run it. He is skilled and caring, and it does not matter whether his patients are rich or poor, he does his best for them. They know that and they love him for it.' Anne knew she was becoming heated and everyone was looking at her with curiosity. Her defence had been a little too spirited to be disinterested. She modulated her voice. 'What happened in the past, unless it was something unlawful, has no relevance, surely?'

No one offered an argument because the doctor and Professor Harrison had entered the room and none of them had the temerity to say anything to the doctor's face. Anne, who had her back to the door, turned to face them, wondering how much they had overheard.

Both men were impeccably dressed in dark frockcoats and strapped pantaloons and their cravats were elegantly tied, but both had wet hair. Dr Tremayne's was darker and sleeker than usual and the Professor's had sprung into tight unruly curls. Anne supposed they had both been for a dip before dressing to attend the meeting.

'We were on our way here when we saw a commotion on the beach,' the Professor explained. 'There were two ladies running up and down, shrieking and pointing out to sea, and then we observed two heads bobbing in the surf. The sea is very turbulent this morning and not safe for any but the strongest swimmers.'

'Yes, I noticed that on my way here,' Anne said. It was the roughest she had seen the water since her arrival. The waves were taller than a man and the wind was whipping them up into white foam. The bathing machines had been pulled higher up the beach and she remembered thinking that if it continued she would have to forgo her swim the next day. It would be disappointing because she felt sure Justin would be at the cove on the look out for her. 'It was surely foolish to go out in it.'

'To be sure. The dipper cautioned her not to go from the safety of the bathing machine, but either she did not hear or decided to ignore the advice,' the Professor went on. 'The young man had seen her from the male section and went after her and then there were two of them in difficulties.'

'You saved them both?' Aunt Bartrum queried.

'Yes. Doctor Tremayne rescued the young lady. It was fortunate he is a strong swimmer for she was being swept further and further away and she had imbibed a great deal of sea water by the time he brought her ashore. Fortunately, she recovered when he ministered to her. The young man managed to make his way back with a little help from me. But I am afraid it delayed us; we had to go back and change into dry clothes.'

'How brave of you,' Anne said, addressing Justin. Their eyes met and held for a moment of time that could only have been a second or two, but it seemed like several minutes as she recalled their swim together, the pleasure of seeing his muscular body cleaving the water next to hers and then the feel of his kiss on her wet hand as he bade her *au revoir.* Even thinking about it made her shiver.

'Nonsense!' he said, still looking at her. She was in blue sprigged muslin with a silk fringed shawl thrown casually over her shoulders and looked so different from the sea nymph in the clinging wet bathing garment he had laughed with and kissed the day before, he began to wonder if it had been a dream sent to torment him. Her bright eyes and pink cheeks told him she was remembering too, but whether the memory was one of pleasure or shame, he could not be sure.

'Why foolish young ladies should think they know better than the women who spend their lives by the water, I do not know,' he went on a little caustically. How could he maintain the cool, practical mien of a respected doctor when she made him feel like a green schoolboy who had suddenly discovered the enchantment of the fair sex? And had he not promised himself he would not let it happen again? 'She was warned, but I suppose she was too busy trying to impress Lieutenant Harcourt.'

'Harcourt?' queried the Major.

'Yes, did I not say?' He tore his gaze away from Anne to answer. 'The young lady was Miss Barry. It was her mother and younger sister at the water's edge and the Lieutenant who went to the rescue.'

'Jeanette!' Anne exclaimed. 'But she is recovered, you say?'

'Yes, I prescribed a mild sedative and a day in bed to recover from the shock, but she will be none the worse for it. A little wiser, it is to be hoped.'

'I shall call on her as soon as we have concluded this meeting.'

'Then let us make a start,' he said.

Everyone settled down to business. The order of the races and the sporting events was settled. The Major, with whatever help he recruited, was to be in charge of organising the horse racing and curricle racing and Captain

Gosforth would oversee the sporting events, such as sprinting, jumping, skittles and bowling for a pig. Mrs Bartrum was to supply the refreshments with the able help of Mrs Carter and her kitchen staff. Lord Mancroft undertook to see that no one misbehaved themselves and to evict anyone bent on being rowdy. He would not manhandle them himself, of course, but he had two big strong grooms who could be trusted to the task. Her ladyship's role was to present the prizes to the winners; if a certain important personage were to turn up, then it would be her duty to welcome him and escort him round and present those she felt deserved the honour.

'And Dr Tremayne?' queried Anne, afraid they meant to snub him by leaving him out. Whatever he had or had not done, she could not be party to that.

'I shall not be able to attend,' Justin said quickly. 'I cannot neglect my patients.'

'I think perhaps your patients will neglect you.' Professor Harrison laughed. 'They will all be at the sports field, trying to win the pig.'

'Not all of them, some are too ill.'

'Then I will look after them. You will be needed to talk to people about your plans.'

'But do not become too scientific,' Walter added. 'It will only confuse people.'

Somehow the news of the near-drowning had subdued everyone and the matter of the doctor's secret past was not mentioned, much to Anne's relief. She supposed they felt it would be churlish to make accusations against him when he had been instrumental in saving the life of one of their friends. Whether the matter would be raised again she had no way of knowing, but she hoped it would not, certainly not before she had had an opportunity to find out the truth for herself.

When the business on the agenda was concluded, she announced that she had found premises that she thought would be suitable for a hospital if Doctor Tremayne agreed. She risked a glance at him and found him looking closely at her, as if he could read her thoughts in her eyes. Could he see her longing to be close to him, to feel again his kisses on her lips, to run, hand in hand, across the beach and dance once again through those empty rooms, filled now with memories? Or was he thinking about his sister-in-law?

Justin had spent the whole meeting trying not to think about anything except the matter in hand, certainly not Sophie. If it had not been for her untimely arrival, the gabblegrinders would not now be slandering him. He had heard some of what was being said about him as he and George approached the room; the door had not be properly closed and Lady Mancroft had the voice of a drill sergeant. On the other hand, Anne's reply had been spoken quietly and he had not been able to hear it. Had she been championing him? Or was she simply concerned for her hospital? Oh, it was her hospital, there was no doubt in his mind of that, and if she could not have it with him involved, she would proceed without him. As Lady Mancroft had so succinctly put it, there was always Professor Harrison.

Why did that trouble him less than the notion that Miss Hemingford believed ill of him? He could, of course, tell her what had really happened, but that would mean calling Sophie a liar and shaming his brother and he could not do it. If Miss Hemingford was so easily influenced by gossip, then he had been wrong about her all along. He searched her face for a sign, a sign that she was still the compassionate, unprejudiced woman he had believed her to be.

She could not bear that telling gaze and looked away to pick up a sheaf of papers from the table in front of her. 'It is called Cliff House,' she said, making a pretence of consulting them. 'It stands on the top of the cliffs to the east of the town. It is empty and I have ascertained that it is available on a long lease that is very reasonable, considering the price houses are fetching nowadays. If we make a success of the races, then I think we will have enough to secure it, though it will need extra money for refurbishment and equipment.'

'You said nothing of it to me,' Aunt Bartrum said, giving her niece a reproving look. 'When did you find it?'

'Yesterday. I saw it from the sea when I was swimming, so I went ashore to explore it.' She raised her eyes to look at Justin again and saw the wry upturn to the corner of his mouth and knew he was thinking of their time together exploring the house, and her whole body flooded with warmth. She had come so near to abandoning all control of herself; another minute and she would have been completely lost to all reason. Strangely she did not view that as a deliverance, but a disappointment, and admitting that gave her a disgust of herself. If he was the gentleman Walter Gosforth said he was, he would be disgusted with her too. But was he? If the kiss she had seen him give his sister-in-law was anything to go by, he was far from a gentleman. Nor did he seem to have any compunction about duping his own brother, cuckolding him perhaps. How could she think twice about such a man?

She made herself return her attention to the papers in her hand and continued. 'This morning I ascertained it is owned by a Mrs Bolton who lives in Islington. I also discovered the name of the agent acting on her behalf.'

'Why is it empty when everyone knows accommodation in Brighton is at a premium?' Mrs Bartrum asked. 'What is wrong with it?'

'It is in want of repair,' Anne said. 'But nothing serious.'

'I know it,' Captain Gosforth put in. 'I pass the end of the lane on my way into town when I come by the coast road and it can just be glimpsed from there. It is in dire condition and reputed to be haunted.'

'Haunted?' her ladyship gasped. 'Then I, for one shan't go anywhere near it.'

'Oh, come, Mama,' the Major soothed. 'Surely you do not believe in ghosts?'

'I neither believe nor disbelieve, but I am not sure I wish to put it to the test.'

'It is nothing to be afraid of,' Walter told her. 'It is only a little child.'

In spite of her conviction that she was practical and not easily frightened, Anne shuddered. Children in distress always aroused her strongest sympathies and if this child had not found peace in death, then she, or he, must have been very unhappy in life. But the house had not struck her as an unhappy house; quite the contrary, she had felt its peaceful ambience. 'Do you know the story, Captain?'

'The house belonged to a Colonel Skipton. His wife died and, having no children or grandchildren, he was lonely and became more and more of a recluse, refusing invitations and never being at home to callers. The house became filthy and the old man unkempt. He had one old military friend who decided to take him in hand. He took it upon himself to advertise for a housekeeper and a young widow applied and was taken on. She had a little daughter and the child changed the old man's life. He doted on her. The house became full of light and laughter, and though there was gossip about the three of them living together like that, he did not let it trouble him and neither did Mrs Bolton. When the old man died, he left the house to her…'

'What happened?' Anne could hardly breathe, so intense was her feeling.

'The child, I think she was called Susan, pined for the old man and was always searching the house, calling his name, pretending they were playing a game of hide and seek and he was simply hiding from her; it was something they had done frequently. One day she went down the cliff path when her mother was busy elsewhere, no doubt because the Colonel had often taken her down there to play. One supposes she was caught by the tide. Her body was washed up further along the coast some days later. The mother could not stand the place after that and left it to stand empty.'

'Oh, the poor thing!' Anne said, completely taken up by the story, feeling the mother's anguish at the loss of her child. 'And so they say the little one still looks for the old man?'

'Yes, people passing by have heard her calling to him.'

'Oh, that is nothing but the wind and the sea,' the Major put in scornfully.

'No doubt you are right,' Anne said, forcing herself back to the matter in hand. 'But what do you think of the idea of taking the house for our hospital? It is large enough to house fifty patients on the first floor, with waiting rooms and accommodation for the doctor on the ground floor. The attic rooms would house the staff.'

'What about drinking water?' the Captain asked.

'I knew water might be a problem, considering that a hospital must use a great deal of it, but the agent assured me there is a well of pure water in the garden that has become overgrown, but it can be cleared out.'

'You have been busy on our behalf,' Justin remarked laconically, pretending, as they had arranged, that this was the first he had heard of it. 'I think we should take a look at it. Can you obtain the key?'

'I have it,' she said, retrieving it from her embroidered reticule. 'No one else has shown an interest in the place. It is too far on the edge of town for anyone of consequence to want it and it is too big and dilapidated for a tradesman. The agent was perfectly willing for me to have the key until we reached a decision.'

'I am not going anywhere near it,' Lady Mancroft said with a shudder.

'Nor me,' said Aunt Bartrum. 'I will leave it to Dr Tremayne and Professor Harrison to decide.'

'If they agree, then it is more than ever important to raise as much money as possible at the games and the ball,' Anne said, handing the key to Justin, touching his hand with hers as she did so. It was no more than a brushing of her fingers on his, but it was enough to send ripples of warmth flowing through her all over again. Whatever this man had done in the past, whether he was a cur or not, did not matter. She wanted him, she wanted him so desperately it was almost a physical ache.

It looked as though she would have her way over the hospital, though whether she would have it on a more personal level she was not so sure. There was still that warning of Mrs Tremayne's echoing in her head. *He has these fancies, you know, but they do not last... It is only when the project, whatever it is, palls and he is off again that the dear people he has involved in it realise his capricious nature. Believe me, it will happen again and you will be left high and dry.*

'It was providential that we stopped to rescue that young lady,' George said, as they strolled back to the doctor's house.

'Yes, she might have drowned,' Justin said. 'And even if someone had dragged her ashore, they might not have known how to revive her.'

'How did you know? I have never before seen anyone being pumped out like that.'

'I learned to do it at sea. Sailors are always tumbling overboard and very few of them can swim. Turning them over and applying pressure to the chest expels the water and allows air back into the lungs.'

'I agree that was providential, but that was not what I meant. I saw how the wind was blowing with those people; if you had not arrived a hero, you would have been subjected to a quizzing.'

'I know. It has probably only delayed it, not prevented it altogether. Sooner or later, I shall have to give an account of myself.'

'Why not sooner?'

Justin stopped to consider the question. He wanted Miss Hemingford to trust him, to believe in him without calling for explanations about why he had done what he had, or so he told himself. But the other side of the coin was that, if he volunteered the information, she might blame him for what had happened. After all, no gentleman of breeding reneged on an engagement whatever the provocation. The condemnation of society would be enough to make her hold him in revulsion. He could not understand why it mattered; there was never any likelihood they would make a match. He had decided his work would fill his life and marriage was not part of it, certainly not marriage to one of the *ton.* 'I will choose the time,' he said.

'It is your business, my old friend, but I cannot understand the difficulty. Tell the truth and shame the devil.'

'She-devil,' he murmured.

'Surely not Miss Hemingford?'

'Good God, no! Far from it. She is more angel than devil, as well as beautiful and intelligent…'

'Oh, I begin to see. The she-devil is the other one. You have got yourself into a coil, Tremayne. If I can do anything to help…'

'Support me in this hospital idea, that must be my first consideration, before anything else. My feelings have no relevance.'

'You do not need to ask. I will do what I can.'

Justin suddenly became animated and quickened his pace. 'Then let us see to the patients who are waiting, and then go and inspect Cliff House.' They turned the corner and discovered the houses at the sea front end of the street was already falling to the hammers of the developers. The air was filled with noise and dust. 'We have no time to waste.'

The fields to the west of the town were often used for games and military parades and on the Thursday chosen for the sports the weather was fine and warm and long before the opening ceremony the crowds were gathering, some to take part, others simply to watch or wander round the many booths set up to entertain and to tempt people to part with their money. There were booths selling hot potatoes, gingerbread, whelks and lemonade and sections roped off where the populace could try their hands at nine pins, bobbing for apples, archery and boxing, all of which would bring in more revenue. Anne sat at a table, taking the entrance fees as people flocked in.

She had seen Justin only once since the last committee meeting and that was when they met by chance while she and her aunt were promenading the sea front after tea at the Assembly Rooms the previous Sunday. He had been in animated conversation with Mrs Tremayne, but stopped to bow to them both. 'Ladies, your obedient.' His smile had seemed a little forced, as if he would rather not have come upon them.

They had returned his greeting from beneath their parasols. 'Good day, Dr Tremayne. Mrs Tremayne.'

'Good afternoon, Mrs Bartrum, Miss Hemingford.'

Mrs Tremayne's cheeks had been bright pink, as if she were embarrassed at being caught out in some indiscretion.

They had exchanged comments about the weather, which was calm again after the storm, and Justin had told them he had viewed Cliff House and was of the opinion that it would make a good hospital and he had made an offer for the lease. 'Of course, there is a great deal of work to be done before it is ready for its first patient,' he had said.

Mrs Tremayne had made a snort of derision. 'Really, Justin, it is a ruin. I cannot see how you can possibly contemplate making it into a hospital.'

'Oh, I shall,' he had said quietly.

'You know, he is only doing it to win a wager,' Mrs Tremayne had said, turning to Anne and her aunt. 'If he wins, I will make a donation to his hospital, but, if I win, he will come home and make his peace with his family. I am confident of success.' She had smiled and taken his arm. 'I know him so well, you see.'

The memory of the encounter still burned Anne's cheeks whenever she thought of it. The woman had been so sure of herself, so like a cat in a cream bowl, that Anne wanted to scream at her, 'You shall not have him!' And that, looking back, only showed how foolish she had been to be taken in by a handsome face, a muscular body and a couple of kisses. Kisses meant nothing to him; she had proof of that, and the sooner she put him from her mind the better. She had made an excuse that they were in a hurry to be elsewhere and dragged her aunt away. She had not looked back.

Now he was coming towards her with Tildy skipping at his side. The child was not in the least in awe of him and was chattering gaily. Seeing Anne, she broke away from the doctor and ran to stand before her. 'Hallo, lady.'

Anne smiled at the little girl. 'Hallo, Tildy. Are you enjoying yourself?'

'Oh, yes. I am going in one of the races later and Tom is going to bowl for the pig.'

'Then I hope you both win.'

'Will you come and watch?'

'I have to stay here and take the people's money.'

'Can't someone else do it for you?'

'Yes, Miss Hemingford,' Justin said with a smile. She was in pale green gingham today, which seemed to heighten the colour of her chestnut hair and amber eyes; she was vibrantly alive. 'Do shut up shop for a while. I do not think there will be many more coming. It is nearly time for the opening ceremony.'

Everyone was congregating at the end of the field where a platform had been erected and on which were gathered the town dignitaries, Lord and Lady Mancroft, Major Mancroft and Captain Gosforth. 'You should be with them,' he murmured, watching as she closed and locked the money box and handed it to the sergeant whom Major Mancroft had detailed to guard her while she had it in her possession. Pickpockets and thieves would view the occasion as a gift from heaven and no one doubted they would take full advantage of it. The sergeant and another soldier, both big strong men, would see off anyone attempting to steal it. 'Without you, there would have been no hospital project.'

'Oh, I have no desire to be in the limelight, Doctor,' she said, retying the green ribbon that secured her straw bonnet. 'But you should be there. Do not let them crowd you out.'

'Like you, I would rather work behind the scenes, Miss Hemingford.'

He offered her his arm. She put one hand upon the sleeve of his dove-grey frockcoat and was surprised and pleased when Tildy slipped a small grubby hand into hers on the other side and together they made their way towards the platform to stand at the back and listen to the speeches. There were cheers from the crowd when Justin's name was mentioned as the doctor whose work with the poor had inspired the project.

'It is very unfair,' Anne said, when the speeches had ended and Lady Mancroft had declared the event officially open. 'No one said a word about you running the hospital when it is ready…'

'Does it matter who runs it as long as it comes to fruition?' he queried. 'I am not indispensable.'

'Oh.' She was reminded of Mrs Tremayne's contention that he would not see it out and wondered if the woman had been right all along. Was he already losing interest?

She had no time to ask him because her aunt was bearing down on them, with Major Mancroft and Captain Gosforth in tow. 'Come, Anne, I need your help in the refreshment tent,' she said. And to Tildy, with a look of revulsion, 'Run along, child. Find your mama.'

'But you promised…' the little one appealed to Anne.

'So I did and I will not break it.' She turned to her aunt. 'I promised Tildy I would see her run in her race. Can you not spare me a little longer?'

'Oh, very well. I will ask Mrs Barry to help me. No doubt the lieutenants will be glad to lose her for a while.'

The Major laughed. 'I am sure you have the right of it, ma'am, but it is understandable that she would be concerned for her daughters after what happened to Miss Jeanette. I would help you myself, but I have other duties. If you will excuse me.' He seized the lady's hand and kissed the back of it before striding away.

'And I must go too, dear lady,' Walter said, doing the same, leaving Justin and Anne laughing.

'Oh, dear, they are fighting for her hand and she does not even know it,' Anne said, as they wandered among the crowds. 'She pretends she is promoting my prospects…'

'Perhaps she is.'

'No, she is mistaken. I am not looking for a husband.'

'I am surprised to hear you say that. Doesn't every young girl hope to be married?'

'I am not every young girl as you well know, Dr Tremayne. I am a mature woman of seven-and-twenty and I prefer my single state. There! Are you surprised by that?'

'Yes and no.' She was too self-assured to be a giddy schoolgirl. She did not giggle, did not flinch at his touch as a seventeen-year-old might, but her looks did not betray her age; she was still very beautiful with a flawless complexion and a slim figure. But he knew, to his cost, that was not enough. If Sophie was anything to go by, there could be venom behind loveliness. And why would she be so against being wed? She was not frigid, he could tell that from her response when he kissed her, so was she more experienced than he had at first thought? The idea of that both repelled and excited him.

'An enigmatic answer. Tell me what you mean.'

'I cannot say that I know what I mean,' he said carefully. 'Seven-and-twenty is no great age and it gives you a certain poise when dealing with people, be they high or low, and a measure of independence, which you undoubtedly exploit to the full, but you are certainly not at your last prayers.'

'You do not think so?'

'I know it. I am surprised neither of those two gentlemen has offered for you.'

'They are intent on my aunt, who is a dear lady and should not have to spend the rest of her life in lonely widow's weeds. The gentlemen concerned are very perspicacious. They have been bowled over by her and I think it is touching.'

'Listening to you, anyone would think she was the young débutante and you were the aunt.'

Anne laughed. 'There are not so many years between us and she is young in spirit, do you not think? I love her dearly.'

'I envy her,' he murmured, so softly, she thought she had misheard him. 'To be loved by you must be a pleasurable condition to be in.'

'Doctor Tremayne, you are putting me to the blush.'

'What! A mature lady of seven-and-twenty blushing? I do not believe it.' But he did, because her cheeks were fiery and he regretted teasing her.

'I wish I had not told you now.'

'Your secret is safe with me.'

'It is not a secret. Anyone with any intelligence would soon be able to discover my age; after all, I am my brother's twin as anyone in society could soon tell you, but that does not mean I should like my age bandied about among the gossips.'

'I am perfectly able to keep my tongue between my teeth, Miss Hemingford.'

'Secrets!' she exclaimed suddenly. 'How I hate secrets.'

'Sometimes they are necessary to avoid hurting other people.'

'I understand that, but surely if one found someone in whom one wanted to confide…'

'That, Miss Hemingford, would be different.'

Tildy was pulling on her hand in her excitement and could not be ignored. Anne turned to smile at her. 'What is it, Tildy?'

'There's Ma and Tom. Let's go over to them.'

Anne allowed herself to be led towards Mrs Smith, who was watching her son bowling at a row of skittles. Justin followed, but the moment of intimacy had gone and she wondered if she would ever learn his secret. She wanted him to tell her without having to quiz him directly, which she knew instinctively he would resent, yet though the opportunity had been there, he had not taken it.

'Good afternoon, miss.' Mrs Smith gave her a little curtsy.

Anne returned her greeting with a smile. 'The day looks to be a great success. The money is pouring in.'

'I wish I could help,' the woman said. 'But…' She shrugged.

'But you have helped. You paid your entrance fee and I do believe Tom has paid for several tries at the skittles.'

'It is so little.'

'Ah, but every little helps. Remember the parable of the widow's mite? It all adds up.'

'If I cannot give money, I can give my time, Miss Hemingford. I believe the house needs cleaning…'

'So it does. If you are offering to help, then I am sure everyone will be most grateful. Is that not so, Doctor?'

'Yes, of course,' he agreed. 'But only if you can spare the time. You have a home and family to look after and they must come first.'

Tom gave a shout of triumph as he managed to send all the skittles flying and the booth holder offered him the choice of a spotted neckerchief or a small wooden doll. He took the doll and handed it to Tildy, who squeaked with delight.

Anne and Justin left them enjoying the win and strolled on. 'The hospital will be for them and people like them,' he said. 'They should not be denied medical help simply because they are poor.'

'But you do mean to stay and see it to fruition?'

'Of course. Did you doubt it?'

'Mrs Tremayne…' she began and stopped.

'She does not know me as well as she thinks she does,' he said. 'Pay her no heed.'

Her head was full of questions. Why was his sister-in-law so determined to undermine him? Had he really broken an engagement? Had he loved the woman, whoever she was? Did he still love her? Could it be Mrs Tremayne herself? The thought shocked her. The woman was his brother's wife; if he went off with her, it would cause a scandal of monumental proportions. He would be banished from society and would have to live in obscurity. But was he not doing that already until she had dragged him out of it over this hospital idea? What had she done to him?

She did not voice any of her questions, not only because she feared a rebuff, but because they had reached a large open area which had been roped off for a curricle race and Mrs Tremayne was there, standing beside a curricle in which Captain Smollett, resplendent in his blue and gold uniform, was sitting with the reins in his hand. The young horse was skittish and it was taking considerable skill to hold him in check at the starting line.

Anne felt Justin stiffen beside her and risked a glance up at his face. His jaw was rigid and his eyes held that hard, glittering look she had seen in them when she first met him. Whatever had happened between him and his sister-in-law, the sight of her still had a very powerful effect on him

'Justin,' Mrs Tremayne called out to him. 'Where have you been? You promised to be my escort today.'

'I have been otherwise engaged,' he said.

'So I see.' She looked Anne up and down with ill-disguised contempt and only the pressure of Anne's hand on his arm prevented Justin responding. 'But no matter, Captain Smollett has been so kind as to escort me.'

She turned to look up at the Captain and whispered something that made him laugh and then she stood back as the three curricles in the first heat moved to the start line. The starter lowered his flag and they were off, rushing down the course wheel to wheel. It was a rectangular course with obstacles set at the corners round which they were obliged to go to prevent anyone from taking a short cut.

As they thundered past Anne found herself remembering her first day in Brighton. She saw again the flying curricle and the officer driving it as it almost ran Tildy down and she knew with certainty that she was looking at the same vehicle and the same man. That was why she thought she had seen Captain Smollett before. She had.

'Captain Smollett is the man who ran Tildy down,' she said quietly, setting aside her fury at Mrs Tremayne's insult and the doubts the woman had put in her mind about Justin promising to escort her. Such things could wait for a more propitious time. 'I did not realise it until now when I saw him driving his curricle. He was the one.'

'Are you sure?'

'Yes.'

'What do you want to do about it?'

'Tell Major Mancroft. He said if he knew who the man was he would see him punished.'

'What will that achieve?'

'It will stop him and others like him driving through the streets as if they were a race track. It will stop children like Tildy being killed.'

The heat ended with Smollett the winner by a carriage length, which meant he would go forward to the next round. While the vehicles for the next heat were lined up, Anne hurried across to where Major Mancroft stood, together with Mrs Tremayne, congratulating his fellow officer. The skittish pony was being rubbed down by a soldier groom.

'Major Mancroft, a word, if you please,' she said.

He excused himself and turned towards her. 'Miss Hemingford, what can I do for you?'

'You can punish that man.' She pointed to Captain Smollett. 'He is the one who ran the little girl down and left her for dead.'

'Are you sure?'

'I will swear to it. You told me there were rules about not racing in the streets, I want them enforced.'

'I did that as soon as you told me about it, but no one admitted to doing such a thing.'

'They would not, would they?'

'I say, Charles, you are not going to take the word of that filly against me, are you?' Smollett was smiling easily, sure of himself, but he could not have said anything more calculated to raise the Major's ire.

'You will apologise to Miss Hemingford for that remark,' he said coldly.

The Captain looked taken aback and then he laughed. 'Oh, I see the way the wind is blowing, but you should not let your personal feelings cloud your judgement. The accusations of a demi-rep will never stand against the word of a gentleman.'

Justin sprang forward, his fists raised, but Anne tugged on his arm. 'He is not worth it.'

The Major took a step forward too, but, knowing he could not strike a junior officer, he stayed his hand. 'Captain Smollett, Miss Hemingford is a lady of rank, the sister of the Earl of Bostock, and you will offer your apology at once…'

Anne heard Mrs Tremayne's sharp intake of breath and then a tinkling, embarrassed laugh, but she did not turn towards her. She remained resolutely facing Captain

Smollett. He could do nothing but make the apology, though he did it with an ill grace. 'That is not enough,' she said calmly. 'I want recompense, not for me, but for that little girl. You left her lying unconscious in the road…'

'I did not know I had hit anyone.'

'That is no excuse. You were driving recklessly. I was witness to it.'

'Pay up, man, and look good about it,' the Major said.

'I don't want him to pay me,' she said, then turned to Justin. 'Will you fetch Mrs Smith and Tildy? This calls for a personal apology…'

The doctor hurried away, while the protagonists stood facing each other without speaking. Anne hoped no one would see how much she was shaking. The Major, determined to keep his word to Anne, delayed the start of the next heat until the Captain had been dealt with. Time seemed to stand still, although the chattering and laughing of the crowd, the calling of the vendors from their booths, and the neighing of impatient horses, all the sounds of the success of the day still went on around them.

Justin returned, accompanied by Mrs Smith and Tildy, still clutching her new doll. Anne bent to put her arm across the child's shoulder. 'Tildy, this is the man who ran you down when you went to see the monster…'

'She ran into the road,' Smollett said. 'Didn't even look where she was going.'

'I thought you said you did not see her,' Anne said.

'Well, she must have done. How else could she have been hit?'

'Your curricle went on to the walkway, I saw it myself. You were going too fast. Tildy could have been killed. You must tell her you are sorry…'

'Oh, Miss Hemingford, we don't want to make a fuss,' Mrs Smith said.

Justin touched the woman's arm. 'Leave it to Miss Hemingford,' he said quietly. 'Do not give the man a chance to wriggle out of it.'

She lapsed into silence as did everyone else. What Anne was asking was unheard of. For an officer in the Regent's own regiment, used to lording it over everyone not his senior, to be forced to make an apology to a peasant child was asking too much and the bystanders were agog to see what he would do.

'I am waiting,' Anne said imperiously. 'Do as I ask or I will personally put your conduct before the Regent. And do not think I cannot.'

'She can,' the Major assured him.

With a very red face, the Captain took a step towards the child. Tildy cringed a little as he loomed over her, but Anne held her steady. 'If I knocked you down, then I am sorry for it,' he said with an ill grace. 'No harm done, I trust.'

'She has recovered,' Anne said. 'But she still bears the scars and they are worth a hundred guineas of your money.'

There was a concerted gasp at the amount she suggested. What would a child of her class do with a hundred guineas? It was outlandish to suggest it. 'It is too much,' he said.

'Would it still have been too much had you killed her?'

'But I didn't.'

'How fortunate, or you would be looking at a charge of murder.'

He went from turkey-cock red to pale as a sheet in a few seconds. 'Oh, very well, have it your own way. But I do not carry that amount on me.'

'We will wait while you fetch it,' Major Mancroft said.

'But I am in the next heat.'

'You have been disqualified.'

He continued to bluster, but, knowing he was beaten, went to obey. The Major strode over to set off the curricles in the next heat and the little crowd began to disperse. All except the little group involved. And Mrs Tremayne.

'I hope you are satisfied,' she hissed at Anne. 'You have brought a good man down. If you had not been who you are, he would not have succumbed. It was a barbarous way to treat an officer and a gentleman.'

Anne ignored her and turned to speak to Mrs Smith, who was shaking with nerves. 'I know you meant it for the best, Miss Hemingford,' she said. 'But I didn't want a fuss and perhaps it was Tildy's fault…'

'No, it was not. I saw it and the Captain as good as admitted it, so think no more about it. Think instead of what you will do with the money…'

'Oh, that's easy, miss, I'll give it to the doctor's hospital.'

'That is more than generous of you, but surely there is something you want?'

'I have all I want. A good husband, a home…'

'You could move somewhere better.'

'What we have suits us. It is near the sea and my husband's work.' She smiled. 'A lick of paint won't go amiss, though. And the same goes for the boat, so perhaps I'll keep a little back for that and a new dress for Tildy, but the hospital shall have the rest.'

Smiling, Anne turned to Justin, thinking he had heard what had been said, but he was in conversation with Mrs Tremayne. She opened her mouth to speak, but shut it again, when she heard the woman say, 'So she is sister to the Earl of Bostock, is she? Ever since I learned her name I have been puzzling over it and now we know. She has been dallying with you, Justin Tremayne. She is far too high in the instep for you, even if you do leave off this foolish idea of being a doctor. You haven't a hope in hell with her.'

Anne, taken aback by the venom in the woman's voice, watched Justin for his reaction. His face was set, his mouth a hard line and his eyes narrowed and she thought he was about to explode. Instead he bowed and excused himself, then strode away. He did not even look at her.

Not for a second would he admit he had come to the same conclusion himself. Anne Hemingford was not for him; there were too many impediments. His need to earn a living, for a start. The allowance he had as his father's second son and his naval pension would not keep her in the way to which her birth and upbringing had conditioned her. And that took no account of his conviction that he was meant to be a doctor, to heal the sick. He could not ask her to become a doctor's wife; she would not agree to it in any case. If he gave that up, he would have to find something else to do that befitted his role as a gentleman, but he would be miserable if he did and so would she. He had been fooling himself if he had thought differently.

Chapter Nine

It was obvious that Mrs Tremayne's words had sunk deep. The doctor avoided being alone with Anne and when they were obliged to meet in company he was correct and businesslike. She could not believe that the disclosure of her rank could have made so much difference to him. The love she felt for him knew no barriers, certainly not the artificial ones erected by those who considered one's place in life sacrosanct. He could relate to the poor, but he seemed to have no difficulty in associating with the *ton,* so why should he treat her any differently? Why, oh, why did it matter so much? It should not, since she had told him that she did not wish to marry and he had no doubt taken her at her word.

Before coming to Brighton, she had revelled in her spinsterhood, telling herself, and anyone else who would listen, that she was happy and fulfilled; now she knew that was far from the case. There was something missing, something very important. She had become all too aware of it when her body responded so willingly to his caress, turning it to liquid fire, making her forget everything around her, even her own identity. It was like a hunger and thirst that must be assuaged. Was she to go to her grave never having tasted the delights of physical love? Never having experienced motherhood either? She went about in a half-dream, living again every word they had said, every nuance of meaning, every touch, however slight.

When she thought about the times they had been together at his consulting rooms, and, more poignantly still, roaming half-dressed through that empty house, hand in hand, she could have cried with disappointment and frustration. She had had a foretaste then, had known for a brief moment the tenderness of his touch with its promise of more. Much more. And she yearned for it. Just when she decided she would have to do something to ease the pain, even if it were to humiliate herself by telling him how she felt, she remembered Mrs Tremayne's words about his inconstancy and held her tongue.

'Anne, what is the matter with you?' her aunt asked on one occasion when they were sitting over the remains of a late breakfast. 'If I did not know better, I would say you were sickening for something. Or in love.'

'Neither, Aunt. I am perfectly well.'

'Then do look more cheerful, dearest. I am going to the mantua-maker this afternoon to bespoke a new ball gown. I have decided to come right out of mourning for the Grand Ball and need something with a little colour. Will you come too?'

'I think not.' Anne put on a bright smile for her aunt's sake. 'But I am glad to hear you are coming out of mourning. You are too young to spend the rest of your life in widow's weeds, but I do not need to buy a gown. One of those we bought in London will do me very well.'

'But supposing the Prince were to come…'

'It will still do. I certainly have no wish to charm the prince.'

'What will you do if you do not accompany me?'

'I am going to walk to Cliff House. Mrs Smith has been working there for days now and I want to see how she is doing.'

'It is a long walk. Why not take a cab?'

'No, I feel the need of exercise.'

'Then be sure to take Amelia.'

Anne agreed, but she knew the walk was too far for her middle-aged companion; they had hardly reached The Steine before Miss Parker was complaining that she was fagged out and her feet were hurting her. 'Then you must go back at once,' Anne said. 'I shall go on alone.'

'Miss Hemingford, you should not, really you should not. You might be set upon.'

'And if I were, what could you do about it?'

'I don't know. Scream, I suppose.'

'I can scream myself, louder than you, I'll wager. Now, don't argue. Nothing will happen to me, I am not a silly chit just out of the schoolroom. I am not carrying valuables or wearing any jewels, and I am wearing my oldest clothes, so no one will bother me.'

'But Mrs Bartrum said—'

'I know what she said, Amelia, she worries too much, but I can wind her round my thumb, so do not trouble yourself about what she will say.'

Reassured, Miss Parker turned to retrace her steps,

leaving Anne to stride on alone, smiling to herself. Amelia was a dear, but sometimes it was hard work dissuading her from what she considered her duty.

It was extraordinary how much work Mrs Smith had managed to do in the few days she had been working at Cliff House. Anne suspected she had given up her job as a dipper in order to devote more time to it, in which case she must be recompensed, especially as she had given three-quarters of her compensation money to the fund.

'What a difference you have made,' Anne told her. 'But who replaced the missing tiles and the broken glass in the windows?'

'My husband, Miss. He can turn his hand to most things and the doctor helped him. He said it was no good cleaning the rooms if the roof let the rain in, so the repairs must come first. He is getting a man in to see to the rotten treads on the stairs. If you go up there, do be careful.'

Anne was reminded she had climbed the stairs hand in hand with Justin and for a moment she was sad, but she pushed the heartbreaking memory from her and looked around. 'Right, what would you like me to do?'

'You, Miss Hemingford? Oh, no, that would not be proper.'

'Why ever not? I came in my oldest clothes especially and I am not afraid of hard work.'

Mrs Smith looked at Ann's grey jaconet gown with its trimming of white lace and smiled. Old or not, it was better than anything she had ever owned and that included her wedding dress. 'You are a lady…'

'And so are you, much more a lady than many another I could name. So, tell me what you are planning to do next.' She rolled up her sleeves as she spoke and dragged an apron and a mob cap out of the bag she had brought with her. She hoped Cook would not miss them and report them stolen before she returned.

'I was going to scrub the shelves in the pantry, but if you are sure…'

'I am.'

'Then perhaps you could take that feather duster and fetch down the cobwebs in the bedrooms. We cannot paint the ceilings and walls until they have been dusted.'

'Very well, that is what I shall do.' She picked up the long-handled feather duster and another cloth and made her way carefully up the stairs to begin work. The physical effort drove some of her low spirits away and she started to sing, but the dust she disturbed made her cough and she thought it more prudent to keep her mouth firmly closed. Before she had been going many minutes, she was covered in a film of grey powder. It settled on the mob cap and the wisps of hair that had soon escaped from it. It settled on her shoulders and on her bare arms, along with a spider or two. She was thankful Harry had made sure she was not afraid of the creatures when they were children. She brushed them off with a smile. And that was how Justin found her.

'Good heavens! Mrs Smith said you were working, but I never expected this. What are you about?'

She had been so busy, she had not heard him arrive and turned round with a startled look on her face that made him smile. 'Oh, it's you.'

'Whom else did you expect?'

'No one.' There was nothing she could do to make herself more presentable. If he disapproved, then it was too bad. She laughed, waving the feather duster and smothering him with dust. 'I have been getting rid of cobwebs, years and years of cobwebs. And the spiders are huge.'

'You are not afraid of them?' He was amused to see the filthy state she was in, but if anything it increased her attraction. She had smudges of dirt on her forehead and cheeks and her hair was so thick it had pushed its way out of the confines of the cap she wore, but she was wonderfully alive, bright as a May morning and dear to him as his own life. If she were not Bostock's sister... He shook his treacherous thoughts from him before they could lead him into trouble.

'No, why should I be?' she asked. 'They cannot hurt me.'

'But you should not be doing this work.'

'Why not? Mrs Smith cannot do it all alone.'

'No, which is why Mrs Armistead is here to help her.'

'Mrs Armistead is back?'

'Yes, her sister is fully recovered and as I still have the temporary nurse to help with my patients, she offered to come. I have left her downstairs helping Mrs Smith. So you see, there is no need for you to grovel around in the dirt.'

'But I am enjoying myself.'

He was about to say that, not being used to physical labour, she would overtire herself, but thought better of it. She had more than her share of energy. 'Your aunt would disapprove.'

'Though I love my aunt dearly, she is not my keeper, Dr Tremayne.'

'No, I doubt anyone is.'

She laughed. 'You are probably right. I have had my own way too long.' She paused, but went on before he could comment. 'But see how much I have done. We shall soon be able to paint these rooms.'

'And I suppose you want to do that too?'

'Oh, may I? I have never painted a room before, but I should love to try. A pale apple green I think, so light and bright and cheerful.'

'Not very practical.'

He was smiling and when he smiled, her heart melted and her hard-won composure was severely threatened. The only way she could cope was to turn away and wave her grubby arm to encompass the room she had spent a good two hours cleaning. 'You would rather have a dark colour that did not show the dirt? But surely that does not accord with your insistence on cleanliness? If you can see a thing is not clean, you can do something about it.'

He laughed. '*Touché,* Miss Hemingford. Apple green it shall be. Would you like to choose it and whatever colours you think suitable for the other rooms?'

'Oh, yes, please. This must once have been a very lovely house, and I shall enjoy making it so again.'

'But you have done enough for today. It is becoming late and I am sure you have an engagement for this evening.'

'Goodness, yes. I had forgot. We are promised at Captain Gosforth's for a musical evening. I must go.'

'I am beginning to wonder how are you going to return home,' he said, standing back to survey her critically, one dark brow lifted and a faint smile playing round his mouth. It was strange how they could tease each other and be so easy together one minute and so tense and restrained the next, as if they were constantly battling to be themselves when the proprieties of society demanded quite different behaviour, all stiff politeness. 'You can hardly walk through the streets like that.'

'Oh, once I have taken off this apron and cap, washed my face and hands and put on my bonnet and pelisse, I shall look quite presentable, I think.' She hurried from the room and towards the stairs.

'Mind those treads!' he called out, hurrying after her.

He caught her up when she had almost reached the bottom and was just in time to prevent her falling as one of the treads gave way and her foot went through the rotten board. He supported her as she sank down to sit on the bottom stair. 'Are you hurt?'

'No, I do not think so.' She put her foot to the floor and gave a sharp gasp. 'I have twisted my ankle a little.'

He squatted down to examine her foot. She sat, watching the top of his head as he bent over her, his hands moving gently over her foot and ankle, carefully feeling for injury. The throbbing in her ankle was matched by the throbbing of the pulse in her throat and it was not the accident that made her feel faint. He was being the cool professional, but she wanted to reach out and run her fingers through his dark hair.

'There is nothing broken,' he said, though the sensations he felt with her foot in his hand were decidedly not professional. 'Do you think you can stand?'

'Yes, I think so.'

He helped her to rise, just as Mrs Smith and Mrs Armistead ran through from the back of the house and demanded to know what had happened.

'Miss Hemingford went through the stairs,' he told them. 'I blame myself. I should have forbidden anyone to use them until they had been repaired.'

'It was my own fault,' Anne said. 'I knew about the rotten boards. I should have been more careful. And there's no real damage done.' He was still supporting her with his arm round her and she gingerly put her foot to the ground and tried not to let him see her wince.

'You certainly cannot walk home now,' he said. 'I will go and fetch a cab.'

'I will go,' Mrs Smith offered. 'It is time I went home. My husband and Tom will be expecting their evening meal. Where is Tildy? She said she was going to help you.'

'Tildy?' Anne queried. 'I have not seen her. I did not know she was here.'

'Oh, dear, where has the pesky child got to?' She went to the foot of the stairs and called Tildy's name. After a few moments they heard scampering feet and the little girl appeared at the head of the stairs, even more covered in dust than Anne was. 'Come down very carefully,' her mother told her. 'Watch where you are putting your feet.'

Justin went up to meet her and guided her down. Once she was on the ground floor again her mother turned to scold her. 'Where have you been? You said you were going to help Miss Hemingford…'

'I know, Ma, but I went to play with the little girl.'

'What little girl?'

'The one upstairs. We played hide and seek.'

Justin and Anne looked at each other, each thinking the

same thought. 'What did she look like?' Anne asked her. 'Did she tell you her name?'

'Like me. So high.' She held her hand on the level with her nose. 'She never said nuffin', just waved to me to come, so I went.'

'Where is she now?'

'She went away.'

'Where?'

'Dunno.' The child shrugged. 'I heard you calling, so I came.'

'We can't leave a child up there,' Justin said. 'It is dangerous.' He hurried up the stairs and they could hear him going from room to room and then his footsteps sounded on the narrow stairs to the attics. After several minutes he returned, carrying Tildy's doll. 'There's no one there, no one at all. The dust in the attics is undisturbed.' He handed the doll to Tildy. 'You left this behind.'

Mrs Smith seemed unperturbed. 'Tildy is always inventing friends,' she said. 'Sometimes she insists I give them food.' She laughed. 'I usually pretend I can see them too.' She turned to Tildy. 'Come along. Pa will be wondering what has become of us. And we have to send a cab back for Miss Hemingford.'

'And I had better go too and begin cooking your dinner,' Mrs Armistead said to the doctor. 'The Professor and the nurse will want to be getting along.'

'How strange,' Anne said, after the two women and the child had gone, leaving her alone with the doctor. 'The little girl…'

'Think nothing of it. Children often have fancies like that. There are no ghosts, nothing to be afraid of.'

'I am not afraid, how can I be afraid of a small child? I am curious, that's all.'

'You heard Mrs Smith. She does not exist, except in Tildy's imagination. Now let me help you to the kitchen. There is a pail of clean water there. You can tidy yourself up and I can strap up that ankle.'

'It is hardly hurting at all, now,' she said, but she allowed him to support her as she hobbled down the hall to the back of the house. 'I shall be right as ninepence by the time the cab arrives.'

'Nevertheless we will wait for it.' He helped her to a chair, which Mrs Smith had brought from one of the other rooms to stand on to reach the top shelves of the pantry.

'If you are in haste…'

'I am not.' He poured cold water from the pail into a bowl, then went to the dresser where he had left his doctor's bag and took out a bandage, which he soaked in the water. 'I'll bind this up before you go.'

'Really, there is no need. I am not hurt.'

'I will say whether you are hurt or not,' he said, kneeling at her feet.

She was hurt, more hurt than she could say, but it was more emotional than physical. She had felt sure he felt something for her before Mrs Tremayne had taunted him. They had been close, as close as two people in love could be. Or had she been wrong about that? Was flirting with her just another of his whims?

'There,' he said, tying off the bandage. 'How does that feel?'

'Better, thank you.' She managed to cram her foot back into her shoe.

'I cannot imagine what you hoped to achieve by coming here today.' His tone was brusque.

'I thought I had done rather well.'

'Your job is to charm your friends out of their money, not go grubbing around in the dirt like a scullion. If I had not been here, you might have broken your lovely neck…'

'Fustian! You are making much of nothing.'

'Miss Hemingford…'

'What happened to Anne?'

'I lost her in the sea.'

'No, you did not. You turned your back on her.'

'That would have been a very ungentlemanly thing to do.' He managed a smile. 'I would find it very hard to turn my back on you. You have a way of making people notice you…'

'Oh, I know I am a hoyden.' She laughed. 'You may blame that on my upbringing.'

'Tell me about it.' He was still kneeling at her feet, but as there were no more chairs, it was either that or stand and he did not want to tower over her.

'There is little to tell. Both my parents died in a coaching accident when I was quite small and Harry and I went to live with my grandfather at Sutton Park. He was an important man, too busy to worry over a couple of motherless children, and we were left very much to ourselves. Harry and I would have been close even if we had not been twins, so whatever he did I had to do too. His mischief was my mischief. Nothing much was done to teach me to be a lady until he went away to college and Aunt Bartrum was brought in to school me in the ways of society and bring me out.' She laughed suddenly. 'Every now and again the old Anne comes to the fore, making me the despair of my aunt.'

'Is that why she is trying to make a match for you?'

'Yes, she thinks I need someone strong, someone able to curb me, but I fear the men she thinks are suitable are those she likes herself and inevitably they prefer her. It is little wonder; she is sweet and gentle and knows exactly how to behave in society, while I am as you see me.' She spread her hands to encompass her dishevelled appearance.

'I like what I see.'

'You do?'

'Oh, indeed I do. You are lovely and a man would be a fool not to see it.'

'Lovely and dirty. And you abhor dirt.'

He looked up at her and laughed. 'There is that, of course.'

She joined in his laughter. 'That is the pot calling the kettle black. You are as grubby as I am.'

He looked down at himself, half kneeling on the floor; it was a position he would have adopted if he had been suing for her hand in marriage and for a brief moment he was tempted, but he knew it could not be. He had chosen his life and he could not ask her to share it. It would be too hard, even for a stalwart like her, and if the gossip spread, she would find herself either pitied or the object of derision. His laughter faded and he rose to his feet. 'You are right as always,' he said, attempting to brush himself down.

She watched as he washed his hands in the bowl, then took it outside and emptied it before refilling it with clean water. 'There, I will leave you to wash and tidy yourself. The cab will be here soon.'

The magical moment had gone, vanished as quickly as Tildy's little friend had vanished and she was left so disappointed she was near to tears. Why could he not see what was in her mind? She supposed for the same reason she was not at all sure what was in his. Why could they not speak out?

'Justin,' she said slowly. 'Why have you never married?'

'I am married to my work.'

'I do not believe it. I have heard—' She stopped, seeing annoyance cloud his face. His eyes hardened and his jaw stiffened as if he were having trouble controlling his temper. 'I am sorry, I should not have mentioned it.'

'But you are obviously curious. You wish to know if I am capable of breaking off an engagement to be married. The answer to that, Miss Hemingford, is yes. Now, I will leave you to tidy yourself and will go outside to watch for the cab.'

She watched him fling himself out of the door and slam it behind him, her mind, body and emotions so confused she could not move. She had hoped for an explanation, not that curt admission, and now she had destroyed whatever had been between them. Slowly and painfully, not so much because of an aching foot as an aching heart, she rose, brushed as much of the dust out of her hair as she could, then went to rinse her hands and face in the bowl of water, drying herself on a piece of cloth Mrs Smith had left.

He returned, apparently once more composed, to tell her the cab was waiting outside. She slipped into her pelisse, crammed her bonnet on to her head and picked up her reticule and hobbled out to the cab, disdaining the offer of his arm. 'I can walk.'

He handed her up and climbed in beside her. The cab

jolted as it moved off on the uneven track. She hung on to the strap and said nothing. She continued to hang on to it even when they had reached the road proper and were bowling evenly down towards the centre of Brighton. Ten minutes later they drew up outside her door. He jumped down, let down the step himself and offered her his hand. She could not refuse it and stepped down on to her good foot first. When she had both feet on the ground, he offered her his arm to escort her to the door.

'I think you should rest that foot for a day or two,' he said, as the door was opened and Mrs Bartrum appeared.

'There you are, Anne! Mrs Smith sent Tom to tell us what had happened.' She hurried forward to take Anne's other arm and help her indoors. 'I was going to send the carriage for you, but he said his mother had already despatched a cab.'

'It is nothing, Aunt. Everybody is making such a fuss. I shall be right as rain by tomorrow.'

Mrs Bartrum looked at the doctor, her eyebrows raised. 'Well, Doctor, what have you to say?'

'Miss Hemingford is probably right. It is a slight sprain that should heal itself in a day or two.'

'And how did it happen?'

She was addressing Justin, but it was Anne who answered. 'Aunt, I will tell you once we are inside.'

'Then come in at once.' She bustled her niece indoors, leaving the doctor staring after them.

Anne turned. 'Doctor Tremayne, will you not come in for refreshment? I have not thanked you properly.'

'Thanks are unnecessary. And Mrs Armistead will have my dinner waiting for me, so I will decline refreshment, if you do not mind. I will take the cab back.' He doffed his hat. 'Good day to you, ladies.' And he was gone.

Anne allowed her aunt to help her indoors, knowing she was in for a roasting, not least because Mrs Bartrum had been obliged to send her apologies to Captain Gosforth for their non-appearance at his musical evening, an occasion that she had been anticipating with pleasure. Anne prepared to endure it stoically, to apologise and to try to make up for her aunt's disappointment in any way she could.

The doctor returned just before noon the following day to see his patient, he was at pains to explain to Mrs Bartrum, who received him and accompanied him to the small downstairs sitting room where Anne was sitting with her foot up on a cushion, reading. She put her book down to greet him and assure him she had perfectly recovered, though when he took off her shoe to examine her foot, she could not repress a slight wince. 'I am perfectly able to get about with a stick to lean on,' she told him. 'Before you know where you are, I shall be back at work.'

'Do you think that would be wise?' he asked mildly.

Remembering their conversation, what had been said and what had not been said, and his reaction, she knew it would be far from wise. But when had she ever taken wisdom into consideration when she wanted to do something? Wisdom might have stopped her going to the doctor's house in the first place, wisdom would have prevented her from swimming to the cove; it would certainly have put a stop to their intimacy. 'I have learned my lesson. I will not fall again,' she said.

He put her foot back into her light kid shoe for her, aware of the *double entendre*. 'I am sure you will take great care not to,' he said. 'But these things happen. You can never be sure what is round the corner.'

'If one went about forever worrying what was round the corner, one would never live,' she retorted. 'We have to take some risks.'

'Of course,' Aunt Bartrum put in. 'But not unnecessary ones.'

'I promise you I shall take great care,' she told her, though she was looking at Justin. 'I shall diligently watch where my steps are leading me.' She laughed suddenly; it was a hollow sound, a little hysterical perhaps, and she stopped abruptly. 'I am sure Dr Tremayne has put repairs to the stairs in hand.'

'Indeed, I have.'

'Then I shall purchase the paint and brushes and whatever else is necessary and have it all delivered to the house so that work can begin in three days' time.'

He bowed. 'Very well. I will have the painters ready.'

He had outfoxed her. She could not say she wanted to do the painting herself, not in front of her aunt, and he knew that. Besides, there was far too much for one person and the painters were necessary. But she meant to return to Cliff House. It was where she felt happiest.

He took his leave, knowing his outburst had not shaken her off, which was what he had intended at the time. He had thought that if she knew the worst about him, she would turn her back on him, and then he would be saved the anguish of wondering and wishing, but she had no more turned from him than he had from her. It just could not be done.

He had barely left her door, when he found himself face to face with Sophie and Captain Smollett. The Captain glowered at him, but Sophie gave him a dazzling smile and slipped her hand beneath his arm, to look up into his face with the smile of a tiger. 'Still seeing the lady?' she asked. 'I had thought you would have given up…'

'If you mean Miss Hemingford, she has sustained an injury. I have been treating her.'

'An injury? Oh, dear, nothing serious, I hope?'

'No, a twisted ankle. It will be better in a day or two.'

'I am glad to hear it, but how did she come to do it?'

'She put her foot through a rotting stair tread at Cliff House.'

'Dear, dear! But I warned you it was a ruin, didn't I?'

'The stairs can be mended.'

'Yes, but how many other hidden hazards are there? I should be very careful, Justin, very careful indeed.'

Was it a threat? It sounded like it, but what could she do? He put his hand on hers to disengage her arm, bowed and continued on his way. He could hear her laughter as he went.

Anne had gone to the window to see him leave and had witnessed the scene without being able to hear what was said, but it was clear to her that his sister-in-law still held him in thrall. If they had been engaged, why had he broken it off? Was he still in love with her? It was a sobering thought.

Two days later, Anne was able to walk without a stick and she and her aunt spent a happy morning choosing paint for the new hospital. Then they set off for Bracken Farm to make the postponed visit to Captain Gosforth, though this time there would be no music.

He received them amiably and made a great fuss of Anne, helping her to a chair and putting a small stool beneath her foot, though she assured him the injury was quite cured.

'You cannot be too careful, Miss Hemingford,' he said. 'When I received dear Mrs Bartrum's message, I was all for rushing into town to be with you both, but she had said she would send word if I should be needed and as there was work to be done here, I waited.' He turned to Mrs Bartrum. 'I trust I did not disappoint you?'

'Not at all, Captain.' She smiled. 'There was nothing you could have done and it turned out not to be as serious as I at first thought.'

'I am very glad to hear it.' He paused as a maidservant came in with a tea tray. She set everything out on a small table bedecked with a crisp white cloth and, at a signal from him, withdrew. 'Mrs Bartrum, would you be so kind as to do the honours?'

Aunt Bartrum busied herself with the teapot and the cups while he watched admiringly. Anne was amused and could not believe her aunt was indifferent to him.

'Tell me, Miss Hemingford,' he went on, when they were each balancing a cup and saucer in their hands, 'why were you at Cliff House that afternoon? I thought you had decided not to go near it?'

'My aunt decided she would not, but that did not mean I concurred,' she answered. 'I went to see how Mrs Smith was faring. She has worked so hard and made a vast difference.'

'But it is still in a state of disrepair?'

'Not so much now. The roof tiles and window glass have been replaced and I believe the stairs repaired. It needs only painting before the furniture and equipment can be brought in and then we shall have our hospital.'

'Splendid! It is a shame it was allowed to fall into such a state, but people were reluctant to take on the lease…'

'Because of the ghost, you mean?'

'Yes. I assume you saw no evidence of it?'

'No, I did not, but something strange did happen.'

'You did not tell me that,' her aunt said.

'I did not want to agitate you.'

'Do you mean it was the ghost who pushed you down the stairs?'

'No, no, Aunt. No one pushed me and besides, there is no malice in that house, none at all. If there is a ghost, it is a kindly one.' She smiled at her aunt's expression of shock and eager anticipation as she leaned forward to learn more. Anne proceeded to tell them about Tildy's little friend. 'It is nothing out of the ordinary, so Mrs Smith tells me,' she finished. 'Tildy is sometimes lonely and often conjures little playmates up from her imagination, but to her they are very real.'

Aunt Bartrum shuddered. 'I do not know how you can go near the place, Anne. You have quite overset me.'

'Oh, dear lady, do not be alarmed,' The Captain said, taking her cup from her trembling hand and setting it down on the table. 'Do let me show you round my house; it has no ghosts, I assure you.' He offered his hand and she took it to rise. 'Miss Hemingford, would you like to accompany us?'

Anne smiled; the last thing he wanted was her company. 'No, I think I shall stay here and rest my foot, if you do not mind.'

They were gone a long time. Anne could occasionally hear their footsteps and doors shutting and sometimes a light laugh and when they returned, her aunt had shining eyes and bright pink cheeks. 'It is a lovely house, Anne,' she said, resuming her seat. 'So comfortably furnished, so elegant. You should have come too.'

'Another time, perhaps.'

'Yes, of course,' the Captain said. 'You will always be welcome, especially if my hopes are fulfilled.' He looked straight at Mrs Bartrum as he spoke and left Anne in no doubt that he had again proposed.

'Oh, dear, look at the time.' Mrs Bartrum jumped to her feet, compelling him to rise too. 'We really must be going home. I promised Mrs Barry I would attend her soirée this evening. I think there is to be an announcement of Jeanette's betrothal to Lieutenant Harcourt. Her little adventure seems to have brought it to a head.'

Reluctantly he ordered their carriage to be brought round to the front of the house from the stables where the horses were being rested, and escorted them to it. 'I shall see you again very soon,' he said, handing Mrs Bartrum up. 'Then I shall hope for my answer.' He turned to Anne with a polite smile. 'Miss Hemingford, if you have any influence at all, I beg you to use it on my behalf.'

'So, he has proposed again,' Anne said as they left the

farm behind. 'And from what he said, you are still holding out against him.'

'How can I think of that when you are not yet settled?
What would Harry think of me?'

'What has it to do with Harry?'

'I promised him I would find you a husband.'

'That was a foolish promise, Aunt Georgie. I shall have
words with him when we get home. You must both have
known I would be too headstrong to fall in with your
scheming.' She turned to smile reassuringly at her aunt.
'And it is as well I am, for by now I would be a very disappointed woman. Captain Gosforth has eyes only for you.'

'So he told me.'

'And what do you think of him?'

'He is a fine gentleman. I like him well enough.'

'Enough to accept him?'

'Perhaps.'

'I remember you said you liked a man to be persistent
as a measure of his regard. He certainly seems that.'

'Yes, he is, isn't he? I begin to believe he is in earnest.'

'Of course he is in earnest. But he is not the only one,
there is the Major…'

'Oh, he is too puffed up for me and too influenced by
his mother. She is a friend, but I do not think I should like
her for a relation.'

Anne laughed. 'I am sure you did not tell him that.'

'No, of course not. I said we should not suit.'

'And did he accept that?'

'I believe so. I think he was not serious and prefers you,
after all.'

'Then he will be doubly disappointed, because I know

we should not suit. Aunt, do please give up this crusade on my behalf. If I want a husband, I think I can manage to find one for myself. I am sure Harry will understand.'

They were approaching the town and there was still an hour or so of daylight left. 'Aunt, do you mind if we go to Cliff House? I want to see how Mrs Smith is doing.'

'Very well, but I shall stay in the carriage. Nothing at all will persuade me inside.'

Anne asked the coachman to turn up the lane and leaned forward in her seat to catch her first glimpse of the house, then she gasped with dismay. Plumes of smoke spiralled above the trees. 'It is on fire. Oh, Daniels, do make haste.'

Almost before the coach had stopped, a fair way from the burning building because the coachman did not want to spook the horses, she was out of it and sprinting. 'Anne, do take care!' Aunt Bartrum called to her. 'Remember your promise.'

The words were carried away on the breeze that was fanning the flames. In any case, Anne would have paid them no heed. Her only concern was for Mrs Smith. Had she been in the house? Had she got out safely? Who else might have been inside? Mrs Armistead? Tildy? Justin? Terror filled her whole body, so that she did not feel the increasing heat as she battled her way towards the kitchen door.

Through the open door she could see someone inside; whoever it was seemed to be surrounded by flames. She put her arm up to shield her face, but the heat drove her back. Other people were arriving behind her, she could hear shouts of command, saw men cranking the handle of the well. God in heaven! They could never get enough water that way. And then someone burst out of the house, a body in his arms.

'Justin!' Her voice was a terrified shriek as she saw his blackened face and scorched clothes.

He looked up, still stumbling on with his bundle. 'Get back, woman! For God's sake, get back!'

She retreated, sinking to the ground as others, stronger than her, made a water chain, handing buckets from one to the other. It was a futile exercise, but it was something to do. The flames roared and the windows cracked with a succession of loud explosions. She looked up at it and then back to Justin, who had laid his burden on the ground. 'Get me some water,' he said in a voice so cracked and hoarse it was barely audible. 'Hurry.'

She went to the well, grabbed a pail of water from one of the fire-fighters and ran back with it to Justin. He was bending over the still figure of Mrs Smith. 'Oh, no! Oh, Justin…'

He grabbed his cravat from his neck, but it was so black he could not use it. Anne lifted the hem of her gown and grabbed her underskirt, pulling at the ties to release it. She stepped out of it quickly and handed it to him. He tore it up and dipped one of the pieces in the water and squeezed it over Mrs Smith's lips. Her clothes, though scorched, had saved her body, but her hands, which she had used to shield her face, looked raw. He tore up more cloth, wetted it and laid it across her hands and arms. She moaned.

'Thank God!' Anne said.

'Tildy,' the woman gasped, trying to sit up. 'Tildy…'

'Tildy?' Justin repeated. 'Tildy was with you?'

'Yes. She was playing upstairs. I 'eard 'er talking to her little friend.'

He looked up at the inferno, wondering if he could get back in and try to find the child, but he knew it was not possible. Strong as he was, used as he was to the carnage of war, this was too much and he felt his eyes fill with tears. The little girl had embodied all his hopes for the future of the poor children of Brighton, poor children everywhere, and now she was gone. And so was his dream. He could hear it crashing about his ears. He looked bleakly across at Anne. The tears were coursing unchecked down her face. Mrs Smith saw them too, and understood. She struggled to rise, saw the burning house and fell back in a deep swoon.

He reached out and touched Anne's hand. 'Look after her.' Then he ran back towards the house and, seizing one of the buckets, tipped it over himself before trying to re-enter the building. Heat drove him back. 'Leave it,' he told the men. They were at least two dozen, drawn by the sight of the flames to come and help. 'Leave it to burn itself out. I don't want anyone else to die.'

'Someone died?' one of the men asked.

He nodded. 'Tildy. A little girl.'

'There's a curse on this house, right enough,' another said. 'Two little girls…'

Justin could hardly bear to talk about it. 'Thank you for your help. I will stay until it is safe.'

He suddenly noticed Mrs Bartrum sitting in her carriage, her face a white mask of terror. He went over to her. 'Madam, are you all right?'

She turned slowly from gazing at the flames to look at him. 'Are you hurt?'

'No, a little blackened, that's all, but Mrs Smith is in need of urgent medical attention. Will you take her in your carriage to my rooms, where you will find Professor Harrison? He will know what to do.'

'Of course I will Oh, how dreadful it all is. How very dreadful.'

But he did not hear her last words; he had hurried to where Anne sat over Mrs Smith, shielding her with her body from the sight and heat of the furnace. 'Mrs Bartrum is going to take Mrs Smith to be looked after. I am afraid there will not be room in the carriage for you, but I will see you safely home later.'

She nodded. Her voice seemed to have dried up in her throat, so that speaking was almost impossible. She could think of nothing but Tildy and the young mother's grief, which she, in some measure, shared. She had taken the little girl to her heart and she would never see her again, never hear her tinkling laugh, nor hear her say, 'Hallo, lady.' She looked down at the woman, lying on the ground and a huge sob escaped her. She could not weep, not in front of the woman who had lost so much more than she had. She choked her tears back and tried to find a wobbly smile as she dipped the cloth back into the water, squeezed it out and mopped the woman's face.

'Where am I?'

'You are safe. You are going to be taken Dr Tremayne's in my aunt's carriage.'

'Tildy?'

She looked up at Justin, then back again. 'We will find her.'

The fire-fighters had all left. Justin called Mrs Bartrum's coachman over to help him carry the woman to the carriage, followed by Anne whom, after reassuring her aunt she was not even the slightest bit hurt, Mrs Bartrum reluctantly agreed to leave behind.

'How are we going to tell her?' Anne asked, as the carriage rumbled out of sight.

'I do not know.' He was looking at the building, now a smoking shell. 'I looked all over the house. I thought Mrs Smith was alone. I should have guessed, done more.' His voice was cracked.

'What happened?'

'I came up to see how everything was going and found the place already alight. I cannot for the life of me understand how it happened. Mrs Smith had not lit a fire, there was no naked flame that I know of. It is a mystery. I rushed in and went from room to room, trying to find the seat of the fire. Then I heard Mrs Smith screaming in one of the bedrooms and fetched her out.' The account was spoken flatly, but she could easily imagine the scene.

'Tildy must have been playing somewhere, perhaps she wasn't in the house at all. She might be hiding in the garden or the sheds, too frightened to come out.'

It was a long shot, but they set about systematically searching the grounds, but without any luck. The fire was almost out and Justin was tempted to go inside to try to find the child's body. It was something he dreaded doing, something he did not want Anne to witness.

'Could she have gone down to the cove?' Anne asked.

'Possible. I suppose.' He did not want to give up hope, though he had never had much to start with. 'Let's see.'

They went down the steep path, not speaking, their hearts too full for words. The tide was coming in and there was only a thin strip of beach still dry. It seemed to be another turn of fate, that the child might have come down here, escaped the fire and been drowned. Anne began to run along the shore line, leaving Justin to go in the opposite direction. And then she saw her, sitting on a rock about six feet from the ground. 'Justin!' she shrieked. 'Over here.'

She clambered up, scraping her hands and knees. 'Oh, Tildy, Tildy, we have been looking everywhere for you.'

'Hallo, lady. Have you come to take me home?'

'Yes.' She was sobbing with relief as she gathered the child to her

Justin was climbing up behind her. 'How on earth did she get up here?'

'I didn't climb up,' the child said. 'I came that way.' She pointed behind her and for the first time, Anne saw that she was sitting at the entrance to a cave.

'It must go back to the house,' Justin said, bending over the child. 'No time to explore it now, we have to get out of here before the tide cuts us off.' He clambered back down the steep slope and once he was standing at the bottom, held up his arms. 'Let her down gently. I'll catch her.'

They were soon all three on the beach. Justin picked up the child and splashed his way back through the rising water to the cliff path, with Anne close behind him. Once safely at the top, he put Tildy down and dropped on to the grass beside her. Anne, coming fast behind, sprawled beside them.

'Thank God you would not give up,' he said, breathlessly. 'If you had not insisted…'

She knew what he meant. The poor child could have been there on the ledge all night, might even have tried to jump down and been drowned. 'She is safe, that's all that matters.'

'It was a big fire,' Tildy said, gazing up at the ruin. She did not seem surprised.

'Yes, a very big fire,' he said. 'But what happened to you? Were you in the house when it started?'

'Oh, yes, I heard the flames and I tried to get out, but I couldn't. It was so hot and smoky and I didn't like it.'

'How did you get out?'

'The girl showed me. She did this…' She stopped to make a beckoning motion with her hand and arm. 'So I went after her. She went through a door and down a tunnel. It was dark and wet, but I knew she was helping me so I didn't mind. It came out by the sea. But I couldn't get down.'

'Was it the same little girl you saw before?' Anne asked.

'Course it was.'

'What happened to her?'

'I dunno. I reckon she went back. I didn't see her no more.' She looked round. 'Where's Ma?'

'She is at Dr Tremayne's, waiting for you. Do you think you can walk that far?'

'Course I can. I walked here, didn' I?'

Justin and Anne smiled at each other; they had been touched by magic that afternoon, divine intervention. Taking a hand each, they led the child away from the ruin and back to the real world.

Chapter Ten

Tildy's dramatic rescue was the talk of the town—not only that she was saved but the manner of it. There was much speculation about the little girl who was supposed to have led her to safety and the story of little Susan gathered fresh credence. Anne was ambivalent, but both Dr Tremayne and Mrs Smith maintained that the little girl was the product of Tildy's imagination and that Tildy had somehow found the tunnel by accident and escaped down it. Whichever it was, Mrs Smith was overjoyed to have her daughter back safe and sound.

Her hands were badly burned and her hair scorched, but if it had not been for the doctor she would have died and she could not find words enough to thank him. He did not want thanks, he wanted answers and, as soon as she was well enough, he questioned her closely.

'I did not light a fire,' she told him. 'I only did that if I needed hot water and that day I had decided to clean the upstairs windows.'

He had gone to visit her at her home where she was

convalescing to find Anne already there, shrouded in an apron, administering beef tea to the invalid, in spite of her protests that a lady like her should not be doing such a thing. 'And there was nothing inflammable about?'

'No, I do not think so.'

'Paint,' Anne said suddenly. 'I was told it would be delivered that day. That would burn well, would it not?'

'Yes, and so would wood shavings. The men had been to repair the stairs…'

'I swept it all up,' Mrs Smith said. 'And the paint was in the front hall, ready to be taken up by the workmen when they arrived.'

'Where did you put the shavings?'

'In a heap beside the fireplace in the kitchen. I thought it would be good for kindling. But there was no fire, I swear it.'

'Did you see anyone? Apart from the delivery men?'

'I do not think so. Why do you ask?'

'I don't know,' he said, looking grim. 'But someone had a naked flame. Houses do not usually combust on their own.'

'I swear I didn't do it.' Mrs Smith was becoming agitated.

'We know it wasn't you,' he said, bending to touch her hand. 'Why, if it had not been for you, the house would not have been ready…'

'Now it's gone.'

'Yes.'

'What are you going to do?'

'I don't know. It is too soon to say. But I shall think of something. What is more important is that you should get well, let those hands heal. No housework or working with the bathing machines. If you need help…'

'No, thank you. I have my husband and Tom and good friends nearby. And Tildy does her best…'

'Where is she?' Anne asked.

'In the yard, I think. I sent her to fetch water.'

Anne left them and went in search of the little girl. She was struggling to carry a pail which, in spite of being only half-full, was more than she could manage. The water was slopping everywhere. Anne took it from her. 'Tildy, come and say goodbye to the doctor. We are leaving now.'

She ran into the house ahead of Anne and scrambled on to her mother's bed, being very careful not to knock her bandaged hands. 'Ma will soon be better, won't she?' she asked Justin.

'Yes, very soon,' he answered, smiling. 'I am sure you are a great help to her.'

'Yes, but I wish she had come down the tunnel with the girl and me, then she wouldn't be burnt, would she?'

'No.' He paused, wondering whether it might upset her to question her, but she seemed none the worse for her adventure, and was bright as a button. 'Tildy, did you see anyone near the house before the fire started?'

'There was a cart—'

'The men delivering the paint,' Mrs Smith put in.

'To be sure. Any others, Tildy?'

'Two men came up the path from the sea. I saw them from a window upstairs.'

'Did you see them again?'

'I heard Ma calling me, but there was smoke and flames and I was frightened. Then the little girl took me down the tunnel…' She paused before adding, 'They got in a boat…'

'You saw them while you were waiting for us to find you?'

'Yes. They were running. I shouted, but they didn't hear me. I wanted to go home…'

'Of course you did. Do not think any more about it. You are safe and so is your mother.' He patted her head. 'Now we must go, but I want you to promise to come for me if you need me. Will you do that?'

'Yes.'

He extracted a guinea from the pocket of his tailcoat and laid it on the table beside the bed, smiling at Mrs Smith. 'Your wages.'

'But I can't take all that.'

'I shall be offended if you do not. You were injured working for me and for that you must be recompensed.'

'Take it,' Anne whispered, bending over her as Justin made for the door. 'I'll see he does not lose by it.' She hugged Tildy and followed Justin from the house.

'You think it was arson, don't you?' she said as they walked. It was only two days since the fire, but their relationship had subtly changed. It was as if the raging furnace in their hearts had burned itself out, just as the house had done. No longer were they consumed by heat one minute and coolly distant the next. Passion and resentment had given way to a calm acceptance of their destiny, whatever that might turn out to be. Without needing to speak of it, they had both realised that life was too short, too ephemeral, to waste it in quarrelling. They were left with the knowledge of each other as people who cared.

Whether the caring was for the sick, the poor, or each other, was of no consequence, it was simply part of the whole.

Another result of the fire and its aftermath was that Aunt Bartrum had ceased to rail against Anne's hoyden- ish ways. She had been terrified by the conflagration and knew how easily she could have lost her beloved niece, and that gave her pause for thought. Anne was Anne and there was no sense in trying to change her. Her friends, like her, must learn to accept that. And so Anne did her visiting and came and went to the doctor's house, with- out a word said against it. Even today, clad in a service- able gingham dress the colour of a summer sky, a dark blue pelisse and a plain bonnet, she was walking beside him without the benefit of a chaperon.

'I fear so. What Tildy said seems to confirm it.'

'But who were the two men? Have you any idea?'

'No, but their identity is not important. They would have been paid to do their mischief by someone else.'

'But who would want to prevent you opening your hospital? Who wants you to fail so badly they are willing to risk lives to bring it about?'

'I don't know.'

She risked a glance at him. He was looking grimly de- termined and she could not help feeling that he did know, even if he did not intend to tell her. 'What are you going to do?'

'Nothing I can do, is there? Without proof…'

'I meant about the hospital.'

'There is no hospital. Perhaps it was never meant to be.'

'How can you say so? It is needed. The house can be rebuilt.'

He gave a cracked laugh. 'What with? We have spent nearly all the money the good people of Brighton donated. There is nothing left.'

'Justin Tremayne, I am surprised at you. The people gave their money for a hospital and some of them could ill afford it. Are you saying they might as well have set fire to it themselves? Shame on you.'

He turned in surprise at her vehemence. 'What would you have me do? Start all over again?'

'Why not? I had not taken you for a quitter, not even when Mrs Tremayne said you were.'

He stopped in his tracks to turn towards her. 'When did she say that?'

'The night of Lady Mancroft's rout. She said you had wild fancies to do things, which did not last. She implied being a doctor was one and you would give up the idea of a hospital at the first hurdle…'

'Do you believe that?'

'I do not want to, but what I believe is unimportant. It is what the people believe, people like Mrs Smith. She gave what to her would have been a fortune and you owe it to her to carry on.'

He laughed suddenly. 'You know, George Harrison said, "Once Miss Anne Hemingford goes on the march, there is no stopping her." I begin to believe him.'

She was amused rather than angry. 'Then let us march on together. There is the Grand Ball next Monday, that will make a start.'

They walked on towards his house, now one of the few

still standing in the street. Where would he go when it was demolished? Cliff House could not be rebuilt in time. 'I will find temporary accommodation,' he said, as they picked their way over rubble. 'Someone will take pity on me.'

Anne knew better than to offer financial help; he was too proud to take it from her, but she could send an anonymous donation to the fund, though not so substantial as to arouse suspicion. The whole idea of the hospital from the start was that it was to be funded by public money. The people of Brighton also had their pride.

She stayed only long enough to exchange pleasantries with Professor Harrison, who had been true to his word and was working with the patients, then set off for home.

Mrs Bartrum was entertaining Lady Mancroft and the Major. The Major was looking rather put out and silent, while his mother was trying to quiz Mrs Bartrum about the fire. 'There has not been so much excitement in town since the Regent cast off Mrs Fitzherbert to marry Caroline,' she was saying as Anne came into the room 'And what a disaster that turned out to be.'

'Ah, there you are, Anne,' her aunt said, apparently relieved to have support. 'I have been telling her ladyship that we do not know how the fire started. Have you learned any more this morning?'

'No, but Mrs Smith is adamant she had no fire in the grate and two men were seen running away down the cliffs to a boat.'

'Arson?' queried the Major, emerging from his brown study.

'Doctor Tremayne thinks it may be.'

'But who would do such a thing?' Mrs Bartrum queried. 'Having a hospital can surely not harm anyone. It was meant for the benefit of all.'

'Smollett,' he said. 'I'll wager it was revenge. He was very angry…'

'Oh, surely not?' Anne said. 'If he wanted revenge, he would surely have taken it against me. I am the one who accused him.'

'Oh, no!' Mrs Bartrum put both hands to her heart. 'He must have thought you were in the house. Oh, Anne!'

'This is pure conjecture,' Anne said, refusing to be rattled. 'You are no doubt maligning the man. And you cannot accuse people without proof.'

'All the same, I think I will make some enquiries,' the Major went on. 'In the meantime, Miss Hemingford, please do not go out without an escort.'

'This is ridiculous,' Anne said. 'No one is out to harm me. It is the hospital they attacked, *if* they attacked it, and we cannot even be sure of that, and we mean to rebuild it as soon as we can raise more funds.'

'But will the people give again, do you think?' Lady Mancroft questioned.

'If it is put to them that to give up would be to waste what had already been donated. We must simply redouble our efforts. The Grand Ball will afford us an opportunity to judge the mood of people.'

'Charles, you must speak to the Regent again,' her ladyship commanded him. 'If we could obtain his public support…'

'More than that, his financial backing,' Anne added.

'To be sure, with his backing, we might encourage the more well-breeched among our friends to be generous.'

'I will do what I can. It depends on his mood…'

'Oh, then I will do it,' his mother said, with a light laugh. 'He is known to be susceptible to the more mature woman and I can turn on the charm when I choose.'

'Thank you, my lady,' Anne said. 'You are kindness itself.'

It was only after they had gone that her aunt said, 'I wonder if she will be as kind when she discovers I have rejected her son?'

'He asked you again? I thought you said he had accepted your first refusal?'

'I thought he had, but he arrived today before her ladyship in order to press me. Anne, I had to be most strict with him.'

'And is he convinced?'

'Oh, yes, he is now.' She blushed prettily. 'I told him I had accepted Captain Gosforth.'

'Aunt Georgie! Is this true?'

'Yes. He was here earlier.'

'Then let me felicitate you and wish you happy.' Anne left her seat to hug her aunt. 'I am so happy for you. When shall you announce it?'

'Oh it does not need announcing, we shall simply tell our friends when we meet. I do not want to puff myself up when you are still single. Everyone will think me a very poor matchmaker when I look to myself before my charge.'

'Gammon! I am as pleased as punch.'

'Anne, I wish—'

'No more, Aunt.'

'You are still determined to help raise more money for Dr Tremayne and the hospital, are you?' she asked, with a strange switch of direction.

'Yes. I cannot desert him now, even if it means staying in Brighton a little longer than we planned, but I do not suppose you mind that now, when there is so much to keep you here.'

Aunt Bartrum laughed. 'Yes, but I must go back to Cumbria before long to settle my affairs. There is the house… I can see no reason to keep it. Unless…' She paused. 'Would you like it? It would delight me to sign it over to you, to give you a home of your own.'

'Oh, Aunt, how can you be so generous to me when I cause you nothing but grief?'

'My dearest girl, I cannot change you and it was wicked of me to think I could. But if you are determined to remain single…' She let the word die on the air.

Anne loved the house in Cumbria. She and Harry had spent many happy times staying with their aunt there. It would make a wonderful bolthole for when all this fuss about the hospital died down. If Justin did not want her for a wife, and it seemed he did not, she would need somewhere to lick her wounds. 'Oh, Aunt Georgie, thank you, thank you so much. But do you mind if we leave the decision until after the ball?'

The ball was becoming the kingpin of everything: the fund-raising for the hospital, judging the mood of the donors, and her hope for a happy outcome with Justin. He had to be made to see that she cared more for him than protocol and etiquette and whether society approved. He evidently did not care for such things himself, so why should she? If only Mrs Tremayne would go home and leave them alone.

Sophie had no intention of leaving well alone. While pretending to commiserate, she was triumphant. 'I told you it would not work,' she told Justin when she met him on The Steine the next day. He had been to visit a patient who was too ill to visit his consulting rooms and was on his way back. She had evidently been shopping because she was followed at a distance by a manservant and her maid, both laden with packages. 'Now the house has been destroyed, you will perhaps come to your senses.'

'I was never more in possession of my senses.'

Her false laughter trilled. 'You cannot possibly hope to raise all that money again. People are not so foolish as to give twice and, without it, how can you hope to go on?'

'Nevertheless, contrary to what you told Miss Hemingford, I intend to stick with it.'

'So she told you, did she? I thought I had rattled her. But why don't you ask her for the money? She has so much she would not even miss it.'

'No.'

'Your stubborn pride, is it?'

'If you say so.'

'Naturally, I say so. I know you, you see. You would like to come home with me, but your stubborn pride will not allow you to admit it.'

'Rubbish! I am staying in Brighton.'

'Are you?' she said, smiling slyly from beneath the

brim of her fashionable bonnet. 'Your hospital is no more and your house is being pulled down. There is nothing left for you here.'

'Go home,' he said wearily. 'Go before you are publicly shamed. You paid no heed when I warned you against Captain Smollett and now he will be under examination, might even be drummed out of the regiment.'

'What for?'

He knew he had startled her and gave her a wry smile. 'Arson. And the disgrace will encompass those around him, including you.'

She did not need to ask him if he were referring to the fire at Cliff House. 'Why would he do that?'

'Perhaps because you asked him to. What I cannot understand is why. You surely did not think it would change anything, did you?'

'Why?' She flung back her head, her voice a squeak of hysteria. 'Because I need you at Sevenelms. It is where you belong.'

'I am not interested in your needs. Let Andrew take care of them.'

'He can't,' she shrieked. 'He's dead.'

'What?' He could not have been more shocked if she had plunged a knife into his gut.

'It's true.' Her voice dropped to its usual pitch. 'You are the heir now and I—'

He seized her shoulders as if he would like to shake her, but, realising what he was doing, dropped his hands to his sides. 'Is this the truth?'

'Of course it is. Why would I lie about such a thing?'

'When? How?'

'His horse threw him…'

'And you left my father to his grief?'

'Only to fetch you home.'

'But you did not tell me the real reason. You taunted me, threatened me, humiliated me, did everything except tell me the truth…' He paused suddenly. 'You said you were not happy in your marriage.'

'I wasn't. I wanted you.'

He gave a cracked laugh, as the implication of what she had said suddenly hit him. 'I am the heir and you are desperate to be the Viscountess. I see it all now. Well, it will avail you naught. Good day to you, madam.' And he strode away, almost running in his anxiety to go to his father.

They did not have to wait for the ball to judge the mood of the populace. Suddenly Dr Tremayne and his hospital achieved the status of a crusade and donations began to pour in. Even the Regent, his eye to his waning popularity, sent a generous donation by Lady Mancroft. As soon as she heard, Anne hurried to tell Justin, only to discover he had left Brighton. 'He had to go home,' Mrs Armistead told her.

'Did he say when he was coming back?'

'No. It was sudden. Doctor Harrison is here. Shall you see him?'

'No, do not disturb him.' She had never felt so miserable. Mrs Tremayne was right. Justin had abandoned the project at the first hurdle, not only abandoned the project and his patients, but her. Just when she was beginning to hope. She felt let down, humiliated, foolish.

She did not want to go home; her aunt always knew

when there was something wrong and would be bound to quiz her about it. She was fighting tears and needed to be more in control before she faced anyone. Turning away from the town, she walked up the road to Cliff House. She had been happy there, had even imagined living there with Justin, his wife and helper, content to be simply Dr and Mrs Tremayne. Aunt Bartrum and Harry would have accepted it in the end. But it was not to be.

She stood and looked at the blackened shell of the house, living again that first visit to it, when she and Justin had roamed all over it, their hands entwined, their wet bathing clothes sticking to their skins, revealing every contour of their bodies. She relived every moment, the kisses and the look in his eyes as he searched her face; his heroic actions at the time of the fire, his misery when they thought they had lost Tildy. It had brought them closer, as close as two people could be, and when Tildy was found alive, they had cried together with sheer relief. And since then… She thought she had persuaded him to carry on, but she had failed. He had left her without a word of fare-well.

Slowly she made her way back down the hill to the town, her spine stiffening as she walked. The hospital must not fail. She would redouble her efforts to get the project up and running again. They would find other doc-tors, nurses, helpers. And when that was done, she would retreat to Lake Windermere and nurse her broken heart, her shattered self-esteem; perhaps, one day, it might heal sufficiently for her to face the world again. But she doubted it.

* * *

Sevenelms had not changed. It was still the same solid mansion, set in several acres of parkland, where he had played as a boy, always in the shadow of his older brother. He had not minded that. He had loved his brother. Until that last final quarrel. And that had been Sophie's fault. She had used him, consented to be his wife so that he would bring her to Sevenelms and she could worm her way into Andrew's affections and into his bed. It had all been planned. And now Andrew was dead and she was still scheming.

The journey had not been an easy one. Unless he were prepared to take the rumbling slow coaches that went from town to town, which would have taken several days, or bespoke a post-chaise, which was horrendously expensive, there was no direct route from Brighton to Exeter, the nearest town to his father's estate. In the end he had taken one of the frequent stage coaches to London and arrived there at six in the evening. He had only enough time to eat a quick meal before making his way to the *Bull and Mouth* where he boarded the overnight mail to Exeter. He had slept very little in the jolting coach as it sped through the dark countryside, stopping only long enough to change the horses, in which time the passengers were expected to stretch their legs, relieve themselves and grab whatever food could be eaten on the move. He was stiff and ragged with tiredness when he left it at two the following afternoon. Nevertheless he would not rest, but immediately hired a hack to take him the last half-dozen miles, dreading what he would find.

He dismounted at the solid front door and lifted the

knocker, but the door was flung open before he could use it. 'Master Justin! I saw a horseman coming up the drive and knew it was you.' The old butler, who had known both boys since they were in leading strings, was beaming with pleasure.

'Hallo, Jarvis.' Justin stepped inside the hall. 'Where is my father?'

'In the conservatory. His lordship will be overjoyed. And Master Andrew too.'

'Andrew?' He was puzzled. 'Andrew is...'

'Why, getting better every day, Master Justin, and now you are home he will soon be himself again.'

She had lied. Why? Just to get him home? He was sure that was not all.

He followed the butler to the large glass adjunct to the house that housed hothouse plants from all over the world, brought back by the Viscount when he was a naval officer. 'I'll announce myself,' he said, pushing open the door.

The room was over warm and smelled of damp earth. His father was standing by a large fern, a pair of clippers in his hand. Andrew was in a bath chair, his legs covered by a rug. His face was pale and he was a great deal thinner than the robust man he had been. They both looked round as he entered. 'Justin!' they said in unison.

He smiled as his father flung down the clippers and hurried to embrace him. 'Oh, my boy, how glad I am to have you home.'

He returned his father's embrace and then went to shake Andrew by the hand. 'What happened to you?' He tried to keep his voice light. 'Take a tumble, did you?'

'Something like that.'

'It was all the fault of that wanton he married,' their father put in. 'How we were taken in by her!'

Justin pulled up a chair and sat down beside his brother. 'What happened?'

'We had a quarrel. We were always fighting. She was being her usual vicious self, taunting me with my failure to get her with child, though what sort of mother she would have made, I do not know. I slammed out of the house. My mare was already saddled because we had intended to ride out that morning. I simply jumped on her back and rode off without checking the girth. It had been cut almost through. By the time I had reached the wall, the one that separates the park from the moor—you know where I mean, we often jumped it when we were young—I put the horse to the wall, the saddle slipped and I was thrown…'

'He broke his leg, but that was not the worst,' their father added. 'He was unconscious for days with an injury to his head. The doctor despaired of him, told us he would never recover.'

'Sophie said he was dead.'

'You have seen her?' Andrew queried in surprise.

'Yes, she came to Brighton. She had been there over two weeks before she told me. She said you were dead and I was the heir and she wanted me back…'

'Good God! Did she think I would let her over the threshold after what she has done?' the old man said. 'We cannot prove she cut the girth, but she was seen near Andrew's horse only minutes before he set out.'

'I imagine she thought if I were with her, you would

allow it,' Justin said. He had had plenty of time to think about it while he had been travelling. Sophie had meant to seduce him, make him fall in love with her all over again and then she would accompany him home to a grieving household, pretending all she had wanted was to bring the family together again.

'She is devious,' Andrew said. 'I learned that over the years. How I wish you had never brought her to Sevenelms.'

'You do not wish it any more than I do. But I am happy to see you are making a recovery, Andrew. No one regretted our quarrel more than I did.'

'I know. We were both duped.'

'Where is she now?' the Viscount asked.

'In Brighton, wreaking her usual havoc.' He went on to tell them all about his work and the hospital project, which he had every intention of returning to. 'It is what I do best,' he said. 'And now I know I am not needed here…'

'Of course you are needed.'

'But not as the heir. Andrew is alive and recovering. I shall still be the second son and that pleases me more than I can say. But we shall see each other often, I promise. Will you do me the honour of attending the opening of the new hospital? There is someone I should like you to meet.'

'Oh?' The Viscount lifted one dark brow in a query. 'There is a lady?'

'A very lovely lady. One who is compassionate, caring, hardworking and I love her very much…'

'Lucky man,' Andrew said.

'I have not yet declared myself and she may not have me.'

'Why not?'

'Oh, there are many reasons, Sophie's poison, my way of earning a living, the fact that she is a Hemingford, sister to the new Earl of Bostock, and is guarded by an aunt determined to make a suitable match for her.'

'All of which can be overcome if she wishes it,' Andrew said. 'I pray for your happiness. I was the one who made you miserable. I was blind…'

'Think no more of it. I am content with my life. But what about you?'

'I shall sue for divorce. I may not succeed and, even if I do, I shall probably never marry again, so it will be left to you to keep the line going.'

'I am sorry for that, but you are still young. There are good women in the world, they are not all like Sophie, though there was a time when I thought so.'

'You will be anxious to return to Brighton?'

'Yes. Tomorrow. But I will come back. Often now.'

They spent a pleasant afternoon and evening, talking over old times and their hopes for the future, until exhaustion overwhelmed Justin and he begged leave to retire. The next day he set off for the long journey home. Brighton was home now and the people there his people and there was Anne… He was suddenly reminded of the Grand Ball. In his anxiety to reach Devon, he had forgotten all about it. But it was to take place the very next night. Could he possibly be back in time?

Everyone who was anyone was expected to attend the ball. Hearing that the Regent might attend, people had been vying for tickets and cheerfully paying over the odds to obtain them. It promised to be the occasion of the year. Aunt Bartrum and Lady Mancroft were in a flutter of excitement and both the Misses Barry were almost delirious with anticipation.

Anne sat at her mirror in her shift and petticoat while Amelia brushed her hair and put it up in swirls of thick loops at the back of her head, fastening it with jewelled combs and a small stand of feathers. Her ballgown was spread out on the bed, ready for her to slip over her head. It was made of forest-green taffeta, with a full-length train falling from the back of the high waist. The hem of the train and the skirt was decorated with pleated satin in the same colour, which also filled the low décolletage. The sleeves were short and puffed. Tonight she was putting off the hoyden, the woman who wielded a feather duster, to become the society belle.

She could not look forward to it with quite the excitement she might have done if Justin had been escorting her. This was for show only, to let everyone know that she was the grand lady, above the vulgar emotions of those lower down the social scale. She smiled a little ruefully as Amelia tugged at a stray curl that would not stay in place. She could rise above disappointment and rebuild her life, just as Cliff House would be rebuilt. It would not be the same, nothing would ever be the same, but it would be functional, useful. The sweet ghost had gone, had done her good deed, had saved Tildy and disappeared for ever. Even Tildy had accepted that.

'She had to go away,' the child had said when Anne had questioned her. Anne would go too, but not before she had seen the project to fruition and witnessed her aunt's marriage to Captain Gosforth. She must remain strong until then.

'There!' Amelia said, laying down her brush and comb. 'How is that?'

Anne surveyed herself in the mirror. The coiffure was a masterpiece, but the face beneath it was a little too pale, the eyes a little too bright. She pinched her cheeks to give them some colour and gnawed at her lips. 'Thank you, my dear. You have worked a miracle.'

'Fustian! You are a natural beauty. You will turn everyone's head.'

Except the one she wanted to turn. He had left her. She stood up so that Amelia could slip the gown over her head. It fitted perfectly around her bosom and fell in rustling folds to her feet. There were white lace gloves, a jewelled reticule, white silk stockings and satin shoes that, together with her emerald necklace, completed her ensemble.

'Time to go,' she said, picking up a silk-fringed shawl and taking a last look at her reflection before making her way downstairs where her aunt and their escorts waited. She had heard them arrive a few minutes previously.

Her aunt, magnificent in deep rose pink, with a satin turban and feathers, was standing beside Captain Gosforth, who was clad in a simple black evening suit, enlivened by a yellow brocade waistcoat and a complicated lace cravat, whose folds quite obliterated his shirt front. Major Mancroft, who was to be Anne's escort, was in the blue-and-silver dress uniform of the Regent's own regiment. He bowed to Anne.

'Miss Hemingford, you quite take my breath away. Such loveliness! I shall be the envy of every man there.'

She smiled and took his arm. 'Shall we go?'

It became apparent as soon as they entered that the ball was going to be the great success everyone had predicted. The Castle ballroom was packed with excited noisy people, all dressed in the most extravagant gowns and evening suits money could buy. Jewellery glittered at the ladies' throats, on their arms and in their hair. Chicken-skin fans fluttered, quizzing glasses were raised and lowered as each new entrant was examined and commented upon. Men stood beside their ladies or, leaving them to gossip in little groups, stood apart, watching with amusement.

But there was no sign of Justin. Anne, looking about her, admitted she had been hoping against hope that he might return, even though she had been told Mrs Tremayne had also left town. But it had been a vain hope. Everyone who was anyone in the town, with the exception of the Regent, was there. It was a magnificent climax to their fund-raising and she was congratulated by many people on the organisation, the music, the flowers, the sumptuous food, but their praise meant nothing when all she really wanted was a kind look, a smile of understanding, a few words of love from a certain gentleman who had not deigned to be present.

The orchestra was playing for the next dance. The Major turned and bowed. 'Miss Hemingford, will you do me the honour?'

She rose, smiling a little stiffly, and took his hand to

be led into a country dance. Her aunt was smiling broadly when they returned to her at the end of it. 'You make a handsome couple,' she murmured to her niece. 'Everyone has been saying so.'

Anne laughed. 'Do you never give up?'

'Oh, I have. I was simply making an observation.'

The evening wore on. Anne did not want for partners and was not left to sit out any of the dances. She was glad of that. To sit, like a wilting flower, waiting for someone to take pity on her would have been too mortifying.

'Miss Hemingford, did I tell you how handsome you are looking tonight?' Charles said during their second dance of the evening.

'Yes, Major, I believe you did.'

'And have I said how much I admire you?'

She looked up at him, startled. 'Do you?'

'Oh, indeed, yes. More than that. I have developed a deep affection for you.'

She wondered what was coming next. Surely he did not mean to propose? But it seemed he did, for he whirled her out of the centre of the ballroom into a quiet alcove, where he stopped and took both her hands. 'Miss Hemingford, will you do me the greatest kindness of all and marry me?'

She searched his face, wanting to laugh, to tell him how ridiculous the idea was, but she could not hurt him by mocking him. 'Major, you have quite taken my breath away,' she said.

'Will you?'

'But I thought you were quite set on marrying Aunt Bartrum.'

'I thought I was to begin with, but she made me realise, in the gentlest of ways, that it would not do. She convinced me that I had been mistaken in wishing it and that my affection for her was that towards an aunt, no more, and if I looked into my own heart I would acknowledge it and realise that it was you I have wanted all along. She said she would be very happy to be my aunt.'

Anne was having a hard job keeping a straight face, but he was so in earnest, she made the effort. She wanted to tell him that she was impervious to her aunt's matchmaking, but that would have been unkind. 'Major, you do me great honour…'

'You will say yes?' His face was all eagerness and Anne wondered how a man of nearly thirty could behave in such a boyish fashion. It was his mother, of course. She had never released the leading strings, allowed him to grow up. If he had served in battle and not at home, he might have been hardened. But he would make someone a gentle wife. If his mother let him.

She smiled. 'No, Major, I think not.'

'Do not dismiss me out of hand. Give yourself a little time. After all, you cannot wish to remain single all your life. You were born to be a wife and mother—'

'How do you know that?' she asked sharply. 'Could it be that my aunt said it?'

'Perhaps she did, but she has the right of it, has she not?'

'How can I tell?'

'Marry me and you will soon see.'

'No, thank you, Major. Now, I think we should go back to the ballroom before tongues start wagging. There has been enough of that already.'

Reluctantly he led her back to her aunt and then took himself off in a miff.

'Well?' her aunt demanded.

'I am out of countenance with you, Aunt Georgie. How could you have put me to the blush like that and mortified the poor man so? You said you had given up matchmaking.'

'But, Anne, he is your last chance.'

'Then so be it,' she said, looking up as a stir by the door indicated a latecomer had arrived. She wondered idly if it was the Regent, but then the crowds suddenly parted and she saw him.

Their eyes met and held. The people and music faded to nothing. There was no one in the room but the two of them, reaching out to each other across yards of shining floor, drinking in the sight of each other like thirsty animals at a desert pool. Neither moved for several seconds. And then he began to walk towards her, his steps slow and measured, his limp hardly showing. He was dressed in his naval dress uniform, just as he had been at the first ball. She waited, though she longed to run to meet him and throw herself into his arms.

He seemed to take an age to reach her and never in all that time did his gaze shift from hers. And then he was standing over her, bowing, and she suddenly became aware that the musicians were playing a waltz. He reached out one hand. 'Miss Hemingford, may I?'

Without speaking, she took his hand and stepped towards him and then they were dancing, just as they had that first time, their feet moving in rhythm, their bodies swaying in unison, their eyes still searching each other's faces. And all she could think was, *He has come back. He has not deserted me.* She felt so languid, so boneless; it was as if she were floating on the sea.

The dance had nearly ended when he broke the spell. 'You are quiet, Anne.'

'What is there to say?'

'What indeed?'

'Time for talking later. I am enjoying the dance.'

'But we must talk.'

'Oh, indeed we must. Not now.'

The music came to an end. He bowed. She curtsied. He offered her his arm and they strolled back to Aunt Bartrum. 'Aunt, look who is here,' she said.

Her aunt looked from one to the other. 'And about time too. Where have you been, young man? We had quite given up on you.'

'I had to return home. My brother had an accident…'

'Oh, I am sorry for that. But he is recovered?'

'Yes, praise be.'

'Had you heard that Captain Smollett has admitted to his part in the fire and has been cashiered?'

'Yes, Professor Harrison informed me when I arrived home. He said he had gone abroad and taken Mrs Tremayne with him.'

Anne, to whom this was welcome news, was glad that it was her aunt doing the quizzing—she did not think she could find the voice to do it. All she wanted was to go somewhere quiet where she could be alone with Justin. She had made up her mind, that if he kissed her she would succumb and let him do what he willed with her. She would taste the forbidden fruit, even if they parted immediately afterwards. She would be an old maid who had known the love of a man. And that would be her triumph, not her shame.

A crowded ballroom was not the place to indulge such fantasies, especially as something was happening at the door. A low murmur turned into applause and the crowds gave way again and this time it really was for the Regent.

He was enormously fat and waddled rather than walked the length of the room. The jacket of his uniform was stretched tight across his chest, which was heavy with decorations. But he had a charming smile. Every man bowed, every woman dropped into a deep curtsy as he made his slow progress. He was met by Lady Mancroft, who sank to the floor. 'Your Highness, you honour us.'

He reached forward to raise her up. 'My pleasure, dear lady. I wish to meet the doctor who began it all.'

Her ladyship was about to say he was not present when she spotted him standing with his hand on Anne's as she clung to his sleeve. 'Doctor Tremayne.'

Almost reluctantly he moved forward to be presented. 'I am merely the figurehead,' he said when the formalities were done with. 'Miss Hemingford…'

'Ah, Miss Hemingford.' He turned to Anne, who came forward and dropped a curtsy. 'We have met before, I think. Your brother, the Earl, was in my regiment. Distinguished himself. Give him my best and tell him I hope to see him at court before long.' And with that he waddled out again to more applause.

There was a concerted sigh as he disappeared and then the Master of Ceremonies called for silence, Lord and Lady Mancroft stepped up on to the platform where the musicians made way for them and his lordship made a speech in which he said the evening and other donations had raised two thousand pounds, an unhoped-for amount, and work could begin on rebuilding the hospital straight away. After the applause had died, he praised those who had made it possible, particularly his wife who had done sterling work, and encouraged the others to keep at it. Anne did not mind in the least who received the accolades. She was happy that Justin was back with her and tomorrow, they would talk, everything would be explained and after that… She tried not to think of what might happen after that in case she should be disappointed.

'I plan to swim in the morning,' he whispered, when the ball came to an end and it was time for everyone to go home.

'Do you know, I had the same idea.'

'Two minds with but one thought.' He lifted the back of her hand to his lips. 'Until then.'

He was sitting on a rock in the cove, waiting for her. She had hardly slept a wink and as soon as daylight filtered through the curtains of her room, she left her bed, dressed in her simplest grey dress and crept from the house. There was a slight on shore breeze, but not enough to deter her. Mrs Smith had resumed her job as dipper and helped her into the plain brown garb before guiding the horse into the water.

'I shall swim to the cove and go up to the house,' Anne told her as she went down the steps into the cold water. 'So do not worry if I am not back soon.'

And here she was, dressed in nothing but a brown shift and a pair of drawers. They clung to her body, revealing every curve. She did not care. She ran up the beach towards him. He rose to meet her, as wet as she was, dressed in nothing but tight breeches. The next minute she was in his arms and being kissed with a thoroughness that took her breath away. He kissed her mouth, her eyes, her hair, her throat, exploring each new place, making her ache with desire. Her whole body opened out like a flower unfolding in the sun. She felt hot, sticky and wild with urgent longing.

He drew back suddenly. 'We have to talk.'

'Later. Later.' She reached up to pull his mouth down on to hers again.

He responded hungrily. He held her close, the curves of her body fitting into his, his manhood hard against the pit of her stomach. 'No,' he said, suddenly. 'First I have a story to tell you. It is a long story and may take a little time.' He sank to the ground, pulled her down beside him and put his arm about her. She laid her head into his shoulder and waited. 'Once, there was a very foolish young man who imagined himself in love with a harpy…'

She lifted her head. 'Did you know she was a harpy?'

'No. Be quiet, or I will never be done.' He had to get it all off his chest. How he had met and lusted after Sophie and asked her to marry him, taken her to his home and introduced her to his brother. 'I blamed Andrew for seducing her. I could see no wrong in her then,' he said, not sparing himself or her. 'There was a terrible quarrel and I left. It wasn't until she came to Brighton that I realised what a blind fool I had been. By then everyone had branded me a jilter.'

She put her finger on his lips. 'Enough, no more. It is of no consequence.'

'But it is. I want you to know everything. I want you to be sure…'

'Of course I am sure. Do you think I make a habit of offering myself to young men as I am offering myself to you now?'

'Before I have even asked?'

She laughed and kissed him. 'The answer is yes.'

'You don't know what I was going to ask.'

'Whatever it was, the answer is still yes. Do I love you? Yes. Do I want to lie with you? Yes. Will I marry you? Yes.' She stopped. 'And even if you were not going to ask the last one, the answer to the other two is still yes.'

'Of course I was going to ask it. Do you take me for a rake? I love you, Anne Hemingford. I love you with all my heart and soul, always and for ever. But it is a big step for you to take, for I mean to carry on with my work…'

'I would not love you half so much if you had wanted anything different. It is what I want too. To live with you in that house up there…' She nodded towards it. Already there were workmen busy rebuilding it. 'To be your wife and helpmate.'

'There will be opposition.'

'Pooh to that. I can deal with opposition.'

'And scandal?'

'That too.'

'Oh, my love, you are wonderful, unique and I adore you.' He took her in his arms again, but his kiss was less frenzied now. He had calmed himself and was once more in control. 'We must marry very soon because I do not think I can keep my hands off you much longer.'

'There is always the second of my answers.'

He laughed, half convinced she meant it, but then sense prevailed. 'No, my love, we will save that for the marriage bed. When it happens, it must be right and I wish us both to savour it to the full as husband and wife.'

'Then you must call at my aunt's house tomorrow, decked out in your best to ask formally for my hand. I shall be waiting.'

And that is what he did. In spite of their impatience they decided to wait until the new Cliff House had risen from the old; after all, it was going to be their home as well as a hospital. Because of all the goodwill Anne had engendered, the money came pouring in and not only money, but offers of practical help from bricklayers, carpenters and painters, and it went up in record time. Six weeks later, the roof was on and the rooms painted and though the wards had to be finished off and equipment brought in, their living quarters were habitable and they could wait no longer.

It was a double marriage ceremony, Walter Gosforth and Aunt Bartrum and Justin and Anne, witnessed by Harry and Jane, who had come down from Sutton Park, Viscount Rockbourne and Andrew, now almost fully recovered, and all their friends, high and low; they made no distinction.

The wedding breakfast was held at Cliff House and that night, when everyone had gone home, Justin kept his promise to make their wedding night the most fulfilled and happy she had ever known. Now she knew why she had remained single so long; she had been waiting for the right man, for Dr Justin Tremayne.

* * *

They spent a week in London and a week at Sevenelms and then returned to Brighton for the opening of the new hospital which had been completed while they were away. 'I was right,' he told her after the ceremony, when the town dignitaries and the watching populace had departed. 'You do make dreams come true.'

'Oh, that was Tildy,' she said, reaching up to kiss him. 'And her little friend.'

* * * * *

MILLS & BOON®

Live the emotion

SUPER *Historical* romance

Look out for next month's Super Historical Romance

IMPETUOUS

by Candace Camp

Ever since 'Black Maggie' Verrere eloped to America, jilting Sir Edric Neville and taking a fortune in jewels with her, the two families have been at odds. Now, over a hundred years later, Cassandra Verrere is curious about the missing dowry. It would provide a future for her young brothers – and for herself. Unfortunately, to find it, she needs one of the hateful Nevilles' help. But trust a Neville? Unthinkable!

'*Impetuous* is a sheer delight. Candace Camp weaves together a charming tale, adding poignancy and enough spice to charm every reader.'
—*Romantic Times*

On sale Friday 7th October 2005

Available at most branches of WHSmith, Tesco, ASDA, Borders, Eason, Sainsbury's and most bookshops

www.millsandboon.co.uk

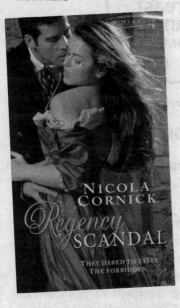

researching the cure

The facts you need to know:

- **One woman in nine** in the United Kingdom will develop breast cancer during her lifetime.

- Each year **40,700** women are newly diagnosed with breast cancer and around **12,800** women will die from the disease. However, survival rates are improving, with on average 77 per cent of women still alive five years later.

- **Men can also suffer from breast cancer**, although currently they make up less than one per cent of all new cases of the disease.

Britain has one of the highest breast cancer death rates in the world. Breast Cancer Campaign wants to understand why and do something about it. Statistics cannot begin to describe the impact that breast cancer has on the lives of those women who are affected by it and on their families and friends.

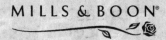

FREE!

2 Books
and a surprise gift!

We would like to take this opportunity to thank you for reading this Mills & Boon® book by offering you the chance to take TWO more specially selected titles from the Historical Romance™ series absolutely FREE! We're also making this offer to introduce you to the benefits of the Reader Service™—

- ★ **FREE home delivery**
- ★ **FREE gifts and competitions**
- ★ **FREE monthly Newsletter**
- ★ **Exclusive Reader Service offers**
- ★ **Books available before they're in the shops**

Accepting these FREE books and gift places you under no obligation to buy, you may cancel at any time, even after receiving your free shipment. Simply complete your details below and return the entire page to the address below. You don't even need a stamp!

YES! Please send me 2 free Historical Romance books and a surprise gift. I understand that unless you hear from me, I will receive 4 superb new titles every month for just £3.65 each, postage and packing free. I am under no obligation to purchase any books and may cancel my subscription at any time. The free books and gift will be mine to keep in any case.

H5ZEF

Ms/Mrs/Miss/Mr .... Initials ....
BLOCK CAPITALS PLEASE
Surname ....
Address ....

.... Postcode ....

Send this whole page to:
UK: FREEPOST CN81, Croydon, CR9 3WZ